THE BROKEN SWORD

THE BROKEN SWORD

POUL ANDERSON

This edition contains the author's original text.

Cover design by Jason Gabbert

978-1-5040-5495-9

This edition published in 2018 by Open Road Integrated Media, Inc.
180 Maiden Lane
New York, NY 10038
www.openroadmedia.com

INTRODUCTION

"Perhaps the finest American heroic fantasy"—so E. F. Bleiler, the great scholar of supernatural and fantasy literature, summed up *The Broken Sword.* Poul Anderson himself felt that the original version of the book was too "savage" and, for a revised edition published in 1971, smoothed out its sentences and slightly altered one important section. Yet most readers prefer the brutal, lyrical excess of the 1954 text and it is that which is reprinted here. In the era of *A Game of Thrones* we can handle a bit of savagery.

Most critics characterize *The Broken Sword* as an homage to "the Northern thing," as W. H. Auden called his own fascination with the Icelandic sagas and Norse *Eddas.* (A character named Audun actually appears in the novel.) But this simple label isn't quite right. Yes, overall the book may be, to borrow Tolkien's words about *Beowulf,* "a drink dark and bitter; a solemn funeral-ale with the taste of death." But Anderson actually recreates nearly all the primary forms of medieval literature—French romance, Celtic fairy tale, Norse myth, Teutonic epic.

The Broken Sword begins with the same kind of sentence one finds at the start of *Njal Saga* or *Laxdaela Saga*: "There was a man called Orm the Strong, a son of Ketil Asmundsson who was a great landsman in the north of Jutland." After this brisk introduction to Orm, we follow him briefly on his Viking adventures until he decides to settle down in England:

"He found a green and fair tract beside a little bay where he could keep his ships. An Englander already dwelt there, but Orm ringed his house with men one night and burned it. The man, his brothers, and most of his household perished then. Some say that the man's mother, who was a witch, escaped the fire. . . ."

Thus Anderson quietly signals the source for all the bloodshed and heartbreak that will blight the family of Orm. Later, however, he hints that there is more to the story than just an evil crone's desire for revenge. The Aesir themselves, especially Odin, may be moving human pawns for dark purposes of their own. "As flies to wanton boys are we to the gods, they kill us for their sport." Not only that; they also manipulate our destinies. In Wagner's *Die Walkure*, Siegmund and Sieglinde must fall in love so that their incestuous union will produce Siegfried.

Shortly before his Christian wife Aelfrida is about to give birth, Orm quarrels with a priest and sends him away, then sails off to do a bit of looting in Ireland and Scotland. As a result, when a son is born, no priest resides nearby to christen the baby—which perfectly suits a sudden impulse of light-hearted Imric, the elf-earl. In short order, the unbaptized infant is swapped for a half troll, half elf changeling, the product of a violent rape. The soulless Valgard will be brought up as Orm's first-born; while the human Skafloc will join the elves.

Imric gives the boy to his sister Leea to nurse. "She was as beautiful as her brother, with thinly graven ivory features, unbound silver-gold tresses floating in the air under a jeweled coronet, and the same moon-flecked twilight blue eyes as he. Tenuous spider-silk garments drifted about the slender white wonder of her body, and when she danced in the moonlight it was a ripple of light and madness to those who watched. She smiled on Skafloc with pale full lips, and her milk was sweet fire in his mouth and veins."

As in Tolkien's *Fellowship of the Ring*, which was first published the same year as *The Broken Sword*, the elves are long-lived and perennially youthful. Anderson's Alfheim—the Other World of Imric and Leea—is a summer realm of sensual pleasure, of love-making and music and poetry. Compared to the hard-scrabble Iron-Age mortals, the graceful, heartless elves are as coolly elegant and amoral as eighteenth-century French aristocrats. In one of several daring developments in the novel, Leea's feelings for the grown Skafloc will be anything but maternal.

Soon after Imric brings his new foster-son home, a messenger of the Aesir appears, bearing a present from the gods: a broken and rusty sword. "The day will come," says the rider, "when Skafloc stands in sore need of a good blade, and this is the Aesir's gift against that time." He also explains that only the giant Bolverk, who originally forged the sword, can make it whole again. Since the elves cannot touch iron, they order two dwarfs to wall up the weapon, then mark the spot with rune signs.

So, two babies, two halves of a sword, two realms of being (faerie and the world of men), two religions (Norse paganism and Christianity)—these and several other dualities run through the novel. Skafloc soon grows up more elf-like than the elves, showing the triumph of nurture over nature; but Valgard proves the opposite, as his brute self overwhelms any tender family feelings. And yet Valgard isn't merely a berserker killing machine: He is prey to tears, regret and even existential angst. When not swinging his axe on the battlefield, he invariably turns inward, brooding on his shattered life and the nature of things. No matter what he accomplishes, it seems hollow. "What am I," he asks himself in agony, "but the shadow of Skafloc?" As for gaining power or even a throne: "What use is that? What use is anything?" At times, Valgard resembles and sounds like his near contemporary, Macbeth.

Skafloc, by contrast, is no deep thinker; he's merry and lighthearted, happy in his skin (or even the skins of animals when he transforms himself into a wolf or eagle). To convey the sensual dream-like ambiance of faerie, Anderson abandons the hammer-blow prose of the sagas for a Lord Dunsany-like lyricism. The growing Skafloc plays with gnomes and brownies, and one afternoon even encounters a lonely faun exiled by Christianity from his sunny Mediterranean groves. Other signs of a pagan world on the wane are hinted at in the sea-faring adventures of Imric and his fosterling:

"Sailing north and then east through a weird white land of mist and cold and drifting icebergs, Imric and Skafloc and their men at last rounded the cape and went south. Here they fought dragons, and harried among the demons of the land. They followed the continent westward again, until it turned south, and then north anew. Their hardest fight was on a desert island with a troop of exiled gods, grown thin and shrunken and mad in their loneliness but still wielding fearsome powers. Three elf ships were burned after the fight, there being none left to man them, but Imric was the victor."

Meanwhile, back in our harsh world, a green-eyed beauty

with lips as red "as new-spilled blood" has completely enthralled the now grown Valgard. She readily persuades him that he will rule all England and revenge himself on Imric if he unites with the trolls in their war against the elves. Of course, he will first need to win King Illrede's favor with gifts. Such as? The trolls are lustful, whispers the temptress, and Valgard's two sisters are not really his sisters. Lovely Freda, especially, will do quite nicely for the troll-king's insatiable appetite.

Revenge may be the driving force in *The Broken Sword,* but Anderson never overlooks its bigger brother, politics (including sexual politics, at which Leea excels). When war approaches, both elves and trolls seek allies. Who will side with whom? And when? At the same time, the gods are playing a desperate game of their own, one that involves their ancient enemies, the giants of Jotunheim. The broken sword is obviously a crucial element in some long foreseen design.

When that mysterious gift is finally reforged, the blind giant Bolverk tells Skafloc, in suitably archaic diction: "Many heroes have owned this sword, because it brings victory to the wielder. There is naught on which it does not bite, nor does it ever grow dull of edge. Venom is in the steel, and the wounds it gives cannot be healed by leechcraft or magic or prayer. Yet this is the curse on it: that every time it is drawn it must drink blood, and that in the end, somehow, it brings the bane of him who uses it." It will, in short, turn on its owner.

No matter. By this time, a desperate Skafloc is as weary and broken-hearted as Valgard: Despite his elfin upbringing, he has been undone by love, by deep human love, and cares little whether he lives or dies. When Skafloc grasps the evil weapon a strange energy flows into his arm and body. "The sword," says Bolverk, "is loose and the end of the world is nigh."

There is much more in Anderson's magnificent, fact-paced novel: diabolical pacts, the depiction of a seemingly endless winter, a moving love story, the resurrection of the dead (an episode derived from the eerie Norse poem known as "The Awakening of Argantyr"), a perilous voyage into a land of ice and mist, the gathering of the Irish fairies (the Sidhe), a sea battle as thrilling as those of Patrick O'Brian, scenes of seduction and torture, and finally . . .

When Poul Anderson ended *The Broken Sword* he hinted strongly at the likelihood of a sequel. Alas, he never wrote it. But, as I said, he did later revise the novel and rework one scene. At one point a witch summons the Devil, who grants her the power she needs to set up what crime writers call a honey trap. Such an encounter isn't out of place, given that major plot developments turn on the opposing ethics of paganism and Christianity. But in this instance Anderson neatly reconfigures the implications of the scene, while also tying it in more tightly with the rest of the story: When the Devil leaves, the witch peers out her window "and what she saw departing was not what she had seen within. Rather the shape was of a very tall man, who strode swiftly albeit his beard was long and wolf-gray. He was wrapped in a cloak and carried a spear, and beneath his wide-brimmed hat it seemed he had but a single eye. She remembered who also was cunning, and often crooked of purpose, and given to disguise in his wanderings to and fro upon the earth; and a shiver went through her."

But then Odin—if it is indeed he--is soon gone and, of course, it might all have been just "a trick of the starlight."

Poul Anderson, as prolific a writer as any in science fiction and fantasy, was once asked to name his five favorites among his books. He didn't choose this one. As a minor character in another fine, albeit quite different fantasy—William Goldman's

The Princess Bride—was wont to exclaim: "Inconceivable!" *The Broken Sword* is a masterpiece, as bleakly beautiful as the northern landscape in winter.

—Michael Dirda

Michael Dirda, a Pulitzer Prize–winning book columnist for the *Washington Post*, is the author, most recently, of *Browsings: A Year of Reading, Collecting, and Living with Books* and the 2012 Edgar Award–winning *On Conan Doyle.* He is at work on a book about late nineteenth- and early twentieth-century popular fiction.

THE BROKEN SWORD

1

There was a man called Orm the Strong, a son of Ketil Asmundsson who was a great landsman in the north of Jutland. The folk of Ketil had dwelt in Himmerland as long as men remembered, and were mighty landowners. The wife of Ketil was Asgerd, who was a leman-child of Ragnar Hairybreeks. Thus Orm came of good stock, but as he was the fifth living son of his father there could be no large inheritance for him.

Orm was a great sea-farer and spent most of his summers in viking. When he was in his twentieth winter, he went to his oldest brother Asmund and said, "Now you have been sitting in Himmer-land and having the use of the farm for some years, and your brothers grow restless for a share. But it is plain that if we divide it five ways our family will sink from great landsmen to smallholders, and soon be lost and forgotten."

"That is true," replied Asmund, "and if you will not yield the inheritance it were best we steered it together."

"I will not be fifth man at the rudder," said Orm, "and so I will make you this offer: give me three ships, and outfit them, and supply arms to all who will follow me, and I will find my own land and quit all claim on our father's."

Asmund was well pleased with this, the more so since two more of the brothers said they would go with Orm, and ere spring he had bought longships and all their outfit and found many of the younger and poorer men of the neighborhood who would be glad to fare westward. On the first clear day of spring, when the seas still ran high, Orm took his ships out of the bay, and that was the last Asmund ever saw of him.

The dragons turned their tails to the low gray moors and the high cloudy sky of Himmerland. With wind piping in their riggings and sea-gulls screaming about the mastheads and the strakes foaming, they pointed their heads westward. Orm made a verse:

White-maned horses
(hear their neighing!),
gray and gaunt-flanked,
gallop westward.
Wild with winter
winds, they snort and
buck when bearing
burdens for me.

By starting thus early, Orm reached the western islands ahead of most other vikings and had a good plundering. With this he bought more ships and gathered a following while he lay in Ireland over the winter.

Now for some time Orm harried the western lands and had a great booty. But he wished for land of his own, and so one summer joined his fleet to the great one of Guttorm, or Guthrum as the English called him. For some time he was with Guthrum ashore as well as at sea, and when peace was made with Alfred, Orm went into the Danelaw to seek land.

He found a green and fair tract beside a little bay where he could keep his ships. An Englander already dwelt there, but Orm ringed his house with men one night and burned it. The man, his brothers, and most of his household perished then. Some say that the man's mother, who was a witch, escaped the fire—for the burners let all women and children and thralls that wished leave first—and laid the curse on Orm that his eldest son should be fostered beyond the world of men, while Orm should in turn foster a wolf that would one day rend him.

Now Orm built a great house and other buildings on his newly gained land, and with the wealth and fame he had he was accounted a mighty chief in the Danelaw. When he had sat there a year, he felt it were well if he had a wife. He rode with a great following to the English ealdorman Athelstane and asked for his daughter Aelfrida, who was said to be the fairest maiden in England.

Athelstane dared not refuse, but Aelfrida said to Orm's face: "Never will I wed a heathen dog, nor indeed can I. And while it is true you can take me by force, you will have little joy of me—that I swear."

She was small and slender, with soft ruddy-brown hair and flashing gray eyes, while Orm was a huge bulky man with face burned red and hair nearly white from years of sun and sea. But he felt she was somehow the stronger, so after thinking for a while he said: "Now that I am in a land where folk worship the White Christ, it might be well if I made peace with him as well as his followers. Indeed, most of the Danes have already done so. I will be baptized if you will wed me, Aelfrida."

"That is no reason," she cried.

"But think," said Orm slyly, "if you do not wed me I will not be christened, and then, if we may trust the priests, my soul is lost. And you will have to answer heavily to your God for losing a human soul." He whispered to Athelstane, "Also, I will burn down this house and throw you off the sea-cliffs."

"Aye, daughter, we dare not lose a human soul," said Athelstane very quickly.

Aelfrida did not hold out much longer, for indeed Orm was a not ill-looking man, and he was known to be rich and powerful. So Orm was christened, and the next day he wed Aelfrida and bore her home to the Danelaw. They lived together contentedly enough, if not always peacefully.

There were no churches near, so at Aelfrida's wish Orm kept a priest on the land, and for atonement of his sins he paid the priest well. But being a careful man with no wish to offend any of the Powers, Orm continued to sacrifice to Thor in midwinter and to Freyr in spring for peace and good harvests, as well as to Odin and Aesir for luck before each sea-voyage.

All that winter he and the priest quarreled about this, and in spring, not long before Aelfrida's child was born, Orm lost his temper and kicked the priest out the door and bade him begone. Aelfrida reproached him greatly for this, until he cried that he could stand no more of that woman-chatter and now would have to flee it. A few days later, earlier than he had planned, he left with his ships and spent the summer harrying in Ireland and Scotland.

Scarce were his ships out of sight when Aelfrida was brought to her bed and gave birth to a child. It was a fine big boy who after Orm's wish she called Valgard, a name old in that family. But now there was no priest to christen the child, and the nearest church lay a good two or three days" journey away. She sent a thrall there at once.

Meanwhile she was proud and glad of her son, and often she sang to him as her mother had to her—

Lullaby, my little bird,
of all birds the very best!
Hear the gently lowing herd.
Now the sun is in the west
and 'tis time that you should rest.

Lullaby, my little love,
nodding sleepy on my breast.
See the evening star above
rising from the hill's green crest.
Now 'tis time that you should rest.

Lullaby, my little one.
You and I alike are blest.
God and Mary and their Son
guard you, who are but their guest.
Now 'tis time that you should rest.

2

Imric the elf-earl rode out one night to see what had happened in the lands of men. It was a cool spring dark with the moon nearly full, rime glittering on the grass and the stars still hard and bright as in winter. The night was very quiet save for the sighing of wind in budding branches, and the world was all sliding shadows and cold white light. The hoofs of Imric's horse were shod with an alloy of silver, and there was a high clear ringing in the gloom as they struck the hard ground.

The elf-earl rode into a darkling forest. Night lay heavy here, but from afar he saw a ruddy glimmer of fire. When he came there he saw it shone through cracks in a little hut of mud and wattles huddled under a great gnarly oak from whose boughs Imric remembered the Druids cutting mistletoe. He could sense that a witch lived here, so he dismounted and rapped on the door.

A woman who seemed old and bent as the tree opened it and saw him standing there, the broken moonlight sheening off his helm and byrnie and his horse shimmering-white and mysterious, cropping the frosty grass behind him.

"Good evening, mother," quoth Imric.

"Let none of you elf-folk call me mother, who have borne tall sons to a man," grumbled the witch, but she let him in and hastened to pour him a horn of ale. Imric had to stoop inside the tiny hovel and clear away a litter of bones and other trash ere he could sit.

He looked at her with the strange slant eyes of the elf-folk, all cloudy-blue without pupil or white. There were little moonflecks drifting in Imric's eyes, and shadows of ancient wisdom, for Imric had dwelt long in the land when the first men came. But he was ever youthful, with the broad forehead and high cheekbones, the narrow jaw and the straight thin-chiseled nose of the elf lords. His hair floated silvery-gold, finer than spider silk, from under his horned helmet down to his wide red-caped shoulders.

"'Tis long since the elves have been abroad among men," said the witch.

"Aye, we have been too busy in the war with the trolls," answered Imric in his voice that was like a wind blowing through ancient trees far away. "But now there is truce, and I am curious to find what has happened in the last hundred years."

"Much, and little of it good," said the witch. "The Danes have come from the east, burning and plundering and breaking English lords. They are nigh to overrunning all the western islands."

"That is not bad." Imric stroked his long mustache. "Before them the Saxons came with fire and death, and before them the Picts and Scots, and before them the Romans, and before them the Brythons and Goidels, and before them—but the tale is long and long, nor will it end with the Danes. And I, who have watched it almost since the land was made, see naught of evil in it, for it helps pass the time. I were fain to see these new folk."

"Then you need not ride far," said the witch, "for Orm the Strong has taken land here and his hall is but the ride of a night or less to the east on a mortal horse."

"A short trip for my windy-maned stallion. I will go."

"Hold—hold, elf!" For a moment the witch sat muttering, and only her eyes had life, gleaming red out of the firelight's monster shadows. Then of a sudden she cackled in glee and screamed, "Aye, ride, ride, elf, to Orm's house by the sea. He is gone a-roving, but his wife will guest you gladly. She has but newly brought forth a son, and he is not yet christened."

At these words Imric cocked his long pointed ears forward and his ivory-white face tautened. "Speak you sooth, witch?" he asked then, low and toneless like wind blowing through unpeopled heather.

"Aye, by Sathanas I swear it." The old woman rocked to and fro, squatting in her rags before the dim coals that spattered her face with red. The shadows flowed out of corners and chased each other across the walls, huge and misshapen and noiseless. "Go see for yourself."

"I would not venture to take a Dane-chief's child. He might be under the Aesir's ward."

"Nay, elf, nay. Orm is a Christian, but an indifferent one, and his son has yet been hallowed to no gods at all."

"Ill is it to lie to me," said Imric thinly.

"I have naught to lose," answered the witch. "Orm burned my sons in their house, and my blood dies with me. I do not fear gods or devils, elves or men. But 'tis truth I speak."

"I will go see," said Imric, and stood up. The scales of his byrnie rang together like little silver bells. He swept his great red cloak around him and went out and swung onto the moon-white stallion.

Like a rush of wind and a fleeting blur of moonlight he was out of the forest and across the fields. Far and wide the land stretched, shadowy trees and silent hills and rime-whitened meadows asleep under the moon. Here and there stood a lonely croft, dark now, huddled beneath the great star-crusted sky. There were presences moving in the night, but they were not men—he sensed a distant wolf-howl, the green gleam of a crouched wild-cat's eyes, the scurry of furtive feet under the mighty oak-roots. They were aware of the elf-earl's passage and shrank deeper into the shadows.

Erelong Imric rode up to Orm's garth. Here the barns and sheds and houses were big, of rough-hewn timbers. The great hall stood with its carven dragon heads like a hill-ridge against the shining star clouds, but after Imric had overleaped the fence it was to a lesser dwelling that he rode. The dogs smelled him and snarled, hair a-bristle, but ere they could bark he had turned his terrible blind-seeming gaze on them, and they crawled off whimpering in fear.

He rode like a wandering night-wind up to the house and looked in a window. Moonlight shafted in over the bed, limning Aelfrida's lovely slumbrous face in soft silver and a cloudiness of unbound silken hair. But it was on the babe beside her that Imric gazed.

The elf-earl laughed within the locked mask of his cold beautiful face, and rode north again. Aelfrida moved in her sleep, woke, and looked at the little one beside her. Her eyes were still clouded with uneasy dreams.

3

In those days the elves and other folk of faerie still dwelt upon the earth, but even then a strangeness hung over their holdings, as if these wavered halfway between this world and another; and there were places which might at one time be a simple lonely hill or lake or forest and then at another gleam forth in all the ancient splendor of the true dwellers. Now and again the gaunt bare crags of the northern highlands known as the elf-hills might be seen by men as halls and castles, and thus they were shunned.

Imric rode to the grim form of Elfheugh, which he saw as a castle tall and slender-spired, having gates of bronze and floors of marble, hung with the fairest shifty-patterned tapestries of magic weave and crusted with great blazing gems. In the moonlight the faerie folk were dancing on the green before the castle, but Imric rode by into the courtyard. His horse's hoof-beats echoed hollowly from the massive outer walls, and the dwarf thralls hurried forth to attend him. He swung to the ground and hastened into the keep.

The clear unwavering light of the tapers was broken into a shifting, tricky dazzle of many colors by the gems and the gold in the walls. Music breathed through the vaulted rooms, rippling harps and keening viols and the voices of flutes like mountain brooks under darkling pines. The patterns on the rugs and tapestries moved slowly, like live figures. The very walls and floors, and the groined ceiling in its dim blue twilight of height, had a fluid quicksilver instability, they were never the same and yet one could not say just how they changed.

Imric went down a staircase, his byrnie chiming in the stillness. Of a sudden it grew dark about him, save for the occasional bloody light of a guttering torch, and the cold dark air of the inner earth filled his lungs. Now and again a clash of metal or a shuddering wail echoed down the rough-hewn water-dripping corridors, but Imric paid no heed. Like all elves, he had a rippling liquid cat-grace in his movements, he went swift and silent and easy as a questing wind down into the dungeons.

Finally he paused before a great door of brass-barred oak. It was green with moss and dark with age and cold with the dew of the inner earth, and only Imric had the keys to the three mighty locks. These he opened, muttering certain words, and swung the ponderous door back. It groaned, for three hundred years had passed since last he had opened it.

A woman of the troll race sat within the little cell. She wore only the bronze chain, heavy enough to anchor a ship, which fastened her by the neck to the wall. Light from a torch ensconced outside the door fell dimly on her huge squat mighty-muscled form. She had no hair, and the green skin moved on her bones. As she turned her great hideous head to Imric, her wolf-toothed mouth snarled. But her eyes were empty, two deep pools of utter blackness in which a soul could drown, sinking down forever into nothingness. For nine hundred years she had been Imric's captive, and she was mad.

The elf-earl looked down at her, but not into her eyes. He said softly, "We are to make a changeling again, Gora."

The troll-woman's voice rumbled like thunder out of the earth's inmost deeps. "Oho, oho," she said, "he is here again. Be welcome, you, whoever you are, out of night and unending chaos. Ha, will none wipe the sneer off the face of the cosmos?"

"Hurry," said Imric. "I must make the change ere dawn."

"Hurry and hurry, autumn leaves hurrying on the rainy wind, snow hurrying out of the sky, life hurrying to death, gods hurrying to oblivion." The troll-woman's crazy voice boomed hollow down the corridors. "All ashes, dust, blown on a senseless screaming wind, and only the mad can gibber the music of the spheres. Ha, the red cock on the dunghill!"

Imric took a whip from the wall and lashed her. She cowered and lay down, and quickly, because he liked not the slippy clammy cold of her flesh, Imric did what was needful. Thereafter he walked nine times widdershins about her where she squatted, singing a song no human throat could have formed, a song which certain beings had sung once, shambling around a strangely carved monolith, to bring forth the fruits of a quaking steamy world. As he sang, the troll-woman shook and swelled and moaned in pain, and when he had gone the ninth time around she screamed so that it pierced his ears and rang in his skull, and she brought forth a man-child.

It could not by the human eye be told from Orm Dane-chief's son, save that it howled fiercely and bit at its mother. Imric cut its cord and took it in his arms, where it lay quiet.

"The world is flesh dissolving off a dead skull," mumbled the troll-woman. She clanked her chain and lay back, shuddering. "Birth is but the breeding of maggots in the crumbling flesh. Already the skull's teeth leer forth, and black crows have left its eye-sockets empty. Soon a barren wind will blow through its bare white bones." She howled as Imric closed the door. "He is waiting for me, he is waiting on the hill where the mist blows ragged on the wind, for nine hundred years has he waited. The black cock crows—"

Imric locked the door anew and hastened up the stairs. He had no liking for making changelings, but the chance of getting a human baby was too rare to lose.

When he came out into the courtyard he saw that a storm was brewing. A rising wind drove a wrack of clouds across the heavens, great flying black monsters from which the moon fled wildly over the sky. Like mountains in the east, the lightning-veined storm clouds boiled darkly over the horizon. The wind hooted and howled.

Imric sprang to the saddle and spurred his horse south. Over the crags and hills they went, across dales and between trees that writhed in the gale. The fleeing moon cast fitful white gleams over the world, and Imric was like such a wind-swift flitting phantom.

Swiftly, swiftly he raced, with his cloak blowing like bat-wings and the moonlight glittering briefly on his mail and his eldritch eyes. He rode along the eastern sea-cliffs with the surf roaring and snarling at his feet and spindrift blowing cold on his cheeks. Now and again a lurid lightning flash showed the waste of running waters and the storm marching out of the east. Thunder bawled ever louder in the darkness that followed the boom and bang of great wheels across the sky. Imric spurred his horse to yet wilder flight—he had no wish to meet Thor, out here in the storming dark with naught but loneliness around for many miles.

Into Orm's garth he leaped and up to Aelfrida's window. She was awake, holding her child to her breast and whispering comfort to him. Her hair blew around her face, almost blinding her.

There came a sudden glare of lightning like white fire. She could not see in that terrible flare, and the thunder that went with it was like a hammer-blow. But she felt the baby fall from her arms, she snatched for him, and then she felt the dear weight again as if it had been laid there.

Imric laughed aloud as he rushed back through the storm. But of a sudden he heard his laughter echoed, a howl in the raving darkness, and he reined in with his breast gone cold. Through a last break in the clouds came a shafting icy-white moonbeam, limning the figure which galloped with the east wind across Imric's path. A brief glimpse he had, seated on his plunging horse, of the mighty cloaked form that outran the wind, the huge eight-legged horse and its rider with the long gray beard and the shadowing hat. The moonbeam gleamed on the head of his spear and on his single eye.

Hoo, halloo, there he went through the sky with his troop of dead warriors and the fire-eyed hounds barking like thunderclaps. His horn screamed in the storm, the hoofbeats were like a rush of hail drumming on the roof; and then the whole pack was gone and the rain came raving over the world.

Imric snarled, for the Wild Hunt boded no good to those who saw it and the laughter of the one-eyed huntsman had been mockery. But—he had to get home now, lightning was cracking all around him and Thor might take a fancy to throw his hammer at an elf. Imric held Orm's son in his cloak and struck spurs into his stallion.

Aelfrida could see again, and she clutched the yelling boy in her arms. He should be fed now, if only to quiet him. He suckled her, but bit until it hurt.

4

Skafloc, Imric named the stolen child, and gave him to his sister Leea to nurse. She was as beautiful as her brother, with thinly graven ivory features, unbound silvery-gold tresses floating in the air under a jeweled coronet, and the same moon-flecked twilight-blue eyes as he. Tenuous spider-silk garments drifted about the slender white wonder of her body, and when she danced in the moonlight it was as a ripple of light and madness to those who watched. She smiled on Skafloc with pale full lips, and her milk was sweet fire in his mouth and veins.

Many great lords of Alfheim came to the naming of the child, and they brought goodly gifts: cunningly wrought goblets and rings, dwarf-forged swords and axes, byrnies and helms and shields, garments of silk and satin and cloth-of-gold, charms and talismans. Since elves, like gods and giants and trolls and others of that sort, know not old age, they had few children, perhaps centuries apart, and the birth of one was a great event; still more portentous to elves was the fostering of a human.

As the feast was in progress, there came a tremendous clatter of hoofs outside Elfheugh, until the walls trembled and the brazen gates sang an answer. Sentries on the moonlit towers winded their clear-throated horns, but none wished to contest the way of that rider and Imric himself met him at the portals, bowing low.

It was a great fair figure in flashing byrnie and eagle-winged helm, with a blaze in his eyes like lightning, and the earth trembled under his horse's hoofs. "Greeting, Skirnir," said Imric. "We are honored by your visit."

The messenger of the Aesir rode across the moon-white flagstones. At his side, jumping restlessly in the scabbard and glaring like fire of the sun itself, was Freyr's mighty sword, given him for his journey to Jötunheim after Gerth. He bore another sword in his hands, a huge rusted one still black with the earth in which it had long lain, and broken in two.

"I bear a naming-gift for your foster-son, Imric," he said. "Guard well this glaive, and when he is old enough to swing it tell him the giant Bölverk who forged it can make it whole again. The day will come when Skafloc stands in sore need of a good blade, and this is the Aesir's gift against that time."

He threw the broken sword clashing on the ground, whirled his horse about, and in a roar of hoofbeats was lost in the night. The elf-folk stood very still, for they knew the Aesir had some purpose of their own in this, yet Imric could not but obey.

None of the elves could touch iron, but Imric shouted for his dwarf thralls and had them pick up the old weapon. Under his direction they bore it down to the inmost dungeons and walled it into a niche near Gora's lonely cell. Imric warded the spot with rune signs, and then left it and avoided the place for a long time.

Now some years went by and naught was heard from the gods.

◆ ◆ ◆

Skafloc grew apace, and a bonny boy he was, big and gay, with great blue eyes and hair like spun gold in the sunshine. He was noisier than the few elf children, and grew so much swifter that he was a man when they were still unchanged. It was not the way of the elves to show over-much fondness for their young, but Leea often made much of Skafloc, singing him to sleep with the wild ancient lays that were voices of sea and wind and soughing forest. She taught him the courtly manners of the elf lords, and also their corybantic dances when they were out in the night, barefoot in the dew and drunk with streaming moonlight. Much of what wizard knowledge he had came from her, songs which could blind and dazzle and enchant, songs which the rocks and trees sang back in shivering echoes, songs without voice to which the auroras danced on winter nights.

While yet a child, Skafloc had a merry time, at play with the elf young and with their strange fellows. Many were the presences haunting the hills and glens of that wild land; it was a place of sorcery and the men and beasts who wandered into it rarely returned. Not all the dwellers were safe or friendly, but Imric always had some warrior of his guard following Skafloc about.

There were sprites dancing and whirling in the rainbowed mists about cataracts tumbling into the dells, with their voices shouting and booming back from the cliffs. Skafloc could dimly see them, a cloudy glimpse of white, graceful, water-gleaming bodies leaping in the foam and spray, haloed with rainbows. Of moonlit nights, drawn like other denizens of faerie by the cold mystic beams, they would sometimes come out and sit on the mossy banks, white and naked and streaming water, with weeds twisted into their long hair and garlands of cool pale water lilies; and elf children could then talk to them. Much could the sprites tell, of flowing rivers and the quick silvery gleam of fish in them, of the frog and the otter and the kingfisher and what those had to say to each other, of sunlit pebbly bottoms and of secret places where the water was still and green and alive with presences—and then the wild rush over cliff edges in a roar and a rainbow, shooting down to dance in the whirlpools!

Other watery places there were from which Skafloc was warned away, certain quaking bogs and silent dark tarns, for the dwellers there were not good.

Often he would be out in the forest to speak with the little old folk who lived there, the humble gnomes and brownies, with their gray and brown homespun clothes and their long stocking caps and the men's beards down to their knees. They lived under trees, with a gnarly comfort to their simple abodes, and were glad to see the elf children. But they feared the grown elves, and thought it well that they were so small none of these could get into their dwellings. Unless of course he had shrunk to their size, which none of the haughty elf lords cared to do.

There were a few goblins about. Once they had been powerful in the land, but Imric had entered with fire and sword, and those who were not slain or driven out had been broken of their might. They were furtive cave dwellers now, but Skafloc managed to befriend one and from him got much curious goblin lore.

Once the boy heard a piping far off in the forest, and he thrilled to its eerie enchantment and hastened through the twilit trees to the glen from which it came. So softly had he learned to move, like a flitting shadow, that he stood before the creature ere it was aware of him. It was a strange being, man-like but with the legs and ears and horns of a goat. It blew a melancholy air on its reed pipe, and its eyes were great and sad and liquid.

"Who are you?" asked Skafloc wonderingly.

The being lowered his pipe, seeming for a moment ready to flee, then he relaxed and sat down on a log. His accent was odd as he said, "I am a faun."

"I have heard of no such beings." Skafloc sat down cross-legged in the grass before him.

The faun smiled sorrowfully in the twilight. The evening star blinked forth above his head. "There are none save me hereabouts," he said. "I am an exile."

"Whence came you hither, faun?"

"I came from the lands of the south, after great Pan was dead and the new god whose name I cannot speak was come to Hellas. There was no more place for the old gods and the old beings who haunted the land. The priests cut down the sacred grove and built a church—Oh, I remember the dryads" screams, quivering voicelessly on the still, hot air and seeming to hang there forever. They ring yet in my ears, they always will." The faun shook his horned head. "I fled north," he said, "but I wonder if those of my ancient comrades who stayed and fought and were slain with exorcisms were not wiser. Long and long has it been, elf-boy, and lonelier than it was long." Tears glimmered in the faun's eyes. "The nymphs and the fauns and the very gods are dead, dust blowing on desolate winds. The temples stand empty, white under the sky, and slowly they topple to ruin. And I—I wander alone in a foreign land, scorned by its gods and shunned by its people. It is a land of mist and rain and soul-freezing iron winters, angry gray seas and pale sunlight spearing through hurrying clouds. No more of blue sky and sapphire ocean, creamy-white in its gentle swells, no more of little rocky islands and the dear warm groves where the white nymphs waited for us, no more of grapes hanging from ancient vines and fig trees heavy with fruit, no more of the stately gods on high Olympus—"

Of a sudden the faun ceased his crooning, stiffened, cocked his ears forward, and then turned and fled into the bushes. Skafloc looked around and saw the elf-guard approaching to take him home.

Skafloc, who could stand the daylight which the elves hated, was much more about in the hills and dales than the other children, and came to know the land far better than a man who had lived there for a lifetime might.

Of the wild beasts, the fox and the otter were most friendly to elves, it being held that there was some kind of kinship, and insofar as these had a language the elves knew it. From the fox Skafloc learned the secret ways of the forest, the hidden trails through sun-spattered shadow and the myriad tiny signs which told a story to one who knew the full use of his senses. From the otter, he learned of the world about lake and river, he learned to swim like a living arrow and to sneak through cover which would scarce hide half his body.

But he grew friendly with nigh all the other animals, even the most timid of birds would come sit on his finger when he whistled in its own tongue, even the grim old bear would grunt a welcome when he came to its cave. Deer and elk and rabbit and other game became wary of him as he took up hunting, but with some special ones he made friends. And the story of all his farings among the beasts would be a long one.

And the years swung by, and he was borne on their resistless current. He was out in the first shy green of spring, when the forests woke after their sleep and grew clamorous with returning birds, when the rivers brawled with melting ice and a few little white flowers in the chill moss were like remnant snowflakes. The summer knew him, a naked brown form with flying sun-bleached hair, chasing butterflies up the windy hills toward the sky, rolling over in the long grasses with sheer joy of life; or out in the light nights which were like a dreamy ghost of day, stars overhead and chirring crickets and dew glittering under the moon. The cold thunderous rains of autumn washed him, or he wove a crown of flame-colored leaves and stood in the breathless sharp air listening to skies gone clangorous with the calls of departing birds. Even in winter he was about, flitting through the dance of snowflakes, crouched under a windfall while the storm roared like a mad bull through the groaning forests; sometimes of nights when it grew so numbingly cold that trees broke open like thunderclaps far away, he would be standing on the moon-white snowfields, listening under the hard brilliance of the stars to a voice of winter, the deep vibrant tone of ice-bound waters shivering in the cold with thunders that rolled between the hills.

5

When Skafloc's limbs began to lengthen Imric took him in charge, only a little at first, but more and more with time until he was being raised wholly as a warrior of Alfheim. Being short-lived, humans could learn more quickly than the folk of faerie, and Skafloc's knowledge grew even faster than his body.

He learned to ride the horses of Alfheim, white and black stallions and mares of an eerie quicksilver grace, swift and tireless as the wind, and erelong his moonlight gallops were taking him from Caithness to Land's End with the cloven air singing in his ears. He learned the use of sword and spear and bow and the slender long-shafted ax which rang like a great bell on splitting skulls. He was less quick and supple than the elves, but grew to be far stronger and could bear helm and hauberk as many days on end as needful; and any other human was like a clumsy clod beside his weird flitting movements.

He hunted far and wide over land, alone or in company with Imric and his warriors. His bow twanged death to many a tall-antlered stag or mighty wild boar, he could put an arrow whither he would at any distance it could reach. There was other and trickier game, hunted crazily through the forests and across the crags swifter than stormwinds, the unicorns and griffins which Imric had brought from the edge of the world for his pleasure.

Skafloc learned also the manners of the elves, their courtly grace and their guileful intriguing and their subtle speech. He could dance in the drenching moonlight to the wild harps and pipes, naked and drunken and abandoned as any of them. He could himself play, and sing the strange lilting lays older than man. He learned the skaldic arts so well that he spoke in verses as easily as in ordinary speech. He could discriminate between the rare and subtle viands of the elves, and drink the liquid fire which smoldered in dusty spider-shrouded bottles below the castle, but for all that his taste for the hunter's black bread and salt meat, or the rainy sunny earthy savor of berries, or the clear cool springs in distant woodlands, was not spoiled.

As he grew up, he had much attention from the supernally lovely elf women. Without gods, and with few children, the elves know not marriage, but their nature was such that their women had more wish of love and their men less than among humans. Thus Skafloc found himself in great favor, and many a good time did he have in the light nights of summer.

But the most difficult and perilous part of his training was in magic. Imric had him wholly in hand for this, and, while he was not able to learn as much as his foster-father, both because of his human nature and his short life, he came to be as adept as most elf chieftains. He learned first how to shun and sidestep the iron no elf, troll, or goblin could endure; even when he became aware of his nature and his ability to touch the metal without harm, he left it alone out of habit. Then he learned the runes for healing wounds and illness, warding off bad luck, or wishing evil on foemen. He learned the songs which could raise or lay storms, bring good or bad harvests, and move rock and wood and metal. He learned the use of the cloak of darkness, and of the skins he could don to take the form of a beast. Near the end of his training he learned the mighty runes and songs and charms which could raise the dead and read the future and compel the gods; but save in time of direst need no one cared to be shaken to his inmost being by these and risk the utter destruction they could wreak on him.

Skafloc was often down by the sea, he could sit hour upon hour looking out over its restless wastes to the cloudy line where the water met the sky, he never wearied of its deep voice or its thousand moods or its clean sharp tang of salty depths and windy distances. He came of a seafaring breed, and the running tides were in his blood. He often spoke to the seals in their barking, grunting tongue, and the wheeling gulls brought him news from the earth's ends. Sometimes when he was in company with other warriors, the white sea maidens would rise from the foam, wringing out their long green hair as they came up on the beach, and then there would be a gay time. They were cool and wet to the touch and they smelled of the sea; afterward Skafloc would have a faint fishy taste on his lips, but he liked them well.

When he was fifteen he stood nearly as tall as Imric, broad of shoulder and taut of sinew, with his long hair bleached almost white against his brown skin. He had a straight, blunt, strong-boned face, a wide merry mouth, and large eyes set far apart and blue as the summer sea. A mystery hung about him, veiling itself behind his eyes which had looked on more than mortals saw, revealing itself in his cat-lithe movements.

Imric said to him: "Now you are big enough to have your own weapons rather than old ones of mine, and also I have been summoned by the Erlking. We will fare overseas."

At this Skafloc whooped for joy, cartwheeled out into the fields, and galloped his horse madly through the lands of men, making magic out of sheer need to do something. He caused pots to dance on the hearth and bells to ring and axes to cut wood of their own accord, he sang cows up onto the peasant's roof and a wind into being which scattered his hay over the shire and a rain of gold out of the sky into his yard. With the Tarnkappe about his shoulders, he kissed the girls working at twilight in the fields and rumpled their hair and tossed their men into a ditch. For many days thereafter, masses were sung to exorcise the spate of witchcraft, but by that time Skafloc was on the sea.

Imric's black longship sped over moonlit waves with her sail taut under a wind he had raised. There was a picked company of elf warriors along, for the chance of meeting trolls or sea monsters was not to be ignored. Skafloc stood by the dragon prow peering eagerly forward—he could see by night as well as by day, given witch-sight. He spied the leaping porpoises, silver-gray under the moon, and hailed an old bull seal he knew. Once a whale broached, water roaring off his mighty flanks. Things which mortal sailors only glimpsed or dreamed were plain to the cloudy slant elf-eyes and to Skafloc: the sea maidens tumbling in the foam and singing, the drowned towers of Ys far below the moon-rippling billows, a brief gleam of white and gold and a hawk-scream of challenge overhead—Valkyrs rushing to some battle in the east.

Wind sang in the ship's rigging and the sea roared at the strakes. Ere dawn the vessel had reached the other shore, been drawn up on the beach, and lay hidden by spells.

The elves took shelter in a cave, but Skafloc was about during much of the day. He climbed a tall tree and looked in wonder at the strange land rolling southward. He spied the gaunt gray hall of some baron, and thought briefly and pityingly of the narrow human lives that flickered in its gloom. He would not trade.

When night came, the elves mounted their horses and rode inland swift as a winging storm. Ere midnight they were in rough wild mountain country where the moonlight cast its thin-etched silver and crouching shadows on bleak pinnacles, swooping cliffs, and the far green shimmer of glaciers. The elves rode easily along a narrow treacherous trail, harnesses chiming, lances high, plumes and capes streaming. Hoofbeats rang on the stones and echoed back through gulfs of night.

A horn sounded hoarsely from above, another from below. The elves heard a clank of metal and a tramping of feet, and when they came to the end of the trail they saw a dwarf host guarding a cave mouth.

The little bandy-legged men scarce came up to Skafloc's waist, but they were immensely broad of shoulder and long of arm. Their dark bearded faces were angry, their little eyes smoldered red and bitter under tangled brows. They held swords and axes and shields, but their power of handling iron was of little use against the elves" arrows and long spears.

"What will you?" asked their leader, his voice cavernously deep in his hairy breast. "Have the elves and trolls not wrought us enough ill, harrying our lands and bearing our folk off as thralls? This time our force is larger than yours, and if you come nearer we will slay you."

"We come in peace now, Motsognir," replied Imric softly. "We wish only to buy of your wares."

"I know your trickery, Imric the guileful," said Motsognir harshly. "You would make peace only to put us off our guard."

"I will give hostages," offered Imric, and this the dwarf king grudgingly accepted. Leaving several elves disarmed and surrounded, Motsognir led the others down into his caverns.

Here glowed red coals, lighting the rocky walls with bloody shadow-beset dimness, and over their forges the dwarfs labored unceasingly. Their hammers rang and echoed and boomed down the dark dank corridors until Skafloc's head seemed to ring in answer. Here were made the most tricky works of all the world, rare goblets and beakers ablaze with gems, rings and necklaces of ruddy gold cunningly fashioned; weapons were beaten out of metals torn from the mountain's heart, weapons fit for gods—and indeed the dwarfs had done much work for the gods—and other weapons cursed with evil. Mighty were the runes and charms the dwarfs could grave, and strange were the arts they had mastered.

"I would have you make an outfit for my foster-son here," said Imric.

Motsognir's little red mole-eyes searched Skafloc's tall form in the wavering light. His voice rumbled through the hammer-clashing: "So you have been up to your old changeling tricks again, Imric? Someday you will overreach yourself. But since this is a human, I suppose he will want arms of steel."

Skafloc hesitated. The elves used brass, copper, bronze, gold, silver, and certain metals which men did not yet know but which gave alloys as hard and tough as steel itself. But such weapons had not quite the weight demanded by Skafloc's growing strength.

"Aye, steel," he said firmly.

"'Tis well, 'tis well," growled Motsognir, and turned to his forge. "Let me tell you, boy, that you humans, weak and short-lived and ignorant, are yet stronger than elves and trolls, aye, than giants and gods. And that you can touch cold iron is only one reason. Ho!" he called. "Ho, Sindri, Dyrin, Dvalin, come to help!"

Now the forging went apace, sparks flying and metal shouting so that it was a marvel, and erelong Skafloc wore winged helm and shining byrnie, shield on back and sword at side and ax in hand, all of wondrous hard, blue-gleaming steel. He yelled, fierce with exultation, and swung high his weapons and shrilled the screaming war-cry of the elves.

"Ha!" he cried, clashing the sword back into its sheath. "Now let trolls or goblins, aye, giants dare approach Alfheim, we shall smite them like the lightning and carry fire into their own lands!" And he made the verses:

Swiftly goes the sword-play
singing in the mountains.
Clash of steel is calling,
clanging up to heaven:—
arrows flying angry;
axes lifting skyward,
banging down on byrnies,
breaking shields and helmets.

Swiftly goes the sword-play:
Spears on hosts are raining;
men run forth in madness,
mowing ranks of foemen;
battle tumult bellows;
blood is red on ax-heads;
greedily the gray wolf
gorges with the raven.

"Well spoke," said Imric coolly, "but remember not to touch elves with those new arms of yours. Now let us begone." He gave Motsognir a sack of gold. "Here is payment for the work."

"Rather had I been paid by the freeing of your thralls of our race," said the dwarf.

"They are too useful," declared Imric, and left.

Again at dawn his troop sheltered in a cave, and then the next night rode on into the mysterious great forest in which was the Erlking's castle.

Here was a weaving of witchery which Skafloc did not yet know how to unravel. He was dimly aware of high slender towers against the moon, of a deep blue twilight in which many stars wavered and danced, of a music which seemed to sing through flesh and bone to thrill in the very soul, but it was not until they were in the throne room that he could see again.

The elf lords stood tall and silent in the blue dusk, their beautiful pale faces closed and secret, their strange eyes seeming blind and yet looking deeper than mortal. In a throne of shadow sat the Erlking. Golden were his crown and scepter, and his robes of a purple that blent with the spacious gloaming. His long hair and beard were white, and he alone of the elves showed any sign of age, in that his high noble forehead and his cheeks were lined. His face was as if carved in marble, but eldritch fires smoldered in his eyes.

Imric the elf-earl bowed, and the warriors in his train bent the knee to the king. When the ruler spoke it was like a wind rushing through far-off trees: "Greeting, Imric, earl of Britain's elves."

"Greeting, lord," answered the chieftain, and he met the Erlking's terrible gaze.

"We have summoned the elf-earls to council," quoth the king, "since word has reached us that the trolls make ready to go to war again. It cannot be doubted that 'tis us they arm against, and we may look for the truce to end in the next few years."

"That is well, lord. Our swords were moldering in the scabbards."

"It may not be so well, Imric. Last time the elves drove back the trolls and would have entered their lands had not peace been made. Illrede Troll-King is no fool, and he would not attempt war if he did not think he was stronger than formerly."

"I will ready my lauds, lord, and try to send spies and raiders to their lands."

"That is well." Now the Erlking turned his eyes on Skafloc, who grew cold about the heart but met that blind fire-flickering stare readily enough. "We have heard tell of your changeling, Imric," he murmured, soft and chill and deadly. "You should have asked us."

"There was no time, lord," defended the elf-earl. "The babe would be baptized ere I could come here and back. Hard is it to steal a child these days."

"And risky too, Imric."

"Aye, lord, but worth it. Humans may do much which is barred to elves and trolls and other beings—they may use all metals, they may touch holy water and the cross and speak the name of that new god who is our greatest foe—aye, the old gods themselves must flee some things which humans use. We elves need such a one."

"The changeling you left in his place could do all that."

"Indeed, lord. But you know the wild and evil nature of such half-breed beings, they are surely not to be trusted with magic such as this human knows. Were it not that men must never be sore their children are stolen, so that they would call their gods to avenge it, elves would make no changelings at all."

"Can this human be trusted? Let him but turn Christian and he is beyond our reach—already he grows strong—"

"No, lord!" Skafloc stood forth in all that proud assembly and looked directly into the Erlking's face. "I am but thankful to Imric for rescuing me from the dull blind round of a human life. I am elf in all but blood, it was elf breasts I suckled as a babe and elf tongue I speak and elf girls I sleep beside." He lifted his tawny head, almost arrogantly. "Give me leave, lord, and I will be the best of your hounds—but if a dog be driven out, he will become a wolf and feed on his master's flocks."

Some of the elves were aghast at this boldness, but the king nodded, and smiled a grim smile. "We believe you," he said, "and indeed earlier men adopted into Alfheim proved good warriors. What worries us about you is the story of the Aesir's naming-gift. They have a hand in this somewhere, and their purpose is not like to be our own."

A shudder ran around the gathering and some made rune signs in the air. But Imric said: "What the Norns have ordered, not even the gods may alter. And I would count it shame to lose the most promising of men because of a dim fear of the future."

"Indeed it would be," quoth the Erlking, and there the council ended.

A great and lavish feast was held ere the meeting of the earls dissolved. Skafloc's head swam with the magnificence of the Erlking's court. When finally he came home, his contempt and pity for humans were so great that he had naught to do with them at all.

Now some half-dozen years went by. The elves showed no change, but Skafloc grew until his outfit had to be altered by Imric's dwarf thralls. He stood even taller and broader than the elf-earl, and was the strongest man in the realm. He wrestled bears and wild bulls, and often ran down a stag on foot. No other in Alfheim could bend his bow, or could have swung his ax even had it not been of iron.

He grew leaner of face, and let a mustache the wheaten color of his long hair grow on his lip. But he became, if anything, merrier and more unruly than before, a lover of madcap pranks and breakneck stunts, a mischievous warlock who would raise a whirlwind just to lift a girl's skirt, a mighty drinker and brawler.

Restless with his own strength, he prowled the land, hunting the most dangerous game he could find. Monsters of the Wood of Grendel he sought out and slew in their desolate fens, sometimes suffering frightful wounds which only Imric's runes could heal, but ever ready for another bout. Then again he might lie idle for weeks on end, staring dreamily into clouds high above, scarce stirring himself. Or in some beast shape, with senses strange to man, he would seek forests and waters, to gambol as an otter or hunt as a wolf or wing in fierce lonely pride as an eagle.

"Three things have I never known," he boasted once. "Fear, and defeat, and love-sickness."

Imric looked at him strangely. "Young are you," he murmured, "not to have known the three ultimates of human life."

"I am more elf than human, foster-father."

"So you are—now."

One year Imric outfitted a dozen longships and went a-roving. The fleet crossed the eastern sea, and harried goblins dwelling along the rocky coasts. Then the warriors rode inland and made a raid on a troll town, burning it after they had slain its folk and taken their treasure. Sailing north and then east through a weird white land of mist and cold and drifting icebergs, Imric and Skafloc and their men at last rounded the cape and went south. Here they fought dragons, and harried among the demons of the land. They followed the continent westward again, until it turned south, and then north anew. Their hardest fight was on a desert shore with a troop of exiled gods, grown thin and shrunken and mad in their loneliness but still wielding fearsome powers. Three elf ships were burned after the fight, there being none left to man them, but Imric was the victor.

They saw somewhat of humans, but paid no great heed, the more so since their warring was with beings of faerie; and the humans never saw them at all, or only in frightened glimpses.

Only four ships returned of that fleet, three years after it set out, but they had a huge booty of wealth and captives. It had been a glorious voyage, of which great report went about in Alfheim and the neighboring lands, and the fame of Imric and Skafloc was high.

6

The witch dwelt alone in the forest with only her memories for company, and over the years these fed on her soul and left their castings of hate and vengeance-lust. She began to increase her powers, raising spirits out of the earth and speaking with demons of the upper air. To the Black Sabbath on the Brocken she rode, high through the sky on a broomstick with her rags streaming in the wind. A monster feasting it was, with ancient hideous shapes chanting about the dark altar, with steaming kettles of blood from which they drank deep, but perhaps the most frightful of all were the fair white young women who joined in the rites and in the fearful matings.

Wiser the witch returned, with a rat for familiar who suckled blood out of her withered breasts with his sharp little teeth and at night crouched on her pillow and chittered in her ear as she slept. And so at last she was given strength to raise the Dark One by herself.

Thunder and lightning rolled about her hovel, with blue phosphorescent glare and the stink of Hell's pits. But the vast shadowy presence before which she groveled was beautiful in its inhuman way, for all evil is luring and this was the fount of it.

"O thou of the many names, Prince of Darkness, Evil Companion," cried the witch, "I would thou did my wish, and for that I will pay thy ancient price."

The one for whom all men in all lands had names, but whom she called Sathanas, spoke, and his voice was slow and deep and endlessly patient: "Already you have gone far down my road, but not yet are you mine. The mercy of God is infinite, and only if you yourself reject it can you be lost."

"What care I for mercy?" asked the witch bitterly. "It will not avenge me. I stand ready to give my soul unto you if you will deliver my enemies into my hands."

"That I may not do," quoth the Dark One, "but I may give you the means to entrap them yourself if your cunning be greater than theirs."

"That will be enough, Lord."

"But think you now, have you not had revenge on Orm already? 'Tis your doing that he has a changeling for eldest son, and the ill that being will wreak on him can scarce be averted."

"'Tis not enough. Orm's true son prospers in Alfheim, and his other children grow apace. I would wipe out his accursed seed altogether, as he wiped out mine. The Aesir will not answer me, therefore you, Black Majesty, must be my friend."

The Devil's strange deep eyes, in which were little flickering flames colder than winter itself, brooded long on her. "The Aesir are not out of this matter," he said slowly. "Odin, who knows the future, has some purpose of his own . . . I knew him of old, in my incarnation of Loki, and I liked it not . . . But you shall have my help. Power and knowledge and strength will I give you, until you become a mighty witch. Also I will tell you the only way to strike, and that way is certain unless your enemies are wiser than you think.

"There are three Powers in the world which not gods nor demons nor men can stay, against which no magic shall prevail and no might shall stand, and they are the White Christ, Time, and Love.

"From the first, and mightiest, you may wait only enmity, and you must be careful that this Power in no way enters the struggle. The second, which has many names—Fate, Destiny, Law, Wyrd, the Norns, Necessity, Brahm, and others beyond counting—is scarce to be appealed to, for it is not to be swerved in its way. But the third is a two-edged sword which may bring harm as well as help, and this you must use."

Now the witch swore a certain oath, and there the council ended for that time.

Save that the changeling was fierce and noisy, he could not be told from the true babe, and though Aelfrida puzzled over the sudden change in her little son's manner she had no thought it was not him at all. She christened the child Valgard as Orm wished, and often she sang to him and was gladdened by sight and touch. But he bit so hard that it was pain to nurse him.

Orm was sheerly delighted when he came home and saw so fine and strong a boy playing in the yard. "A great warrior will he be," cried the chief, "a swinger of weapons and a rider of ships, a leader among men." He looked about the place. "But where are the dogs? Where is my trusty old Gram?"

"Gram is dead," said Aelfrida tonelessly. "He sought to leap on Valgard and rend him, so I had the thralls slay the poor mad beast. But it must have given notions to the other dogs, who growl and slink away when the child comes near."

"That is strange," quoth Orm, "for my folk have ever been good with hounds and horses."

But as Valgard grew it was clear that no beast liked to have him around, horses snorted and shied away, cats spat and climbed a tree or wall, and the boy early had to learn the use of a spear to ward himself against dogs. He himself was no friend in return, but gave kicks and curses, and grew to be a relentless hunter.

He was sullen and close-mouthed, given to wild tricks and refusal to obey. The thralls hated him for his ill will and the cruel jests he had with them. And slowly, fighting it all the way, Aelfrida came to have no love for him.

But Orm was very fond of Valgard even if they did not always agree. When he had to strike the boy, he could draw no cry of pain however hard his hand fell. And when he had sword-play and his keen blade whined down as if to split the skull, Valgard never even blinked. He grew up swift and strong, taking to weapons as if born with them, and he showed no fear or pain whatever happened. He had no real friends, but there were many who followed him.

Orm had other children by Aelfrida—two more sons, red-haired Ketil and dark Asmund, who were both promising boys, and daughters Asgerd and Freda, of whom the last was nigh an image of her mother. These grew up like other children, glad and sad by turns, playing about their mother and then later rambling all over the land, and Aelfrida loved them with a deep and aching love. Orm was fond enough of them, but Valgard was his darling.

Strange, aloof, silent, Valgard grew up. He was outwardly little different from Skafloc, save that his hair was a shade darker and his skin whiter and that there was a flat hard shallowness to his eyes. But his mouth was ever sullen, he smiled only when he drew blood or otherwise gave pain, and then it was a wolfish skinning of teeth. Taller and stronger than other boys of his age, he had little use for them. He would rarely help with the work of the farm, and often went out for long lonely walks.

Once Aelfrida had the priest come to talk to him, and Valgard laughed in his face. "I have no use for your snivelling god," he said, "or for any other gods for that matter. Insofar as appealing to them makes any sense at all, I think my father's sacrifices to the Aesir are of more use than whatever prayers he or you give to Christ. For if I were a god, I might well be bribed by blood and burnt offerings to send good luck, but any who dared annoy me with a mealymouthed prayer I would stamp on—so!" And he brought his heavy-shod foot down on the priest's.

Orm roared with laughter when he heard of it, and Aelfrida's tears were of no avail, so the priest got no satisfaction out of the matter.

Valgard liked best the night. Then he would often slip from his bed and go outside. He could run till dawn with his loping wolfish gait, swift and tireless and driven by some strange moon-magic glimmering inside his head. He knew not what he wished, save only that he was driven by a sadness and a yearning for which he had no name, a black gloom lighting only when he slew or maimed or brought to ruin. Then he could laugh, with the troll-blood beating in his temples and drowning all else in its dark rush!

But one day he took notice of the girls working in the fields with their dresses clinging to their big fair bodies, and thereafter he had another diversion. He had, for his part, strength and good looks and a glib elf tongue when he cared to use it. Sometime thereafter Orm had to pay goodly sums for thralls or daughters wronged.

This the chief did not care about, but it was another matter when Valgard quarreled in his cups with Olaf Sigmundsson and afterward waylaid and slew him. Orm paid the weregild, but saw that his son was not safe to have around. That summer he took Valgard in viking.

This was very pleasing to the boy, who soon won the respect of his shipmates by prowess and reckless daring in battle, though not all liked his wholesale killings and burnings. But soon the berserkergang began to come on Valgard, he trembled and frothed and gnawed the rim of his shield, he rushed forward howling and slaying. His ax was a red blur, he did not feel weapons bite on him, and the sheer terror of his rage-twisted face froze many men even while he cut them down. When the fit was over he was weak, but he had heaped corpses high.

Thus only the rougher and more lawless men cared to have much to do with him, and these were the only ones he cared to lead. He was out plundering every summer, even when Orm did not go, and as his full growth and strength came to him he won a frightful name. He bought his own ships and manned them with the worst of evil-doers, until even Orm forbade him to land his crew.

The other children of Orm grew apace, and they were fine youngsters who were much liked by all folk. Ketil was like his father, big and merry, ever ready for fight or frolic, and often went a-roving when he was old enough; but he quarreled fiercely with Valgard and so sailed his own way. Asmund was more slender and quiet, a good archer but no lover of battle, and came to take over more and more the running of the farm. Asgerd was a big fair may with blue eyes and gold hair and cool strong hands, but Freda was growing up with all her mother's beauty.

Thus matters stood when the witch decided it was time to draw the threads of the web together.

7

On a blustery fall day, with the smell of rain in the keen air and all the forest leaves turned to gold and copper and bronze, Ketil rode forth with a few comrades to hunt. They had not gone far into the woods when they saw a white stag of so huge and noble an aspect they had scarce ever dreamed its like.

"Ho, a kingly beast!" shouted Ketil, spurring his horse, and away they went over stock and stone, leaping fallen logs and dodging trees, crashing through brush and crackling the fallen leaves, with wind roaring in their ears and the forest a wild blur of color. Strangely, the hounds were not very eager in the chase, and though Ketil was not riding the best of horses he drew ahead of the dogs and the other hunters.

Before him in the dim forest evening glimmered the white stag, leaping and soaring like a misty wraith, with his antlers towering tree-like against the sky. Rain came for a time, sluicing icily through the bare limbs, but in the blindness of the chase Ketil did not even feel it. Nor did he feel time or distance or aught but the wind of his gallop and the eagerness of the hunt.

Then at long last he burst into a little clearing, nigh caught up with the stag. The light was dim, but he launched his spear at the whitely looming shape. But even as he made the cast the stag seemed to shrink, to fade like a wind-blown mist, and then he was gone and there was only a rat scuttering through the dead autumn leaves.

Now Ketil grew aware that he had outstripped his companions and become lost from them. It was growing dark, with a thin chill wind whimpering through bare branches, and his horse stood trembling with weariness. He had come into a part of the forest unknown to him, far west of Orm's garth. And the eeriness of the wind and the dusk ran coldly along his backbone.

But just here, on the edge of the clearing, a cottage stood under a huge gnarled oak. Ketil wondered what manner of folk would live so far out—but at least here was shelter for himself and his horse, in a neat little cottage of wood and thatch with firelight glowing cheerily from the windows. He dismounted, picked up his spear, and rapped on the door.

It creaked slowly open, showing a well-furnished room. But it was on the woman that Ketil's eyes rested, nor could he tear them away. And he felt his heart turn over and then slam within his ribs like a beast attacking its cage.

She was tall, and the thin dress she wore clung lovingly to every curve of her wondrous figure. Dark unbound hair streamed to her knees, framing a perfect oval of a face white as sea foam. Her wide full mouth was red as new-spilled blood, her nose delicately arched, her eyes long-lashed under finely drawn brows. They were a fathomless green, those eyes, with little golden flecks in their lustrous depths, and they seemed to look into Ketil's soul. Never, he thought wildly, never before had he known how a woman might look.

"Who are you?" she asked in a soft voice. "What will you?"

The man's mouth was dry and the thudding blood nigh drowned out his hearing, but he made shift to reply: "I am—Ketil Ormsson . . . I lost my way hunting, and would ask a night's shelter for my horse and . . . myself . . ."

"Be welcome, Ketil Ormsson," she said, and gave him a smile at which his heart almost left his breast. "I have little company, and am glad to see guests."

"Do you live here—alone?" he asked.

"Aye—but not tonight!" she laughed, and at that Ketil threw his arms about her.

After three days were past, Orm became sure that something ill had happened to Ketil. "He may have broken a leg, or met robbers, or otherwise come to grief," he said. "Tomorrow, Asmund, we will go look for him."

Valgard sat sprawled on the bench with a horn of mead in one hand. He had come back from a summer's viking work two days before, left his ships and men at a garth he had bought some distance from Orm's, and come home for awhile, more because of his father's good mead and ale than any love for his kinfolk. The red firelight seemed to stream like blood off his shadowed sullen face. He spoke slowly: "Why do you say this only to Asmund, Orm? I am here too."

"I knew not there was any great love between you and Ketil," quoth Orm.

Valgard grinned and emptied the horn. "There is not," he said, "but none the less I will hunt for him, and I hope 'tis I who finds and brings him home. Naught would seem worse to him than being beholden to me."

Orm shrugged, but tears glimmered in Aelfrida's eyes.

They set out the next day, many men on horses, with dogs barking in the crisp cold air, and scattered into the forest.

Valgard went alone and afoot as was his habit, loping swiftly and silently with his crouched wolf-pace. He carried a great ax for weapon, and had a helmet on his tawny mane, but otherwise in his hairy garments he might have been a hunting beast. He snuffed the air with his inhumanly keen nose and circled about looking for signs. Erelong he found faint remnants of a track. He grinned again, and did not sound his horn, but set off at a long easy lope.

As the day went on, he came west into thicker and older forest where he had not been before. The sky grew gray and cold, with swollen clouds flying low over the bare trees. A bitter wind whirled dead leaves through the air like ghosts hurrying down hell-road, and its shrill whine gnawed at Valgard's nerves. He could smell a wrongness here, but having no training in magic he did not know what it was that bristled the hairs on his neck.

At dusk he had gone far, and was tired and hungry and angry with Ketil for giving him this trouble. He would have to sleep out tonight, with winter on the way, and he vowed revenge for that.

Hold—Far, far ahead he saw a glimmer through the thickening twilight. No will-o'-the-wisp that, it was fire—shelter, perhaps, unless it was a robber lair. And were that the case, Valgard snarled to himself, he would have great joy in killing them.

It was utter night when he reached the cottage, and a thin stinging sleet was blowing on the rising gale. Cautiously Valgard edged over to a window. It stood high, but he was tall enough to peer in.

Ketil was there, seated on a bench before a leaping fire, glad and gay. He had a horn of ale in one hand, and the other was caressing the woman on his lap.

Woman—almighty gods, what a woman! Valgard sucked a sharp breath through his teeth. He had not dreamed there could be such a woman as the one laughing on Ketil's knees.

Valgard knocked thunderously on the door with the flat of his ax. It was some time ere Ketil got it open and stood there with spear in hand, and by then the sleet was thick and cruel.

Valgard stood in the door, huge and angry, filling it with his shoulders. Ketil cursed, but stepped aside and let him in. Valgard stalked slowly across the floor with water from the melting sleet streaming off him. His eyes glittered on the woman, crouched on the bench.

"You are not very guest-free, brother," he said, and laughed, a flat mirthless bark. "You let your brother, who has traveled many weary miles to find you, stand out in the storm while you play with your sweetheart."

"I did not ask you to come," said Ketil sullenly.

"No?" Valgard was still looking at the woman with his hard flat eyes. And she met his gaze, swimming in a mist of loveliness, and slowly her red mouth curved in a smile.

"You are a welcome guest," she breathed. "Not ere this have I guested one like you."

Valgard laughed again and swung to face Ketil's stricken stare. "Whether you asked me or not, brother, I am guest here tonight," he said softly. "And since I see there is but room for two in the bed, and I have come such a long hard way, I fear me you will have to sleep outside tonight."

"Not for you would I do that!" shouted Ketil. He poised his spear. "I did not ask you to come. Had it been Father or Asmund or anyone else from the garth, he had been welcome, but you, ill-wreaker and berserker that you are, will be the one to sleep in the forest."

Valgard sneered and chopped out with his ax, splitting the head from the spear. "Get out, little brother," he said. "Get out ere I throw you out."

Blind with anger, Ketil struck at him with the broken shaft. A white rage flamed in Valgard, he leaped forward and his ax shrieked down and buried itself in Ketil's skull.

Still raging, he swung about on the woman. She held out her arms to him. Valgard gathered her to his breast, kissing her so that blood ran from their lips, and she laughed aloud.

But the next morning when Valgard awoke, he saw Ketil lying in a gore of clotted blood and brains, the dead eyes meeting his own in an unwinking stare, and suddenly a mighty remorse welled up in him.

"What have I done?" he whispered. "What have I done?"

"You have killed a weaker man," said the woman indifferently.

But Valgard stood above his brother's body and brooded darkly. "We had some good times together between our fights, Ketil," he murmured. "I remember laughing with you once at a new little calf striving to use its wobbly legs, and the wind in our faces and sun a-sparkle on waves when we went sailing, and deep drinking at Yule when storms howled outside the warm hall, and swimming and running and shouting with you, brother. Now it is all over, you are a stiffened corpse and I gang my own dark way—but sleep well. Goodnight, Ketil, goodnight."

And he picked up the body and bore it into the forest. He did not wish to touch the ax again, so he left it sticking in the skull when he raised a cairn over the dead man.

But when he came back to the cottage, the woman was waiting for him, and he soon forgot all else. Her beauty outshone the sun, and there was naught she did not know about the arts of lovemaking.

It grew bitterly, unrelentingly cold, and the first snow whispered down. The winter would be long.

After a week, Valgard thought it would be best if he returned home, lest others come looking for him or lest fighting break out among his crew. But the woman would not come with him. "This is my place and I cannot leave it," she said. "But come whenever you will, Valgard my darling, and I will always gladly greet you."

"I will be back soon," he promised. He did not think of carrying her off by force, though he had done that to many before her. Somehow he knew she was the stronger.

He came bade to Orm's hall and was joyously greeted by the chief, who had feared him lost too. No one else in the garth was overly happy at seeing him again.

"I hunted far to the north," said Valgard, "and did not find Ketil."

"No," replied Orm sadly, "I fear me he is dead. We searched for days, and at last found his horse wandering riderless. I will ready the funeral feast."

Valgard was but a couple of days among men, then he slipped again into the woods with a promise to be back for drinking Ketil's grave-ale. With a thoughtful eye, Asmund watched him leave.

It seemed strange to the youngest brother how Valgard dodged talk of Ketil's fate, and stranger yet that he should go hunting—as he said—now that winter was come. There would be no bears, and other game was getting so shy that men did not care to go after it in cold weather. Why had Valgard been so long in the forest, and why did he now go back?

So Asmund wondered, and at last, two days after Valgard left, he followed. It had not snowed or blown since, and the tracks could still be seen in the crisp whiteness. Asmund went alone, skiing through silent reaches where no other life stirred, and the deepening cold ate and ate into his flesh.

Three days later, Valgard came back. Folk had gathered at Orm's garth from far around for the grave-ale, and the feast went apace. The berserker slipped grim and close-mouthed through the crowded yard.

Aelfrida plucked at his cloak. "Have you seen Asmund?" she asked timidly. "He went into the forest and has not returned yet."

"No," said Valgard shortly.

"Ill would it be to lose two tall sons in the same month and have only the worst left," said Aelfrida bitterly and turned away from him.

Now evening fell, and the guests met in the great hall for drinking. Orm sat in his high seat with Valgard on his right. Down the length of the long table sat the men, merry with ale, and the women went to and fro to keep their horns filled. Many a man's eyes followed Orm's two daughters through the smoky red firelight, especially Freda the Fair.

Orm was cheerful over his sadness, but Aelfrida could not keep from weeping, quietly and hopelessly, and Valgard sat silent, draining horn after horn until his head buzzed but only deepened his gloom. Away from the woman and the alarums of war alike, he had naught to do but brood on his deed, and Ketil's face swam in the fire-flickering dusk before him.

The feast went apace until all were drunk and making the hall ring with their noise. And then all at once there came a knocking on the door, cutting loud and clear through the racket, and when someone opened it the firelight limned Asmund against the bitter dark.

He stood white and swaying with weariness, bearing in his arms a long cloak-wrapped burden. His hollow eyes swept the hall, seeking one face, and a great silence fell as men grew aware of him.

"Welcome, Asmund!" cried Orm into the taut stillness. "We had begun to fear for you—"

Still Asmund stared before him, and those who followed his gaze saw it fixed on Valgard's face. He spoke at last, tonelessly: "I have brought a guest to the grave-ale."

Orm sat moveless, with his cheeks paling. Asmund set his burden on the floor. It was frozen stiff enough to stand, leaning against his arm.

"It was cruel cold out there in the cairn where I found him," said Asmund. Tears and hate and mockery shivered across his countenance. "It was no good place to be, and I thought it shame that we should hold a feast in his honor and he be out there with naught but wind and the stars for company. So I brought Ketil home—Ketil, with Valgard's ax in his skull!"

He drew aside the cloak, and the leaping firelight was like newly running blood on that which was clotted around the ax. Rime was in Ketil's hair, and his dead face grinned at Valgard and his staring eyes seemed to flame with unearthly lights. He stood leaning against Asmund, stiff and icy cold, and glared into Valgard's eyes.

Orm turned slowly, slowly about to face Valgard, who was looking into the corpse's blind stare with horror riding his back. But on an instant rage came, he leaped up and roared at Asmund: "You lie!"

"All men know your ax," said Asmund heavily. "Now seize the brother-slayer, men, and bind him for hanging."

At this Valgard snatched a spear from the wall and hurled it. Through Asmund's breast it went, pinning him against the wall so that he still stood there with Ketil leaning against him, the two dead brothers side by side glaring at their murderer.

Valgard howled as the berserkergang swept him, his eyes flamed wolf-green and froth was on his snarling lips. Orm roared and sprang at him, drawing a sword. Valgard whipped forth a knife, dodged under Orm's blade, and buried it in the chief's throat.

Blood gushed over him as Orm fell. Valgard snatched the sword and leaped onto the table and then down to the floor. A man rose to stop him, and Valgard hewed him down. His crazy howling rang between the rafters.

Now the hall boiled with men as some sought to flee and some to seize the bloody demon. Valgard's blade sang, and three warriors sank before him. A fourth barred the door, holding an iron shield, and as Valgard smote at this the sword snapped.

"Too weak is your blade, Orm," cried Valgard. As the man rushed at him, he wrenched the ax from Ketil's head and struck out. The man's sword-arm sprang from his shoulder and Valgard went out the door.

Spears and arrows hissed after him. He fled into the forest, gasping, streaming blood. Even after he lost the pursuit he kept running, wolf-gaited, wolf-swift, lest he freeze in the pitiless night. Shuddering and sobbing, he fled westward.

8

The witch sat waiting, alone in the bitter darkness. Presently something slipped through a rat-hole and into her dwelling. Looking down to the shadowed floor, she saw her familiar.

Thin and weary, the rat did not speak ere he had crawled up to her breast and drunk deep of her blood. Then he lay on her lap, watching her with hard little glittering eyes.

"Well," she asked, "how went the journey?"

"Long and hard and cold," he said. "In bat shape, blown on a freezing wind, I fared to Elfheugh. Often as I crept about Imric's Halls I came near death—they are beastly quick, the elves, and they knew I was no ordinary rat. But even so I managed to spy on their councils."

"And is their plan as I thought?"

"Aye. Skafloc will fare to Trollheim to make a raid in force on Illrede's garth, hoping to slay the king or at least upset his readying for war. Imric will remain in Elfheugh to prepare defenses."

"Good. The old elf-earl is too crafty, but Skafloc alone can scarce avoid the trap. When does he leave?"

"Nine days hence. He will take some fifty ships."

"Elves sail swiftly, so he should be at Trollheim the same night. With the wind I will teach him how to raise, Valgard can reach the place in three days, and I'd best allow him another three to busk himself for the journey. So if he is to reach Illrede only a short time before Skafloc, I must keep him here three days—which will not be hard, since he is now an outlaw fleeing hither in despair."

"It seems to me you treat Valgard roughly."

"I have naught against him, he not being of Orm's seed, but he is my tool in a hard and perilous game. It will not be near as easy to ruin Skafloc as it was to kill Orm and the two brothers, or will be to hurt the sisters. My magic and my force alike he would laugh at." The witch grinned in the half-light. "Aye, but Valgard is a tool I shall use to make a weapon that will pierce Skafloc's heart. As for Valgard himself, I give him a chance to become great among the trolls, the more so if they conquer the elves. It is my hope to make Skafloc's downfall all the more bitter by causing the ruin of Alfheim through him."

And the witch sat back and waited, an art many years had taught her.

It was near dawn, with a gray and hopeless light creeping over the snows and the ice-leaved trees, when Valgard knocked on the woman's door. She opened it at once and he fell into her arms. Nearly dead of weariness and cold he was, with great gouts of blood frozen on him and wildness in his eyes and ravaged face.

She gave him meat and ale and curious herbs, and erelong he felt well enough to hold her close to him. "Now you are all that remains to me," he muttered. "Woman of night and mystery, whose beauty wrought all this ill, I should slay you and then fall on my own weapon."

"Why do you say that?" she smiled. "What is so bad?"

He buried his face in her long black fragrant hair. "I have slain my father and my brothers," he said, "and am outlaw beyond hope of atonement."

"As for the slayings," said the woman, "they but prove you stronger than those who threatened you. What does it matter to you who they were?" Her wondrous green eyes burned into his. "But if the thought of murdering your own kin troubles you, I will tell you that you are guiltless."

"Eh?" He blinked dully at her.

"You are no son of Orm at all, Valgard Berserk. I have second sight, and I tell you that you are not even of human birth, but of such ancient and mighty stock that you can scarce imagine your true heritage."

His huge frame grew taut as an iron bar. He clasped her wrists hard enough to leave bruises, and his shout shook the walls of the cottage: "What do you say?"

"You are a changeling, left when Imric the elf-earl stole Orm's eldest son," said the woman. "You are Imric's own son by a slave who is daughter to Illrede Troll-King."

Valgard flung her from him. Sweat gleamed on his forehead. "Lie!" he gasped. "Lie!"

"Truth," answered the woman calmly. She walked toward him. He backed away from her, his breast heaving. Her voice came low and relentless: "Why are you in all your nature so unlike the other children of Orm or any other man? Why do you scorn gods and men alike, and walk in a black loneliness only forgotten in a tumult of slaying? Why, of all the women with whom you have slept, has none become with child? Why do all beasts and children hate and fear you?" She had him backed into a corner now, and her eyes blazed at him. "Why indeed, save that you are—not human?"

"But I grew up like other men, I can endure iron and silver and holy things, I am no warlock—"

"There is the evil work of Imric, who robbed you of your heritage and cast you aside in favor of Orm's son. He made you look like the stolen child. You were raised among the petty rounds of men, and have had naught to rouse the wizard power slumbering within you. That you might grow up, age, and die in the brief span of human life, that the things holy and earthly which the elves fear might not trouble you, Imric traded your birthright of undying life. But he could not put a human soul in you, Valgard. And like him, you will be as a candle blown out when you die, without hope of Heaven or Hell or the halls of the old gods—yet you will live no longer than a man!"

At this Valgard snarled like a wild beast, thrust her aside, and rushed out the door. The woman smiled.

It grew loud and cold with storm outside, but it was not till after dark that Valgard crept back to the cottage. Bent and beaten he was, but his hollow eyes glared at his leman.

"Now I believe you," he muttered hoarsely, "nor is there aught else to believe. There were ghosts and demons riding the storm wind, flying with the snow and howling their mockery as they swept by me." He looked haggardly into the darkened corners of the room. "Night closes on me, the sorry game of my life is played out—home and kin and my very soul have I lost, I see I was but a shadow cast by the mighty Powers who now blow out the candle. Goodnight, Valgard, goodnight—" And he sank sobbing onto the bed.

But the woman smiled her secret smile and lay down beside him and kissed him with her mouth that was like sweet red fire. And when his dazed eyes turned mutely to hers, she breathed: "This is not like Valgard Berserk, mightiest of warriors, whose name is terror from Ireland to Gardariki. I would have thought you would seize on my words with gladness, would hew fate into a better shape with that great ax of yours. You have taken terrible revenges for lesser hurts than this—the robbery of your being and the chaining into the prison which is a mortal's life."

Valgard felt something of strength return, and as he caressed the woman it rose fiercer in his breast. Hate and a steely will flared in his wolf-eyes. But he said at last: "What can I do? Where can I avenge myself? I cannot even see elves and trolls unless they wish it."

"I can teach you that much," she answered. "It is not hard to give the witch-sight with which the beings of faerie are born. Thereafter, if you like, you can take a frightful revenge on those who have wronged you, and can laugh at outlawry, you who will be more powerful than any king of men."

Valgard studied her with narrowed eyes. "How so?" he asked at last, slowly.

"The trolls make ready for war with their ancient foes the elves," she answered. "Erelong Illrede Troll-King leads a mighty host against Alfheim, most likely striking first at Imric here in England. Among Imric's mightiest warriors, because iron and holy things trouble him not, as well as because of great strength and warlock knowledge, will be his foster-son Skafloc, Orm's child who sits in your rightful seat. Now if you sailed quickly to Illrede, and offered him good gifts and the services of your human-like powers as well as telling him your descent, you could find a high place in his army. At the sack of Elfheugh you could slay Imric and Skafloc, and Illrede would most likely make you earl of the British elflands. Thereafter, as you learned sorcery, you would wax ever greater—aye, you might learn how to change Imric's work and make yourself like a true elf or troll, ageless till the end of the world."

Valgard laughed, harshly and mirthlessly, like the yelp of a hunting wolf. "Indeed that is well!" he cried. "Murderer and outlaw, not even human, I have naught to lose and much to gain. If so be I join the hosts of cold and darkness, then I will join them with all my heart, and in battles such as men have never dreamed drown my misery and loneliness. Oh, woman, woman, a mighty thing have you done to me, and it is evil, but I thank you for it!"

Fiercely he loved her, but when later he spoke above the whistling gale it was in a cold and level tone.

"How will I get to Trollheim?" he asked.

The woman opened a great chest and took forth a leather sack tied at the mouth. "When your longship is bound, untie this," she said. "It holds a wind which will blow you thither, and you will have witch-sight to see the troll garths."

"But what of my men?"

"They will be part of your gift to Illrede. The trolls have great sport in hunting men across the mountains."

Valgard shrugged, "Since I am to be troll, let me also be my blood true in such treachery," he said wearily. "But what else shall I give which will please him? He must have enough gold and jewels and costly stuffs."

"Give him that which is more," said the woman. "Orm has two fair daughters, and the trolls are lustful."

"Not those two," said Valgard in honor. "I grew up with them. And I have done them enough ill already."

"Those two indeed," said the woman. "For if Illrede is to take you in service, he must be sure you have broken all human ties."

Still Valgard refused. But she clung to him and kissed him and wove him a tale of the dark splendors he could await, until at last he agreed.

"But I wonder who you are, most evil and most beautiful of all the world," he said.

She laughed softly, cuddled on his breast. "You will forget me when you have had a few captured elf women."

"Nay—nay, never can I forget you, beloved, who broke me as you would."

Now the woman held Valgard in her house for as long as she deemed needful, making some pretense of brewing enchantments to restore the witch-sight to him. Even this was hardly of use, since her beauty could hold him more surely than iron chains.

Snow was falling endlessly through the dusk when she said at last, "You had best start out now."

"We," he answered. "You must come along, for I cannot live without you." His great hands fondled her. "If you come not willingly, I will carry you, but come you must."

"As you will," she sighed. "Though you may feel otherwise when I have given you sight."

She stood up, looking down at his huge seated form, and her slender hand touched the strong lines and angles of his face. Her red mouth curved in a strangely wistful smile.

"Hate is a hard master," she breathed. "I had not thought to have joy again, Valgard, but now it is a cruel wrench to bid you farewell. All good luck to you, my dearest. And now—" her fingertips brushed his eyes "—see!"

And Valgard saw.

Like smoke in the wind, the well-kept little house and the tall white woman wavered to his vision. With a sudden ghastly fear, he willed to see them not with magic-tricked mortal eyes, but as they really were—

He sat in a smoky hovel of mud and wattles, where one tiny dung fire cast a feeble glow on the disordered heaps of bones and rags, rusted metal tools and evilly twisted implements of sorcery. He looked up into the dim eyes of a hideous ancient hag, whose bald toothless head was a fleshless mask of wrinkled skin drawn over a lolling skull, to whose shriveled breast clung a great rat.

Wild with horror, he stumbled to his feet. The witch leered at him, her cackle rising over the screeching storm: "Beloved, beloved, shall we away to your ship? You swore you would not part from me."

Rage leaped up in Valgard's heart and contorted his face until it was scarce human. "For *you* I am outlaw!" he howled, and he grabbed his ax and struck at her. Even as he smote, her body shrank. Two rats sprang across the floor. The ax thudded into the ground just as they went down a hole.

Foaming like a maddened beast, Valgard took a stick and thrust it into the fire. When it was well alight, he touched it to the dry wood of the hutch. He stood outside while it burned, ready to strike with his ax at anything which might show itself. But there were only the leaping flames and the piping wind and the snow hissing as it blew into the fire.

When only ashes remained, Valgard shouted forth into the night: "For you I have lost home and kin and soul, for you I am resolved to forswear my lifetime and league with the lands of darkness, for you I have become a—troll! Very well, witch, if still you live, I will follow your advice. I will become earl of all the trolls in England—perhaps even one night king of all Trollheim—and I shall hound you down with all the powers I have. You too, like men and elves and all else in my way, will feel my vengeance, and never will I rest until I have flayed alive you who broke my heart with a shadow!"

He wheeled about and loped eastward, soon lost in the flying snow. Crouched below the earth, witch and familiar grinned at each other. This was just as they had planned.

The crew of Valgard's ships were the worst of vikings, most outlawed from their homelands and all unwelcome wherever they went. Thus he had bought a garth of his own where they might winter. They lived well, on meat and ale and wine stolen during the summer, with women and thralls likewise reaved, but were so quarrelsome and unruly that only their chief could hold them together.

When word of his outlawry reached them, they knew it would not be long ere all men in the Danelaw came to put an end to them, so they busked the ships and themselves to sail. But they could not agree on whither it should be, now in winter, and there was much dispute and some killing. They might have sat thus till their enemies were upon them had Valgard not returned.

He came late at night into the great hall. It was a wild place, where the huge burly hairy men sat draining horn after horn, growing drunk until their shouting shook the walls. Many snored on the floor beside the dogs, while steel flashed between others, whose comrades were more apt to egg them on than step between them. To and fro in the brawling fire-bloodied company scurried the terrified thralls, and women who had long since wept out all their tears went from hand to hand.

Valgard stepped into the hall and up to the empty high seat—a tall and terrible figure, face set in even grimmer lines than his men remembered, the great ax which had begun to be called Brother-slayer over one shoulder. Silence spread in waves through the hall as folk noticed him, until at last only the crackling flames had voice down its length.

Valgard spoke: "It is plain we cannot stay here much longer, but that may be just as well. I know a place where we can win even greater wealth and fame, and thither we sail the dawn after tomorrow."

"Where is that, and why not leave tomorrow?" asked one of his captains, a scarred old outlaw by name Steingrim.

"As to the last, I have a business here in England which we will attend tomorrow," quoth Valgard. "And as to the first, our goal is Finnmark."

Now a great uproar arose. Steingrim finally raised his voice above it: "That is the worst rede I ever heard. Finnmark is poor and lonely, and lies across seas which are dangerous even in summer. What can we win there save death, by drowning or by the sorcerers who dwell in the land, or at best a few miserable earth huts to huddle in through a long cruel winter? Near at hand are England, Scotland, Ireland, Orkney, or even Valland south of the channel, and in all there is a good booty."

"I have given my orders, and you will follow them," said Valgard bleakly.

"Not I," answered Steingrim. "I think you have gone mad in the forest."

Like a leaping wildcat, Valgard was out of his seat and up to the captain. His ax, already aloft, crashed down into Steingrim's skull.

A man yelled and thrust at Valgard with a spear. The berserker sidestepped, yanked the shaft from his hands, and drove it through him. Pulling the ax from Steingrim's head, Valgard stood looming in the firelight with his eyes like flakes of sea-ice. He asked very quietly: "Does anyone else wish to argue with me?"

None spoke or moved. Valgard stepped back up to his high seat and said: "I know my plan looks foolish, but the fact is I have word of a great garth built in Finnmark just this summer, where all a man could wish is stored. They will not await vikings in winter, so we can take it easily enough. Nor do I fear rough weather on the way, for we have spent all winter at sea before this."

This seemed well to the crew, who remembered how Valgard's leadership had been to their good, so they shouted they would follow him. After the feast was under way again, he gathered his captains.

"We have a place near here to sack ere leaving England," he said. "'Twill be no hard task, and good booty is to be had."

"What place is that?" asked one man.

"That of Orm the Strong, who is now dead and cannot ward it."

Even the outlaws thought this would be an evil deed, but they dared not gainsay their chief.

9

Ketil's grave-ale became also a feast for Asmund and Orm. Men drank silent and sorrowful, for Orm had been a great man and he and his sons well-liked. Despite the frozen ground, the thralls began making a howe the day after the murders.

Orm's best ship was dragged from its house into the grave. In it were laid many costly treasures, and meat and drink for the long voyage, horses and dogs were killed and put in the ship, and all whom Valgard had slain were placed in it with the best of clothes, weapons, and armor, and with hell-shoes on their feet.

When the task was done, some days later, Aelfrida came forth. She stood in the dull gray light of the lowering winter day, looking down at the still, dead faces of Orm and Ketil and Asmund. Her unbound hair swept down to their breasts and hid her own face from those who stood watching.

"The priest says it would be a sin, or I would slay myself now and be laid beside you," she whispered. "Weary will life be. You were good boys, Ketil and Asmund, and your mother is lonely for your laughter. It seems but yesterday I sang you to sleep on my breast, you were so little then, and all at once you were great long-legged youths, goodly to look on and a pride to Orm and me—and now you lie so quietly, with the snow drifting down on your faces. Strange—" She shook her head. "I cannot understand you are slain. It is not real to me."

She smiled down at Orm. "Often did we quarrel," she murmured, "but that meant naught, for you loved me and—and I you. You were good to me, Orm, and the world is all at once so cold, so cold, now you are dead. This I ask all-merciful God: that He forgive certain acts you did against His law. For you were ignorant of much, however wise with a ship or with your hands to make me shelves and chests and little carven toys . . . And if so be God cannot receive you in Heaven, then I pray Him I too may descend to Hell to be with you—aye, even if you go to your heathen gods, even there I would I could follow you. Now farewell, Orm, whom I loved and still love—farewell."

She bent and kissed him. "Cold are your lips, Orm," she said, and looked bewilderedly about her. "Thus did you never kiss me, Orm. This is not you, dead in the ship—but where are you, Orm?"

They led her out of the ship, and the thralls labored long casting earth over it and the grave-chamber built on its deck. When they were done, the howe rose hugely at the edge of the sea and the waves came up the beach to sing a dirge at its foot.

The priest, who had not approved of this heathen burial, would not consecrate the ground, but he did whatever else he could and Asgerd paid him for many masses for the souls of the dead.

There was a young man, Erlend Thorkelsson, who was betrothed to Asgerd. "Empty is this garth now that its men are gone," quoth he.

"So it is," replied the maiden. A cold sea-wind, blowing fine snowflakes, ruffled her heavy locks.

"Best I and a few friends should stay here some days and get the place in order," he said. "Then I would we should be wed, Asgerd, and thereafter your mother and sister can come live with us."

"I will not wed you till Valgard has been hanged and his men burned in their house," she said angrily.

Erlend smiled without mirth. "That will not be long," he said. "Already the war-arrow goes from hand to hand. In a few days the land will be rid of that pest."

"It is well," nodded Asgerd.

Now many of those who had come to the feast went home, but the folk of the garth sat behind, and also Erlend and some half-dozen other neighbors. As night fell, a strong wind came with snow on its wings, howling around the hall. There was hail too, banging on the roof like night-gangers thumping their heels on the ridgepole. The hall was long and dark and cheerless, and all folk on the place huddled together at one end of it. They spoke little, and the horns passed often.

Once Aelfrida stirred from her silence. "I hear something out there," she said.

"Naught can I hear, and naught would be abroad tonight," answered Asgerd.

Freda, who liked not her mother's empty stare, touched her and said timidly, "All alone are you not, Mother. Your daughters have not forgotten you."

"Aye—aye!" Aelfrida smiled. "Now you are all which is left—Orm's seed dies not, and the long dear nights we had are not in vain—" She looked into Erlend's face. "Be good to your wife. She is of the blood of chieftains."

"What else could I be but good to *her*?" he said.

There came of a sudden a great beating on the door. Above the hooting wind rose the shout: "Open! Open or we break in!"

Men clutched for their weapons as a thrall opened the door—and was at once cut down by a flashing ax. Huge and grim, guarded by two men's shields held before him, snow mantling his shoulders, Valgard stood looking in.

He spoke into the silence: "Let all women here come outside and they shall live. But the hall is ringed with men and I am going to burn it."

A cast spear clanged off the iron-bound shields. The sharp reek of smoke in the hall seemed to grow stronger.

"Have you not done enough?" shrieked Freda. "Burn the hall if you will, but I for one would rather stay within than take my life of you."

"Then forward!" shouted Valgard, and ere those in the hall could stop him he and a dozen of his men had come inside. Across the long fire they leaped, and up to the high seats.

"Not while I live!" cried Erlend, rushing at Valgard with drawn sword. The ax Brotherslayer flashed down, knocking the blade from his hand with a mighty clang and burying its beak in his side. He pitched to the floor and Valgard went up to the high seats and grabbed Freda's wrist. Another of his men took Asgerd, and the rest formed a shield-burg about the two. They fought back to the door, killing three men on the way.

The others made a wild rush to follow them, but were hewed down by vikings warding all ways out. Aelfrida cried and ran to the door, and her the men let go through.

Valgard was just straightening up from binding Asgerd and Freda. The roof of the hall was already burning brightly, the roaring flames painting faces bloody. Aelfrida clung to Valgard's arm and shrieked up into his face.

"Beast and monster and unnatural son," she cried, "what new evil are you working on the last of your kin? What madness turns you on your own sisters, who have done you naught but good, and how can you stamp on your mother's heart? Let them go, let them go!"

Valgard watched her with moveless face and pale cold eyes. "You are not my mother," he said at last, and struck her. She fell senseless in the snow and he turned away, dragging the two captive girls aboard his ship.

"Where are we going?" sobbed Freda, while Asgerd spat at him like an angry cat.

He smiled at them, grimly. "I will not harm you," he said. "Indeed, I do you a service, since you are to be given to a great king." He sighed. "I envy him. But knowing my men, I had best watch over you."

Such of the women as did not wish to be burned alive went out to the raiders, but many stayed inside with their men. The hall burned brightly, lighting up the garth for a great ways around, and erelong the other buildings had caught fire.

Valgard summoned his men before dawn, for he knew the neighbors would soon see the burning, if they had not already done so, and arrive in force. The vikings entered the ships and stood out to sea, rowing against a wind which blew icy waves inboard.

"Never will we reach Finnmark like this," grumbled Valgard's steersman.

"I think we will," he answered, and untied the knots of the witch's leather bag. At once the wind swung around until it was coming from astern, blowing directly northeast in a great steady drone. When the sails were set, the dozen ships fairly leaped ahead.

When the folk of the neighborhood reached Orm's garth, they found only charred timbers and smoldering ash-heaps. A few women were about, sobbing in the dreary dawn-light. Aelfrida alone did not weep, or indeed say anything. She sat on the great howe with hair and dress blowing wild in the wind, sat unmoving, empty-eyed, staring out to sea.

Now for three days and nights Valgard's ships ran before an unchanging gale. One of them foundered in the mighty waves, and three others dropped sail in the dark and rowed away, and there was uneasy muttering everywhere. But Valgard overawed all thoughts of mutiny.

He stood nearly all the time in the prow of his ship, wrapped in a long leather cloak, with salt and rime crusted on his helmet, brooding darkly over the sea. Once a man dared gainsay him, and he slew the fellow on the spot and cast the body overboard. He said little, and his crew trembled when his uncanny stare rested on them.

He would not answer the pleas of Asgerd and Freda for word on where they were bound, but he gave them well of food and drink and saw that they were not bothered by the crewmen.

Freda would not eat at first. "Naught do I take from that thief and murderer," she said. The salt streaking her lovely pale cheeks was not all from the sea.

"Eat to keep your strength," counseled Asgerd. "You do not take it from him, since he has robbed it from others, and the chance may come to us to escape. If now we pray God for help—"

"That I forbid," said Valgard, "and if I hear any such word from you I will gag you."

"As you will," said Freda, "but a prayer is more in the heart than the mouth."

"And not very useful in either place," grinned Valgard, wolf-like. "Many a woman has squawked to her God when I got hands on her, and little did it avail. Nevertheless, I will have no more mention of gods in my ship."

He lapsed into his dark thoughts and the sisters into silence. Nor did the men say much, so that the only sounds were the scream of wind in the rigging and the roar of sea past the bows. Overhead flew gray clouds from which snow and hail often whirled, and the vessels were alone on the running waves.

On the third day, near nightfall, with clouds so low and heavy as almost to bring dusk by themselves, they raised Finnmark. Bleak and terrible rose the cliffs from the sea, surf snarling and shattering against them and naught on their heights save snow and ice and a few low wind-twisted trees.

"Ill looks this land," shivered Valgard's steersman, "and I see naught of that great garth whereof you spoke."

"Sail into that fjord ahead," commanded the chief.

The wind blew them directly into it. Under mighty and sullen cliffs the ships sailed, through the thickening snowy twilight to ground on a rocky beach. Looking ahead, Valgard saw the waiting trolls.

They were not quite as tall as men, but nigh twice or thrice as broad, with long arms like tree boughs and clawed splay feet. Their skin was green and cold and slippery, moving on their stone-hard flesh. Few of them had hair, and their great round heads, with the flat noses, huge fanged mouths, pointed ears, and eyes deep buried in their bony sockets, were like skulls. Their eyes were all black, pits of inky darkness and brooding horror.

They were for the most part naked, or wore but a few skins, even in the freezing wind. Their weapons were chiefly clubs, and axes, spears, arrows, and slings using stone, all too heavy for men to swing. But some wore helms and byrnies and carried weapons of the dwarf-forged alloys that were hard as iron.

Valgard could not but shudder at the sight. "Are you cold?" asked one of his men.

"No—no—'tis naught," he muttered. And to himself: "Indeed I hope the witch was right and the elf women fairer than these. But they will make wondrous good warriors."

Now the vikings drew their ships ashore and stood uncertain in the gathering dusk. And Valgard saw the trolls descend on the beach.

The fight was brief and horrible, for the men could not see their foes. Now and again a troll might chance to touch iron and be seared by it, but they knew how to avoid the metal. Their laughter boomed hollowly between the cliffs, great rolling peals of mad thunder, as they dashed out men's brains, or ripped them limb from limb, or hunted them up through the mountains.

Valgard's steersman saw his comrades die and his chief lean unmoving on his ax. The viking roared and rushed on the berserker. "This is your doing!" he shouted.

"Indeed it is," quoth Valgard, and met him in a clamor of iron. It was not long before he had slain the steersman, but by then the rest of the battle was over.

Now the troll captain approached Valgard, the ground quivering ever so faintly under his tread. "We had word of your coming," his deep voice rumbled in the human tongue, "and give many thanks for the sport. Now the king awaits you."

"I come at once," said Valgard.

Asgerd and Freda had swooned, and were not aware of being borne along a deep gorge and up a barren mountainside and past sentries into a cave. They came at last into the great hall of Illrede himself.

It was a huge place, hewn out of rock but furnished with magnificence raided from elves, dwarfs, goblins, and other folk, including men. Great gems blazed on the walls amid rare tapestries, costly goblets and cloths were on the cunningly wrought tables, and the long fires burning down the length of the hall lit the rich garments of the troll lords and their ladies.

Thralls of elf, dwarf, or goblin race scurried about with trenchers of meat and bowls of drink. It was a high feast, for which many human and faerie babies had been stolen, along with cattle, horses, and wines of the south. There was music of the snarling sort the trolls liked, rattling out of the air.

About the walls stood guards, moveless as graven images, the ruddy smoky light glinting on their spears. Down the length of the tables, the trolls were gobbling and guzzling, quarreling with each other in a din of voices. But the great lords of Trollheim sat quiet in their high seats.

Valgard's eyes went to Illrede. The troll king was huge of girth and stature, with a wrinkled massive face and a long beard of green tendrils. There was darkness and horror in the eyes that stared at the newcomer, and a fear he sought to hide ran coldly along the changeling's backbone.

"Greeting, great king," he said. "I am Valgard Berserk, come from England to seek a place in your company. I am told you are father to my mother, and fain would I claim my heritage."

Illrede slowly nodded his gold-crowned head. "That I know," he said. "And welcome, Valgard, to Trollheim, your home." His dreadful eyes swung to the maidens, stirring to wakefulness on the floor. "But who are these?"

"A small gift," said Valgard firmly, "children of my foster-father. I hope they will please you."

"Ho—ho, ho—ho, ho, ho!" Suddenly Illrede's laughter was echoing through the great chill hall. "Ho, a goodly gift! Long is it since I held a human man in my arms—aye, welcome, welcome, Valgard!"

He sprang to the floor, which trembled under his mighty weight, and went over to stand above the girls. Freda and Asgerd looked about them in bewilderment.

"Where are we?" cried Freda. "A dark cave, with echoes that have no voice—"

"You should see your new home," grinned Illrede, and touched the sisters" eyes. And at once they had the witch-sight, and saw the hall and him stooping over them, and then their courage broke and their screams were like those of mad beasts.

Illrede laughed again.

10

The elf raid on Trollheim was to be a strong one. Fifty longships were manned with the best warriors of Britain's elves, and veiled and warded by the sorceries of Imric and his wisest warlocks. It was thought they could under these spells sail unseen into the very fjords of Finnmark's troll lands, but how deeply inland they could thrust thereafter would depend on the strength of the guard. Skafloc thought they could get even into Illrede's own halls and bring back the king's head, and he was wild to go.

"Be not too reckless," cautioned Imric. "Kill and burn, but lose no men in foolish adventures. 'Twill be worth more if you spy out their strength than if you kill a hundred of them."

"We will do both," grinned Skafloc. He stood tall and restless as a young stallion, eyes alight in his lean face, the long tawny hair tumbling from under his gleaming helmet.

"I know not—I know not." The elf-earl shook his head. "I feel, somehow, that no good will come of this trip, and am fain to halt it."

"If you do that, we will go anyway," said Skafloc.

"Aye, so you will. And I may be wrong. Go, then, and luck be with you."

On a night just after sunset, the warriors embarked. A moon newly risen cast silver and shadow on the crags and scaurs of the elf-hills, on the beach from which they rose, on the clouds racing eastward on a great gale which seemed to fill the sky with its clamor. The moonlight ran in shards and ripples over the waves, which tumbled and roared, white-maned and angry, on the rocks. The light flashed off the weapons and armor of the elf warriors, eerie silver in the shouting night. The black-and-white longships drawn up on the beach seemed but fleeting shadows and light-ripples.

Skafloc stood wrapped in his great cape, the wind streaming his hair, and watched his men embark. To him, a white loveliness in the moonlight with her hair like silver and her eyes cloudy with cold mystery, came Leea.

"Now bid me farewell, foster-mother, and sing a song for my luck," cried Skafloc.

"I cannot bid you goodbye properly, for I can come no closer to that iron byrnie of yours," quoth Leea in her voice that was like wind and rippling water and silver bells heard from afar. "And I have a black feeling my spells will avail naught against the ill luck wafting for you." Her eyes sought his in the fleeting moonlight. "I know, with a sureness beyond proof, that you sail into a trap, and I beg you, by the milk I gave you as a child and the kisses as a man, to stay home this one time."

"That would be a fine deed for an elf chief, given command of a great raid that may bring back his foeman's head," cried Skafloc in anger. "Not for you nor anyone else would I do so shameful a thing."

"Aye—aye." Sudden tears glimmered in Leea's eyes. "Men, whose span of years is so bitterly short, rush to death in their youth as to a maiden's arms. A few years ago I rocked you in your cradle, Skafloc, a few months ago I lay out with you in the light summer nights, and to me, undying, the times are almost the same. And no different, in the same blink of years, is the day your bloody corpse will lie stiff awaiting the ravens. I will not ever forget you, Skafloc, but I fear I have kissed you for the last time."

And she sang in her lovely voice:

Seaward blows the wind tonight,
and the seamen, never resting,
rise from house to take their flight
with the gulls" and spindrift's questing.
Woman's arms, and firelit hearth,
kith and kin, can never hold them
when the wind beyond their garth
of the running tides has told them.
Spume and seaweed shall enfold them.

Wind, ah wind, old wanderer,
gray and swift-foot, ever crying,
woman curses, who, from her,
calls forth man to doom and dying.
Seamen, kissed by laughing waves,
cold and salt-sweet, hearts deceiving,
shall be borne to restless graves
when the sea their life is reaving.
And their women will be grieving.

Skafloc liked not this song, which seemed one of ill luck rather than good, but as soon as he was aboard his ship he forgot it in the joy of departure.

"This gale has blown for three days now," said Goltan, a comrade of his. "And it has the smell of a wizard breeze. Mayhap some warlock sails eastward."

"If he has been three days at sea, his ship is but mortal," laughed Skafloc. "We travel faster."

Now the sails were raised and the slim black-and-silver dragon craft leaped ahead. Like the wind itself they went, like flying snow and freezing spindrift white under the moon, waves hissing in their wake, a long bounding over the clamorous waters. Swiftest of all in faerie, afoot or on horse or aboard ship, were the elves, and ere midnight Finnmark's cliffs loomed ahead.

"Now comes a goodly fight," said Skafloc, his teeth gleaming forth. And he quoth:

Elves come early
east to Trollheim,
spears and singing
swords their presents.
Good are gifts they
give, for troll-men:
sundered skulls and
splitted bellies.

Trolls shall tumble
(tumult rages),
fear of firebrands
freeing bowels.
Kin, be kind to
clamoring troll-men:
have they headaches,
hew the heads off.

The elves grinned, along the length of the plunging ship, and readied their weapons. Into the fjord the fleet steered, busked for battle, but no sign of troll guards met their questing eyes. Instead they saw ships drawn up on the beach—eight mortal longships, whose crews were bloodily strewn over the rocks.

Skafloc leaped ashore with sword drawn and cloak flying winglike behind him. "Strange is this," he said, and his hackles rose.

"Belike the ships landed here and were set on by trolls," quoth Goltan. "'Twas but a short time ago—see, the blood is still wet—and so the troll guards may still be at Illrede's garth reporting the matter."

"Why, then, that is wondrous luck!" cried Skafloc, and winded his great lur horn. Not he nor the elves gave further thought to the dead men, who were only humans.

At the bray of the horn, the elves sprang into the shallows and dragged their ships ashore. Some few stood by to guard the vessels, while Skafloc led the main troop along the inland trail.

Through a grim black gorge they went, and came out onto a mountainside where the snow glittered dazzling under the moon and bare peaks snarled at the frosty, galing sky. The wind shrieked and tore at them, cuffing with hands of icy cold, and the ragged clouds still blew across the moon's face. Lithe as cats, the elves made their way over cliff and crag, up the mountain toward the great cave gaping in its front.

Now as they neared the cave they saw a company of trolls come out, belike the sea watchers returning to their posts. Skafloc's cry rose over the wind: "Swiftly, swiftly, and we can cut them off!"

Like a panther he sprang, the elves beside and behind him, and ere the trolls had their wits, metal was howling about their ears. They fell back, and Skafloc's band pushed into the cave itself.

Din of weapons seemed even more clamorous in the narrow descending tunnel. The wild war-shouts of the elves and the booming cries of the trolls rolled in broken echoes down the corridor. Skafloc and Goltan led the way, their swords a blur before them, and troll after troll sank under their feet.

A great warrior thrust at Skafloc with a spear like a young tree. The man smote with his sword, striking the shaft aside, and the iron blade seared into the troll's breast. A mighty club thundered for his head, but he caught the blow on his shield. It rang like a great gong, and the shock sent him staggering back. He fell to one knee, but stabbed upward into the troll's belly. Rising, he swept his glaive in a yelling arc and another troll's head leaped from its shoulders.

Now the retreating trolls came into a great room. The elves cried their delight at having a space big enough for their kind of fighting. Longbows were strung, and the gray-feathered arrows flew in a storm that smote many a troll. Other elves fought hand to hand, leaping, dodging, thrusting in a blur of speed.

Some elves died, with shattered skulls or ripped hides, but the troll corpses were heaped high. At the door warding the way to the king's feasting hall, the royal guards stood in a grim close line, shields before them, and the shock of the elf charge rebounded.

"Let me show you how to get in!" shouted Skafloc. Streaming green troll blood and some of his own red, with dented helm and shield and nicked sword, he laughed in glee as he seized a spear, ran forward, and vaulted over the foemen's heads into the hall beyond.

He struck down three trolls from behind in as many blows of his dreaded iron blade. The guards turned to face him, and the elves rallied and rushed on them—bore them in a living tide into the troll-king's hall!

Skafloc yelled as he saw Illrede himself, sitting rock-like in the high seat but clutching a mighty spear. His sword screamed, mowing trolls like ripe wheat, as he rushed forward. Then a man rose in his path to dispute the way.

For a moment Skafloc stood in utter astonishment, seeing his own face glare at him behind the descending ax. Then with elf swiftness he skipped aside, but the stranger's weapon sundered his battered shield and laid open his left arm.

Skafloc swung, and iron met iron in a clamor of sparking fury. For a short space they traded blows, and deeply did they gash each other. Then a troll attacked Skafloc from the side. He thrust at him, and had a hard fight ere the troll was slain. Meantime the tide of battle had borne the stranger away, but he was doing great slaughter among the elves. He fought his way over to Illrede, and the remaining trolls rallied about the two. In a quick, strong push they cut through their foes to a great door in the rear of the hall. Through this they went.

"After them!" roared Skafloc, mad with battle fury.

Goltan and the other elf captains held him back. "'Twould be foolhardy," they said. "See, the door leads to lightless descending caverns whence we could scarce hope to return alive. Best we bar it on this side instead, that Illrede call not the monsters of the inner earth up against us."

"Aye—you are right," said Skafloc grudgingly.

His eyes swept the hall, and then all at once came to rest in a surprise scarce less than when he had seen his own shape among the trolls. Two mortal women lay bound near the high seat.

Skafloc strode over, and his knife gleamed briefly to unfasten them. They shrank back in horror, and one, a tall fair-haired may with flashing blue eyes, snarled at him: "Traitor and murderer, what new evil do you wreak?"

"Why—" Skafloc was taken aback. Like most folk of faerie, he had learned the speech of men, but had had little use of it. His accent held the strange singing note of the elf-tongue.

"Why, what have I done—?" He smiled. "Unless you like being bound."

"Mock us not, Valgard, on top of all your other evil deeds," said the golden-haired maiden wearily.

"I am not Valgard, nor do I know him unless he is that man with the trolls whom I fought just now—but you could not see that from here. I am Skafloc of Alfheim, and no friend to trolls."

"Aye—aye, Asgerd!" cried the younger girl of a sudden. "He is not Valgard, in truth he is not. See—he wears a different garment and speaks strangely—"

"I know not," mumbled Asgerd. "Was all the clamor and death about us but some new trick? Is this not an evil enchantment to beguile us—? Oh, I know naught save that Erlend is dead—" She began to sob, dry racking coughs that had no tears.

"No, no—" The younger maiden clung to Skafloc's shoulders, searching his face, smiling through a mist of tears like springtime sunshine through rain. "No, stranger, you are not Valgard though you look much like him. Your eyes are warm and bright, your mouth is kind and glad—Oh, I know, I know!"

Skafloc looked long at her. She was only of middle height, but it was all a vision of supple slender youthful beauty gleaming through the rags of her dress. Her tresses were long and lustrous bronze-brown, sparkled with red, her face a sweet molding of broad forehead and pertly tilted nose and wide soft mouth. Under dark brows, her long-lashed eyes were huge and brilliant, a haunting gray waking some dim half-memory which he could not place in Skafloc's mind.

"Who are you?" he asked wonderingly.

"I am Freda Ormsdaughter, and this is my sister Asgerd," she said. "But who are you, warrior—?"

"Skafloc Imric's-Foster, of Alfheim's English lands," he replied.

She shrank back, crossing herself, and somehow he was pained she should fear him.

Now the elves went to work with plundering. They took what they could of the treasures in Illrede's hall, and released his slaves of their own race. Then they set the hall ablaze and went outside in quest of other places. Soon they had found the houses and barns about the cave, great buildings of stone and timber that burned brightly against the star-frosted sky. What trolls they found they put to the sword, but there were not many of these.

"It seems to me Trollheim's strength is naught to fear," said Skafloc.

"Be not so sure," replied Valka the Wise. "Indeed, I would we had seen something of his levies ere this. I like not the silence and emptiness."

"Not all empty," laughed Skafloc. "We have won a rich booty. Now I think if we go back to the ships we can be at home ere dawn."

Asgerd and Freda stood numbly in the bitter cold, watching from their witch-sighted eyes the elves at work. Strange were these tall warriors, moving like rippling water with never a sound of footfall, but byrnies chiming silvery through the night. White and ageless, of thin-carved, high-boned features, with beast ears and eyes of blind mystery, they were a sight of terror to mortal gaze.

Among them moved Skafloc, soft-footed and graceful as they, seeing like a cat, speaking their own eldritch tongue. Yet he was a man to the eye, and Freda, thinking of the warm touch of him, unlike the cool silky-skinned firmness of elf flesh, felt sure he was human even to his soul.

"He is a heathen, to dwell among these creatures," said Asgerd once.

"Aye—perhaps—but he is kind, and he saved us from—from—" Freda shuddered, and wrapped the cloak Skafloc had given her more tightly about her slim form.

Now the elf chief blew his horn for withdrawal, and the long, silent file began wending its way down the mountain. Skafloc walked beside Freda, saying naught but letting his eyes dwell on her.

She was young, younger even than he, the awkward grace of a colt still in her long legs and slim-waisted body. She bore her head high, the bronze sheen of her hair seeming to crackle in the frosty moonlight—but he thought it would be soft to the touch. As they came down the rugged slope he often had to steady her, and her little hand was engulfed in his calloused paw.

But of a sudden there rang between the mountains the bull-bellow of a troll horn, and another answered it and another, with echoes snarling back from the cliffs and blowing raggedly on the wind. The elves stopped dead a moment, ears cocked, eyes flashing, nostrils quivering as they searched the night for sign of their foemen.

"I think they are ahead of us, cutting off our retreat," said Goltan.

"Ill is that," quoth Skafloc, "but it would be worse to go blundering down the black gorge and have rocks hurled at us from above. We will make our way beside it instead of through it."

He blew a battle call on the lur horn carried for him, and said to Freda and Asgerd: "I fear we must fight through a troll guard. But my men will ward you if you speak not those names which hurt them."

"It would not be good to die without calling on—Him above," said Asgerd. "But we will obey you in this."

Skafloc laughed and laid a hand on Freda's shoulder. "Why, how can we but win when such beauty is to be fought for?" he asked gaily.

He told off two elves to carry the girls, and others to form a shield-burg about them. Then, at the head of a wedge formation, he proceeded over the ridge toward the sea.

Lightly went the elves, springing from rock to crag like cats, hauberk scales singing their silver tones and weapons agleam in the moonlight. When they saw the trolls black against the stars, waiting for them, they set up a fierce shout, clashed swords on shields, and leaped to battle.

But Skafloc drew a sharp breath as he saw the size of the troll force. The elves were outnumbered some six to one—and if Illrede could raise that horde so quickly, what might not his full strength be?

"Well," he said, "we will just have to kill six trolls apiece."

Now the elf archers loosed their shafts, and the trolls had naught to match the moon-darkening cloud which sighed over them. Many sank on the spot. But most of the arrows rattled harmlessly off rocks, or stuck in shields, and all were soon spent.

The elves rushed forward, and battle clamored in the night. Roaring troll horns and yelling elf lurs, wolf-howling troll cries and hawk-shrieking elf challenges, thunder of troll axes on elf shields and clash of elf swords falling on troll helmets stormed up to the far stars and the wavering northern lights.

Ax and sword! Spear and club! Cloven shield and sundered helm and ripped byrnie! Red gush of elf blood meeting cold green flow of troll's! Auroras dancing death-dances overhead!

Two tall figures, scarce to be told from each other, loomed over the battle. Valgard's thundering ax and Skafloc's flying sword hewed a bloody way through the battle. The berserker was foaming in his madness, howling and smiting at all before him; Skafloc was silent, but scarcely less wild as he moved speed-blurred in the fight.

But the trolls were hemming in the elves, seeking to cramp them—for in close quarters, where the swiftness and agility of the elves were hampered, the sheer strength of the trolls counted heavily. It seemed to Skafloc that for each gaping grinning face that sank before him, two more rose out of the blood-steaming snow. He had to stand his ground, with sweat rivering off him to freeze on his face, and hew, hew at the enemy.

Thus it was Valgard who came up to him, Valgard mad with the berserkergang and hate for all things elfly—most of all for Imric's foster. They met almost breast to breast, glaring into each other's eyes in the uncertain moonlight.

Skafloc's blade clanged on Valgard's helm, and the mighty blow dented the metal—could have shorn through had the sword not been blunted by use. Valgard's ax bit an edge from Skafloc's new shield, which cried out in metal pain.

Skafloc thrust for Valgard's neck, and laid open his cheek so that the teeth grinned forth. The berserker howled anew and pressed in with a thunderous hail of blows, banging on Skafloc's helm and shield till the man reeled from the blows.

But he thrust again, and as Valgard sought to parry with his ax handle, Skafloc changed in mid-motion to a downward arc that bit deep into the berserker's leg. Howling, Valgard fell back, and Skafloc pressed in on him.

A blow as of a thunderbolt dinned on his helm, and he fell forward to hands and knees. Illrede Troll-King had loomed up beside him and swung his huge stone-headed club. Valgard snarled, and rushed forward with ax descending. Elf-swift, Skafloc rolled aside. The weapon clove where he had been, into the neck of an elf in the shield-burg. As that one fell, Valgard smote a second time, at the one behind, but it was into the burden he bore that the ax sank.

The elf sprang away, being weaponless, and the shield-burg moved after Skafloc, who was now fighting elsewhere. Valgard was alone.

Swaying on his feet and pouring blood, the berserker stood over Asgerd's body. "I had not meant that," he muttered. "But indeed my ax is accursed—or is it me?" He passed a hand over his eyes, puzzledly. "Only—they are not my kin, are they?"

Weak with the passing of the berserkergang, he sat down beside Asgerd. The battle moved away from him. "Now there are only Skafloc and Freda to kill, then all the blood I once thought my own is gone," he said, stroking her heavy golden braids. He took the ax from her side. "And it might be well to do it with you, Brother-slayer. Aelfrida too, if she still lives, I could kill—why not? She is not my mother, my mother is a great hideous monster chained in Imric's dungeons. Aelfrida, who sang me to sleep, is not my mother—"

Ill went it with the elves, but they fought valiantly. In their van, Skafloc shouted to them, rallying them, summoning them, and his blade yelled death to the trolls. None could stand before the whirling steel, and with his men he slowly hewed a dreadful seaward way.

Once he faltered, when Goltan fell with a spear through him. "Now I am one comrade poorer," he said, "and it is a wealth not won back." Then his shout rose again: "Hai, Alfheim! Forward, forward!"

And so at last a remnant of the elves broke through the trolls and retreated to the beach. Valka the Wise, Flam of Orkney, Hlokkan Redspear, and other great elf warriors fell in the rear-guard, but the rest won down to the ships which waited for them, invisible save to the greater warlocks among the trolls.

Half their ships they burned, there on the beach in Finnmark, for they would be empty. The others were all undermanned, and none of the crews but had grievous wounds, but still they made shift to get under way ere the trolls came down to the shore.

Freda, huddled in the bottom of Skafloc's dragon, saw him standing tall and bloody against the sinking moon, and she saw him making rune signs in the air and speaking strange words. A wind sprang up behind the elf fleet, a gale, a storm, and with iron-taut sails and bow-bent masts and groaning wind-harped rigging the ships leaped forward. Faster and ever faster they fled, like the flying spindrift, like the howling storm, like dream and sorcery and moonlight running over the water. Skafloc stood in the spray-sheeting bows, singing his warlock song, with unhelmed hair flying and ragged byrnie chiming, a figure out of myth and worlds beyond man.

Darkness came to Freda.

11

She awoke on a couch of carved ivory, spread with furs and silks. She had been bathed and dressed in a white samite shift. By her bedside stood a curiously wrought table bearing clustered grapes and other fruits of the southland. But save for this she could only see an endless deep-blue twilight all about her, as if she floated in the womb of infinity.

For a time she could not remember where she might be or what had happened to her, then recollection rushed back and she fell to wild sobbing. Endlessly she wept, alone in the vast blue peace, until she had wept herself out, and then she fell asleep.

Awakening again, she felt marvelous rested, but the silence and loneliness weighed heavily on her. Then looking around, she saw Skafloc approaching, seeming to stride through the blue spaciousness toward her.

No sign of his wounds remained, and he smiled eagerly at her. He wore only a brief, richly broidered tunic and kilt, and the great muscles could be seen rippling under his skin. He sat down on the side of the couch and took her hands and looked into her eyes.

"Do you feel better now?" he asked. "You have slept long."

"I feel well, only—only where am I—?" she answered dazedly.

"In Imric's castle of Elfheugh, in the elf-hills of the northern marshes," said Skafloc, and as her eyes grew wide with fear: "No harm shall come to you here, and all shall be as you wish."

"I thank you," she said, "as well as God Who—"

"Nay, speak not holy names here," said Skafloc, "for elves must flee the sound. But else you are free to do as you wish."

"But you are not an elf," protested Freda.

"No, I am human, but raised among the elves. I am foster to Imric the Guileful, and feel more akin to him than to whoever my real father is."

"How came you to save us? We had despaired—"

Skafloc told briefly of the war and his raid, then smiled and said, "But it is better to speak of you. Who could have had so fair a daughter?"

Freda flushed, but told him of what had happened. He nodded. The name of Orm meant naught to him, for Imric, to break his fosterling's human ties, had brought him up not be curious about his parentage. As for Valgard, Freda knew not save that he was her brother gone mad; Skafloc had sensed an inhumanness about the berserker, but with so much else to think over—especially Freda—did not stop to wonder at its reason or why the two of them should be almost twins. Belike, he thought, Valgard was a man who had become devil-possessed.

Nor did Freda think much about the likeness of the two men, for she could never have mistaken them. Eyes and lips and play of features, manner and touch and thought, were so different in them that she scarce noticed the sameness of height and bone structure and cast of face.

She had not finished her tale ere she was weeping again on Skafloc's breast. He sought to comfort her, for it seemed wrong to him that she should ever know unhappiness, and he whispered certain charms which lifted woe sooner than nature could.

"Dead!" cried Freda. "Dead, all dead, all slain save Valgard and myself. I—I saw him slay Father and Asmund when Ketil was already dead, I saw Mother stretched stark and moveless at his feet, I saw him strike down Asgerd—now only I am left, Skafloc, alone— Oh, Mother, Mother!"

"Be of good cheer," said the man awkwardly. "You are unharmed, and I shall seek out Valgard and revenge you and your folk on him."

"Little good will that do. Orm's garth is an ash heap and all his kin dead save one gone mad and one left homeless and alone." She clung to him, shivering. "I am afraid, Skafloc, I am afraid of the loneliness—"

He ruffled her hair with one hand, while the other tipped her chin back so she looked into his eyes. "You are not alone," he said, smiling, and kissed her. Her lips quivered under his, soft and warm and salty with tears.

"Now 'tis time you broke your fast," he said. There was a dress laid out for her, of the filmy flowing spider silk worn by elf women. Freda blushed hotly as she donned it, for it hid little from Skafloc's frank blue eyes. But she could not but laugh with sheer admiration of the heavy gold rings he put on her slender arms and the diamond-twinkling coronet he set on her flowing locks.

They crossed the invisible floor and came into a long hallway which did not appear at once but grew like a mist about them into solidity. Shining colonnades went down its marbled length, and the richly colored figurings of rugs and tapestries moved in fantastic dances.

Here and there scurried goblin thralls, a race halfway between elf and troll, green-skinned and squat but of not unpleasing aspect. Once Freda shrank against Skafloc with a little cry as a huge yellow demon stalked down the corridor bearing a massive chandelier. Ahead of him scuttled a dwarf with a big shield.

"What was *that*?" whispered Freda.

Skafloc chuckled. "One of the Shen, Cathayan devils whom we took captive in a raid," he said. "He is strong and makes a good slave, but as his kind can only move in straight lines unless deflected by a wall, we must have the dwarf with the shield off which he can rebound at corners."

She laughed with him, and he stood listening in wonder to the clear peal of it. Always in the silvery mirth of the elf women was a hint of malicious mockery, but Freda's laughter came fresh and artless as a spring morning.

The two ate of the rare viands, alone at a small table with music sighing from the air around them. Skafloc quoth:

Food is good for friendship,
fairest one, and wine-cups.
Good it is to gladden
gullets in the morning.
But my eyes, bewildered
by the sight of Freda,
sate themselves on sun-bright
southern maiden's beauty.

She dropped her eyes, feeling her cheeks burn, yet she could not but smile.

Remorse came to her. "How can I laugh so soon after my kin are dead? Broken is the mighty tree whose branches sheltered the land, and now the wind blows cold across the barrens—" She ceased looking for words, saying merely, "Ill is it when good folk die."

"Why, if they were good you need not mourn for them," said Skafloc glibly, "for they are safe from this world's sorrows, come home to Him above. I should think, in truth, that only the sound of your weeping could trouble their bliss."

Freda clung to his arm as they left the room. "I cannot help it," she said, tears filming her gray eyes. "I loved them, and now they are gone and I am left alone."

Skafloc kissed her. "Not while I live," he murmured.

As they entered another great room, whose vaulted ceil was hidden in its own awesome height, Freda saw a woman so lovely she had never imagined the like. Elf she was, with an unearthly beauty that was cold and subtle and resistless. Beside that white goddess, Freda felt small and plain and afraid.

"You see I came back, Leea," Skafloc hailed her in the elf tongue.

"Aye," she replied, "but with little booty, and over half your men dead. It was a fruitless quest."

"Not all fruitless." Skafloc laid an arm about Freda's waist. She crept close to him out of fear of the cold white witch who watched her with a deep sullen anger.

"What do you want with mortal women?" taunted Leea. "Unless your own human blood is calling in your veins."

"Belike so." Skafloc was unmoved by her contempt.

She came close to him and laid a cool hand on his arm, searching his face with her eyes of blue dusk and moonlight. "Skafloc," she said urgently, "get rid of this girl. Send her home if you will not slay her."

"She has no home, and I will not let her wander the roads." Skafloc jeered at Leea: "What do you care what two mortals do?"

"I care," she said sorrowfully, "and I see my prophecy was right. Like calls to like—but not her, Skafloc! Take any mortal maid save this one. There is doom in her—I can feel it, deep within myself. 'Twas not mere chance you found her, and she will wreak ill on you."

"Not Freda," said Skafloc stoutly, and then to change the discourse: "When will Imric return? He had been summoned to council with the Erlking when I came back from Trollheim."

"He will be back soon. Wait until then, Skafloc, and it may well be he can sense the doom I feel over this may and warn you."

"Should I, who have fought trolls and demons and men, care aught for danger a woman brings?" snorted Skafloc. "Go to!" And he led Freda away.

Leea looked wildly after them, then fled through the long halls with tears aglimmer in her eyes.

Skafloc and Freda wandered through the mighty castle, talking eagerly. At last he said: "Now come outside and I will show you something I made for you."

"For me?" she cried.

"For you—and perhaps, if the Norns be kind, me too," he laughed.

They went through the great brazen gates into the snow-decked hills. There was bright sunlight, dazzling on the blue-shadowed whiteness, and no elves were abroad. They walked into the ice-flashing forest, Skafloc's great cloak wrapped around them both. Breath smoked whitely into the frosty blue sky and breathing was a sharp clear sting. The sea thundered grayly on eastern cliffs, and a breeze soughed through the darkling firs.

"It is cold," shivered Freda. The hot ruddy-bronze color of her hair was the only warmth in all that frozen world. "Outside your cloak it is cold."

"Too cold for you to wander begging on the roads."

"There are those who would take me in. We had many friends."

"Indeed, but why go forth to find them when you have them here? And now—see."

They topped a high hill, one of a ring about a little vale. And down there Skafloc had created summer. Green were the trees about a little dancing waterfall, and flowers nodded in the fragrant grass. Birds sang in the glen, fish leaped in the clear cool river, and a doe and her fawn stood watching the humans with trustful eyes.

Freda clapped her hands and cried out. Skafloc smiled. "I made it for you," he said, "because you are of summer and life and joy. Forget the winter and its death and hardness, Freda—here we have our own summer."

They went down into the dale, casting off the broad cloak, and sat close by the waterfall. Breezes ruffled their hair and berries clustered heavily about them. At Skafloc's command, the flowers wove themselves into a chain which he hung about Freda's neck.

She could not fear him or his arts. She lay dreamily back on the grass as he quoth:

Laughter from your lips, dear,
lures me like a war-cry.
Bronze-red locks have bound me:
bonds more strong than iron.
Never have I nodded
neck beneath a yoke, but
wish I now the welcome
warmth of your arms" prison.

Life was made for laughter,
love, and eager heartbeat.

Could I but caress you,
came I to my heaven.
Sorceress, you see me
seek your love with pleading:
how can Skafloc help it
when you have ensnared him?

"It is not meet—" she protested feebly, unable to keep from smiling.

"Why, how can it but be meet? There is nothing else so right and proper."

"You are a heathen, and I—"

"I told you not to speak of such matters. Now you must pay the penalty." And Skafloc kissed her, long and lingeringly. She sought for a moment to fend him off, but she seemed to have no strength, and in the end she gave him back his kiss.

"Now, was that so bad?" he laughed.

"No—" she whispered.

The day ended and night came to the vale of summer. They lay by the rushing waterfall and listened to the nightingale.

Suddenly Skafloc knew that the snare that he had laid for Freda, mostly in idle jest, had caught him too. He did not care, and lay drowsily back on the cool soft moss. Never had he had much feeling for an elf woman, but Freda—

Leea was right. Like called to like.

12

A few days later, Skafloc went out alone to hunt. He traveled on wizard skis which bore him like the wind, up hill and down dale, over frozen rivers and through snow-choked forests, far up into the Scottish highlands by dusk. He was about to turn back, for he had a roe deer over his shoulders, when from afar he saw the glimmer of a campfire. Wondering who or what was camped in these desolate hills, he went whispering over the snow with his spear poised.

Coming close through the chill gray twilight, he saw a figure of mighty stature squatted on the snow and roasting horseflesh over the blaze. Despite the freezing wind, he wore only a wolfskin kilt, and the ax beside him seemed to flash with unearthly brilliance.

Skafloc sensed the grim power before him, and when he saw that the other had only one hand his spine felt cold. It was not thought good to meet Tyr of the Aesir alone at dusk.

But it was too late to turn back. The god was already looking in his direction. Skafloc skied boldly into the circle of firelight and looked straight into Tyr's brooding dark eyes.

"Greeting, Skafloc," said the As. His voice was deep and vibrant, as of a storm-wind blowing through a sky of brass. He kept on turning the spit over the fire.

"Greeting, lord." Skafloc felt a little more at ease. The elves, without souls, worshipped no gods, but neither was there any ill will between them and the Aesir—indeed, some elves served in Asgard itself.

Tyr nodded his dark head curtly in sign for the man to be seated. There was silence for a long while, save for the low flames which sputtered and sang and cast weaving highlights over Tyr's gaunt grim face.

He spoke at last: "I smelled war. The trolls make ready to fare against Alfheim."

"So we have already discovered, lord," answered Skafloc. "The elves are prepared."

"It will be a harder struggle than you think. The trolls have many allies this time." Tyr looked somberly into the flames. "More is at stake than elves or trolls know. The Norns spin many a thread to its end these days."

There was silence again for a while, until Tyr said: "Aye, ravens hover low, and the gods stoop over the world, which trembles under the hoofbeats of Time. This I tell you, Skafloc: you will have sore need of the Aesir's naming-gift to you. But the gods themselves are troubled. Therefore I, the war-wager, am on earth."

A wind shook his long black locks. His terrible eyes smoldered into the man's. "I will give you a warning," he said, "though I fear it avails naught against the will of the Norns. Who is your father, Skafloc?"

"I know not, lord, nor have I cared ere now. But I can ask Imric—"

"Do not so. What you must ask Imric is that he say naught to anyone of what he knows, least of all yourself. For the day you learn who your father was will be a dark one, Skafloc, and what will come on you from that knowledge will also wreak ill on the world."

He jerked his head again, and Skafloc took a hasty departure, leaving the deer as a gift in return for the rede. But as he swept homeward with the wind of his passage roaring in his ears, he wondered how good Tyr's warning had been—for now all at once the question of who he really was rose black in his mind, and the night seemed full of demons who shouted at him and howled derision of his ignorance.

Faster he fled and faster, until he was raising a wind that screamed behind him over the hills, but he could not outrun the nightmare saddled on his back. Only Freda, he thought, sobbing for breath in the merciless cold, only Freda could banish the fear from him.

Ere dawn the walk and towers of Elfheugh were before him, rising high against the heavens. He was spied from afar, and the elf guard blew a shrill blast of his war-horn to signal the gatekeepers. Through the opened gateway whizzed Skafloc, into the courtyard and up to the castle steps. Kicking off his skis, he ran into the halls.

Imric, returned early that evening, was just giving audience to Leea. "What if Skafloc be taken with a mortal maid?" he shrugged. "'Tis his affair, and a small matter indeed. You are but jealous, Leea."

"That I am," she answered frankly, "but 'tis more than that. See the girl for yourself, Imric, see if you cannot sense she is in some way meant as a weapon against us."

"Hm—so." The elf-earl scowled in thought. "Know you who she is?"

"She hight Freda Ormsdaughter, of a now broken family south in the Danelaw—"

"*Freda—Ormsdaughter—*" Of a sudden Imric was aghast. "Why, that—that means—"

Skafloc burst into the room, and the haggard face he wore made their eyes turn fearfully to him. But it was a little time ere he could speak, then his tale poured out of him in one flood.

"What did Tyr mean?" he cried at the end of it. "Who am I, Imric?"

"I see what he meant," replied the elf-earl grimly, "and therefore your birth is my secret alone, Skafloc. I will but say that you come of good family, with naught shameful in its blood." And then he put on his most guileful manner and spoke fair words which sent Skafloc and Leea away soothed.

But when alone, he paced the floor and muttered to himself. "Ill is this," he said between his teeth, "and I can see the workings of an enemy in it. Best to get rid of the girl—but Skafloc guards her with all his power. Failing that, the secret must be kept. Not that Skafloc has any more morals than an elf, but if he found out, the girl soon would—and 'tis one of the strongest laws laid on all humans which they have broken. She would be desperate enough to do—anything! And we need Skafloc."

He began turning over plans in his crafty brain. He thought of beguiling Skafloc with other women—but no, over love not he nor the gods had any power; and if Skafloc loved her not, the secret scarce mattered. Then he cast back in his memory, and as near as he recalled—it is not easy to keep thousands of years straight—there was only one besides himself who knew of this matter.

He sent for Firespear, a trusty guardsman, still a youth of some two centuries but cunning and sorcerous. "There was a witch who dwelt in the forest south and west of here some two-and-twenty years ago," he said. "She may now be dead or moved away, but I want you to track her—and if she still lives, slay her."

"Aye, lord," nodded Firespear. "If I may take a few huntsmen and elf-hounds, we shall soon do that."

"Take what you will, and begone as swiftly as may be. The matter will scarce wait."

Freda welcomed Skafloc back with a glad cry. Despite all her wonder at the magnificence of Elfheugh, she was afraid when he left her alone there. The dwellers, tall lithe elves and their unearthly beautiful women, dwarfs and goblins and gnomes and other folk who did the work, the very horses and dogs with their proud grace and quicksilver movements, all were alien to her. Their flesh was cool, their features cast in a strange mold, their speech and dress and heathen ways and ageless centuries of life all sundered from her world. The great dim splendor of the castle which was also a barren crag, the sorceries drifting in the very air of its eternal twilight, the presences haunting hills and forest and sea—all these oppressed her with their strangeness and aloofness.

But when Skafloc was by her side, Alfheim seemed to lie on the borders of Heaven. (God forgive her for thinking that, she whispered to herself, and for not fleeing this heathendom for the holy chill and darkness of a nunnery!) He was laughing and impudent and mischievous until she could not but laugh with him, his verses rushed out of him and all to her praise, his arms and his lips were fierce and sweet and mad with a young craziness she had not known could be. She had seen him fight, and knew there were few warriors in lands of men or faerie who could stand before him, and of that she was proud—after all, she stemmed from warriors herself. But with her he was always gentle. And he took the place of her dead kindred, in her eyes and in her heart.

She knew he loved her—he must, or why would he lie with her when elf women beautiful as angels and skillful after many centuries looked after him as he went down the corridors? What she did not know was how deeply her human warmth had entered his soul which had never before known the like. The elves were cooler of heart than humans, and Skafloc had not been aware of his own loneliness until he came on Freda. He knew that, unless he paid a certain price which he would not, he must sometime die, his life the briefest flicker in the long elf memories. It was good to have one of his own sort by his side.

In their few sweet crazy days together they had done much, ridden the swift horses and sailed the slender boats and walked over many leagues of hill and forest. Freda was a good archer, and when she went through the woods with bow in hand and coppery-bronze hair shining, she seemed a young goddess of the hunt. They had watched the magicians and mummers whose shows amused the elves, but these were often too sly and subtle for human liking. They had been to see Skafloc's friends, little gnomes dwelling under tree roots, slim white water-sprites, an old and sad-eyed faun, and many beasts of the rivers and forests. Freda could not converse, but she was wide-eyed and often a-laugh at sight of them.

She had given only the most fleeting thoughts to the future. Some day, of course, she must bring Skafloc to the lands of men and get him christened, a worthy act for which her present sins would no doubt be forgiven her. But not now, not yet. Elfheugh was timeless, she lost all track of days and nights, and there was so much else to do—

Now she flew into his arms. His troubled mien vanished at sight of her—young, slim, lithe and long-legged, still more girl than woman. He laid his hands on her waist and flung her up into the air and caught her again, both of them laughing aloud.

"Set me down," she gasped. "Set me down so I can kiss you."

"In a moment." Skafloc tossed her up again, making a sign with his hand. There she hung, weightless in mid-air, kicking out and choking between merriment and surprise. Skafloc pulled her to him and she hung above him with her lips on his.

"No sense craning my neck to kiss you," decided Skafloc. He made himself weightless and conjured up a cloud on which they could rest. A tree grew on it, heavy with grapes, and rainbows arched through the misty leaves.

"Some day, madman, you will forget some part of your wizardry and fall and break your neck," she said.

He held her close, looking into her gray eyes. Then he counted the freckles dusting the bridge of her nose, and kissed her once for each of them. "I had best make you spotted like a leopard," he said.

"You know you need no such excuse," she answered softly. "I have longed for you, Skafloc. How went the hunt?"

He scowled as memory returned. "Well enough," he evaded.

"You are troubled, dearest. What is it? All night there have been horns blowing and feet marching and hoofs tramping. I see armed men in the castle, more every day. What is it, Skafloc?"

"You know there is war with the trolls," he said. "We are letting them come to us, for 'twould be hard to invade their mountain fastnesses while they still have their full strength."

She shuddered in his arms. "The trolls—"

"No fear." Skafloc laughed. "We will meet them at sea and break their power. Any who land we will wipe out. Then with its righting strength gone, Trollheim will be easy to subdue. 'Twill be a lusty fight, but Alfheim cannot help winning it."

"I fear for you, Skafloc."

He quoth:

Fear of fairest
fay for chieftain

makes him merry—
means she loves him.
Girl, be gay now.
Gladly take I
gift you give me,
gold-bright woman.

Freda blushed. "Shameless are you," she said, though not able to keep from smiling.

"Why," asked Skafloc in surprise, "what is there to be ashamed of?"

Firespear rode out shortly after sunset of the next night, while a few sullen embers still glowed red in the west. He and his dozen huntsmen wore the green tunics of the chase, but with cowled black cloaks flung over. Their spears and arrows were tipped with silver. About their curvetting horses bayed the pack of savage elf-hounds, great black beasts with eyes like hot coals and slavering fangs, with blood of Garm and Fenris and the Wild Hunt's dogs in them.

Forth they swept as Firespear's horn shouted, with thunder of hoofs and bellow of hounds ringing between the hills. Like the wind they went, through a stormy pit-black night, racing between the ice-sheathed forest trees. A fleeting glint of silver and jeweled hilts and angrily burning red eyes was to be seen, a rush of shadows, and no more, but the clamor of their passage rang from end to end of the great forest. Lonely hunters and outlaws and charcoal burners who heard that racket shuddered and crossed themselves, and wild beasts slunk aside.

From afar the witch, squatting in the shelter she had built by the ashes of her house, heard. She crouched over her tiny fire in the numbing lightless cold while a storm-wind roared in the trees above her, and muttered, "The elves hunt tonight."

"Aye," squeaked her familiar, and as the noise came nearer: "And I think they hunt—us."

"Us?" screamed the witch. "But why—"

"You are no friend to Skafloc or Imric." The rat chattered with fear and cold against her bosom. "Now quickly, mother, quickly, summon aid or we are done."

The witch had no time for ceremonial or sacrifice, but she howled the call for help and a monstrous blackness deeper than the night rose up before her.

She groveled before the Dark One. Faint and cold, the little blue flames of Hell raced across him. "Help," she whimpered. "Help, the elves come—"

The wise inscrutable eyes watched her without rancor or pity. The clamor of the hunt swept nearer. "Help!" she cried.

He spoke, in a voice that blent with the roaring wind but seemed to come from vast and hollow depths unthinkably far removed. "What do you call on me for?"

"I am being hunted by those who wish my death," she quavered.

"What of that? You said once that you do not care for life."

"My vengeance is not complete," she sobbed. "I cannot die now, without knowing whether my work and the price I paid are for naught. Master, help thy servant!"

Nearer came the hunters. She could hear the drumming of hoofs now.

"You are not my servant, you are my slave." The far voice rushed through the groaning trees. "What is it to me whether your purpose is fulfilled? I am the master of evil, which is futility. You have sold me your soul, and wrought enough ill to seal the bargain forever. What more concern have I with this shadow-play? It is time I reaped my harvest."

And the Dark One was gone.

Now the witch screamed and ran. Behind her the hounds, confused by the smell of her visitor, barked in the clearing. The witch turned herself into a rat and crawled into a hole under a great tree.

"She is near at hand," said Firespear, "and— Ha! They have the scent!"

The pack snarled around an ancient tree. Earth flew as they dug after their prey, ripping the deep roots in their monster eagerness. The witch darted past them, changed to the form of a crow, and flew up. Firespear's bow twanged, and the crow sank to earth, becoming a hag at whom the hounds rushed. The rat leaped from her bosom, and a rearing horse brought its silver-shod foot down to crush him.

The hounds tore the witch apart, but as they did she screamed at the elves: "All my curses! All woe do I wish on Alfheim! And tell Imric that Valgard the changeling lives and knows—"

There her words ended. "That was an easy hunt," said Firespear. "I had feared we would have to use sorcery to track her wanderings of perhaps a score of years, even into foreign lands." He snuffed the gale eagerly. "As it is, we will have the rest of the night for better game."

Imric rewarded his hunters well, but when they told him, in some puzzlement, what their quarry had said, he scowled blackly.

13

Valgard found a place of honor at the court of the trolls, grandson of Illrede and mighty warrior as he was. But the lords looked askance at him—after all, he had elf blood too, and came from lands of men; also, they were jealous of a poor and lonely stranger who rose at once so high. Thus Valgard found no friends in Trollheim. But he did not seek any, the aspect and the cold-blooded, barbarous natures of the trolls not being to his liking.

They were, however, fearless warriors of terrible strength, and their great warlocks were masters of tremendous powers. The whole troll nation was stronger than any other in faerie save—perhaps—Alfheim. All this suited Valgard well, for here was the means to his vengeance and the gaining of his heritage.

Illrede told him of the troll power. "We have built our lands for war all during the peace," said the king, "while the elves loafed and intrigued among themselves and took their pleasure. There are not quite so many trolls as elves, but with those who march beside us we outnumber them by a good many."

"Who are they?" asked Valgard.

"Most of the goblin tribes we have either conquered or made alliance with," said Illrede. "They have old grudges against both trolls and elves, who have long harried them, but I have promised them loot, and freedom for such slaves of their race as we have, and a place just below the trolls when we rule all faerie. They are doughty warriors, and there are many of them.

"Then we have companies from distant lands, demons of Baikal, Shen of Cathay, imps of Moorish deserts, adding up to a good number. They have come for the looting and are not all to be relied on, but I will dispose them in battle according to what they can do. There are also stragglers who came alone or in little bands—werewolves, vampires, ghouls, that sort. And we have plenty of dwarf slaves, some of whom will fight in exchange for freedom—and they can handle iron.

"Against this host the elves stand alone. They may be able to scrape together a few odd goblins and dwarfs and whatnot else, but those scarcely count. The very best they can hope for is aid from the Sidhe, but I doubt that those—save one or two, perhaps—wish to join in this struggle. True, the elf leaders are crafty and learned in magic—but so am I and my lords." Illrede's laughter bellowed forth. "Oh, we will break Alfheim—break it like a dry twig across the knee!"

"Can you not call on the Jötuns for help?" asked Valgard. "They are akin to trolls, are they not?"

"Speak not of such matters!" rapped Illrede. "We dare no more call the ice giants to our aid than the elves the Aesir." He shivered. "We do not wish to be more their pawns than we are already—the mighty contending Powers beyond the world. Even if they would answer, not we nor the elves would dare call—because if Aesir or Jötuns should move into Midgard, the other side would move against them, and then the last battle might be joined."

He moved ponderously about the great dark hall. "In like manner," he said, "no creature of faerie dares do much against men, particularly baptized men. A few sorceries, a stolen baby or woman, little else. For they fear us now, but if they came to fear us too much they would send to the gods, under whose protection they are, a call that would be heeded—they might even call on the new white god, and that would be the end of faerie."

Valgard shuddered. And that night he went to Asgerd's shallow grave and dug her up and took her aboard a troll-boat. West he sailed on such a witch-wind as Illrede had taught him to raise, until he came to a village on the eastern English coast.

There were snow-clouds and darkness as he bore Asgerd's stiffened form through echoing, empty streets to the church. Into its graveyard he crept, and in a corner of the wall he scratched another hole, and laid her in it, and covered it up so that none could see he had been there.

"Now you are sleeping in holy ground, sister, as you would have wished it," he whispered. "Evil have I done, but now mayhap you will pray for my soul—" And then looking bewildered about him into the snowing darkness, with a cold fear gripping him who had never been afraid before: "But why am I here? What am I doing? She is not my sister, and I am a creature made by sorcery—I have no soul—"

He snarled his anger and loped back to his boat and sailed eastward as if devils were on his track.

Now came the time of the troll hosting. But Illrede was too shrewd to gather his forces in one spot where elf spies could see how great they were. Each part of his fleet sailed from its own place, with a wizard or other wise one aboard each flagship to see that all came to the agreed meeting place at the same time. This would be somewhat north of the English elflands, so that the trolls could land on empty beaches rather than against powerful forts. Illrede meant to break the elf sea power at that spot, and then move south by sea and land alike to overrun the enemy homeland. He would then leave part of his force in England to root out the elves, while his main fleet went on south across the channel to Alfheim's other provinces. Part of his army would meanwhile have marched overland from Finnmark. Thus the trolls would attack the Erlking from west and east—and, as soon as England was wholly conquered, north—and smash him.

"Swift are the elf warriors," said Illrede, "but I think the trolls will move swifter this time."

"Give me in charge of England," begged Valgard, "and I will see that no elf man remains alive there."

"I have promised the English earldom to Grum," said Illrede, "but you, Valgard, shall sail in my own flagship with me, and in England I will make you second to Grum only."

Valgard said he was well content with this, but his cold eyes measured the lord Grum, and he thought to himself that the troll might easily have an accident in all the fighting there would be—and that would make him, Valgard, earl as the witch had said.

He boarded the flagship with Illrede and the mightiest warriors of the guard. A huge vessel it was, with high sides and a dwarf-made iron beak for ramming, and all dead black save for the white skull which was its figurehead. The trolls aboard had arms and armor of dwarf metals, alloys of great strength and hardness, but most also carried the stone-headed war-tools which had weight enough to suit them. Illrede wore a golden coronet on his black helmet, and rich furs over the somber dragon-skin byrnie on which even iron did not bite. The others were also richly clad, and were a rough, boisterous, arrogant crew. Valgard alone wore naught of ornament, and his face was set in bleak lines; but his great iron ax and the iron he wore made him an object of fear to the trolls.

There were many other ships in the royal fleet, all of uncommon size, and the night rang with the shouting voices and roaring war-horns and tramping feet. Troll vessels sailed more slowly than elf, being larger and heavier and made with less skill in sorcery, and morning found them still at sea. The trolls took shelter under black awnings which shut off the hated sunlight, and let the ships ride, invisible to mortal eyes.

The next night found the grand fleet assembling, and Valgard was awed by its size. It seemed to carpet the sea out to the horizon, and every vessel swarmed with men and the huge shaggy troll-horses. But so well drilled were all in Illrede's plans that each craft went at once to its proper place.

Many and strange were the ships and crews which sailed against Alfheim. The long, high, black troll craft formed the center, at the head of a blunt wedge with Illrede's own ship at the very point. To starboard and port were the goblins, some manning troll-built vessels and some in their own slim red snake-prowed ships; merrier than the trolls were they, clad in fantastical garments over their silvery armor, and wielding for the most part light swords and spears and bows. Then the wings of the fleet spread out into weird creatures: great scimitar-swinging Shen, in painted junks; lithe imps in slave-rowed galleys, with engines of war mounted on the decks; black barges of the winged demons from Baikal; iron-plated dwarfs; savage monsters from lonely hills and swamps and forests. All these were officered by trolls, and only the most reliable were in the first line. There was a second wedge behind the first, and beyond this were still more vessels which would go wherever they were needed.

Horns screamed their commands from troll ships, and were answered by goblin pipes and Shen gongs and imp drums. Dark clouds hung low over the forest of masts, and the sea ran white from many oars under the fitful light of the gibbous moon. Blue will-o'-the-wisps crawled over the ships, casting the faces of trolls and goblins and demons into ghastly highlights, and wavered between them. Strange winds sighed in the rig, and harrying presences rode through the moon-flecked, snow-sullen clouds.

"Erelong now we join battle," said Illrede to Valgard. "Then you may find the revenge you seek."

The berserker said naught, but looked fixedly ahead into the darkness.

14

It was something over a month since the elf raid on Trollheim, and in that time Imric had worked hard. He could not find out much about the enemy, since Illrede and his warlocks had screened their land heavily with magic, but he knew that a mighty force of many nations was being gathered and would most like strike first at England. Thus he strove to assemble all ships and men of his realm, and he sent abroad for all help there was.

Few came from outside, for each province of Alfheim was readying itself alone against the trolls—the elves were too proud to work well in concert. Also, it seemed that all mercenaries in faerie had already been hired by Illrede years before. Imric sent to the Sidhe of Ireland, promising rich booty in the conquest of Trollheim, and got back only the cold word that enough of wealth already glittered in the streets of Tir-nam-Og and the caves of the Leprechauns. Thus the elf-earl found himself standing alone.

But even so his strength was great, and as it swelled day by day in the hosting of the elves the fierce joy of his people grew apace. Never, it seemed to them, had so mighty a force been gathered in faerie, and some of the younger warriors held that not only could England's elves beat off the whole troll fleet, but they could alone carry the war to Trollheim and break the whole enemy kingdom.

From Orkney and Shetland came Flam, son of that Flam who had fallen in Skafloc's raid and wild to avenge his father. He and his tall brothers were among the greatest sailors in faerie, and their dragon fleet darkened the water as it swept southward. Shields blinked on the sides and wind hummed in the rig and the roar of cloven sea at the bows seemed to be the angry snarl of the carven serpent heads.

From the gray hills and moors of Pictland marched the savage chieftains with their flint-headed weapons and their leather breastplates. Shorter and heavier than true elves were they, dark of skin and with long black locks and beards blowing wild about their tattooed faces, for there was also blood of troll and goblin and still more ancient races in them, as well as some strains from Pictish women stolen in long-gone days. With them came certain of the lesser Sidhe who had entered with the Scots centuries ago, strong gnarly leprechauns leaping goat-like, tall beautiful warriors striding in shimmery mail with their spears ahigh or riding in huge rumbling war-chariots with sword-blades on the hubs for mowing of men.

From the south, from Cornwall's wild hills and cave-riddled sea coast, came some of the oldest elves in the island: tall mail-clad horsemen and charioteers whose flying banners told of forgotten glories; green-haired, white-skinned sea-folk, who had always a gray mystery of salt-smelling fog about them for the sake of dampness on land; a few rustic half-gods whom the Romans had brought and afterward abandoned; shy, flitting forest elves, clan by clan.

Saxon lands did not hold so many since most of the beings once dwelling there had been exorcised, but such as still lived came. Nor were these elves, poor and backward though they often were, to be despised in war, for many could trace descent to Wayland or even to Odin. They were the greatest smiths among the elves, since they had some dwarf blood, and many chose to fight with their great stone hammers.

But the mightiest and proudest were those who dwelt in the hills about Elfheugh. Not alone in ancestry, but in beauty and wisdom and wealth, the lords whom Imric had gathered about him outshone all others. Fierce and haughty they were, going to battle as gaily clad as to a wedding, and kissing their spears like brides, and they had hewed many a bloody pathway ere this. They cast mighty spells for the undoing of their enemies and the protection of their own men. All the elves who assembled around Imric's castle stood in awe of them, but were not thereby hindered in enjoying the huge feast they set forth.

Freda was much taken with watching that eerie host gather. The sight of those unhuman warriors gliding noiselessly through dusk and moonlight, their alien visages half hidden to her eyes and all the stranger for that, sent waves of shock and delight, fear and pride, through her. It was a kingly power over which Skafloc had the lordship—but not one of man's world.

And she remembered the brutal strength of the trolls. What if he should fall before them? What then?

The same thought came to Skafloc. "Mayhap it were best I took you to what friends you have in the lands of men," he said slowly, "It may be, though I do not believe it, that the elves will lose—true it is that all omens we took were not good. And if that should happen, this would be no place for you."

"No—no—" She looked briefly at him with frightened gray eyes, then hid her face on his breast. "No, I will not leave you. I cannot."

He ruffled her shining hair. "I would come back for you if we won," he said.

"No—it might happen that someone there, somehow, persuaded or forced me to remain—I know not who it should be, save perhaps a priest, but I have heard of such things—" She remembered the lovely elf women and their eyes on Skafloc. He felt her slim body stiffen in his arms, and her voice came firm: "Anyway, I will not leave you. I stay."

He said naught, but his eyes shone with gladness.

Now word came that the trolls were putting out to sea. On the last night ere their own sailing, the elves held feast in Elfheugh.

Mighty was Imric's drinking-hall. Freda, sitting close by Skafloc up near the earl's high seat, could not see the other walls or get aught but a glimpse of the great rafters. The cool blue twilight loved of the elves seemed to drift like smoke through the hall. Light came from clear silvery-burning tapers in heavy bronze sconces, and it flashed back off the shields hanging on the walls and the great panels of cunningly etched gold. All of gold and silver, and studded with flaming gems, were the trenchers and bowls and horns on the snowy tablecloths. And though she had grown almost used to rare and delicate viands in Elfheugh, Freda felt her head swim at the wondrous food, meat and fowl and fish and fruit, at the sweet fieriness of mead and wine, at this feast.

Richly clad were the elves. Skafloc wore a tunic of white linen over silken breeches, a gold-worked belt with a jeweled dagger in it, a doublet whose colorfully broidered pattern seemed to lead the eye in a trackless maze, and over it all an ermine-trimmed scarlet cloak that was like a rush of blood from his wide shoulders. Freda had on a filmy dress of the thinnest spider-silk, over which rippled all colors in a restless play of molten rainbows and through which shone the sweet curves of her young body; a heavy golden girdle was locked about her slim waist, and golden rings weighted her bare arms. Both of them wore diamond-glittering coronets, as fitting a lord of Alfheim and his lady. The other great elves were no less gay of apparel, and even the poorer chieftains from other districts shone with raw gold.

There was music, not alone the eldritch melodies borne on the dusky air, but the wild harp-lays of the Scottish Sidhe and the pipes of Cornwall's warriors. There was discourse, the quick brilliant cruel discourse of the elves, delicately poisonous mockery and subtle fencing with words, and the silver laughter went up and down the long tables.

But when the feasting was done and the jesters should have skipped forth, the cry went up for a sword dance instead. Imric scowled, not liking to make omens plain to all, but since most others wanted it, he could not but agree.

The elves moved out onto the cleared floor, the men stripping off cloaks and women all their clothes, and each man took a sword. "What is it they do?" asked Freda.

"'Tis the old war-dance," replied Skafloc. "I must be skald to it, I suppose, since no human could dance it unscathed even if he knew all the measures. But they dance to ninety and nine verses which the skald must make up as he goes along, and if no one is hurt 'tis a great omen for victory; but if someone be slain it means defeat, and even a slash is a bad omen. I like this not."

Now the elf men stood in a wide double row, facing each other and crossing swords on high; and behind each man stood a woman, poised and taut. The rows reached far into the dimness of the hall, a long aisle of gleaming blades.

"Hai, go!" shouted Imric so that it rang through the hall.

Skafloc chanted:

Swiftly goes the sword-play,
sweeping foemen backward
to the beach where tumult
talks with voice of metal:
belling of the brazen
beaks of cleaving axes,
smoking blood, where sea kings
sing the mass of lances.

As he called it out, the men danced forward, and a mighty din of clashing swords arose in time to the verse. The women likewise danced lithely ahead, and each man's right hand seized a woman's left and whirled her into the narrowing aisle where the fencing swords flashed and clanged.

Skafloc called:

Swiftly goes the sword-play,
storm-like in its madness:
shields are bloody shimmers,
shining moons of redness;
winds of arrows wailing,
wicked spearhead-lightning
lads will smite who lately
lay by lovely sweethearts.

Through and between the whirring, flickering blades wove the elf women in a measure swift and supple and intricate as the foam-play on a whirlpool. The men danced to each other, beyond, and wheeled about, and each threw his sword in a glittering arc at his opposite number, just missing a lithe lovely body, and caught the weapon thrown at him.

Skafloc quoth:

Swiftly goes the sword-play!
Swinging bloodied weapons,
shields and helms to shatter,
shout the men their war-cry.
While the angry, whining,
whirring blades are sparking,
howl the wolves their hunger,
hawks stoop low for feasting.

Round and about, swifter than mortal eye could follow, whirled the measures of the dance, and leaping and shrieking between the twisting bodies were the swords. Now blades hummed low, and as two clashed points just above the floor, an elf woman sprang over them—the keen edges came up just behind her. Now the dancing men each seized a partner and wove a glitter of metal about her spinning body. Now they fenced again in the dance, and the women danced between the fencers in the bare instants when the blades were not meeting.

Skafloc's verses spilled out unbroken:

Swiftly goes the sword-play!
Song of metal raises
din of blades for dancing
(death for eager partner).
Lur horns bray their laughter,
lads, and call to hosting.
Sweeter game was sleeping
softly with your leman.

Leaping and weaving between the clamorous blades, a flying white frenzy, Leea called out with malice on her lovely face: "Oho, Skafloc, why is not that girl of yours who makes such a pretense of loving you dancing with us for luck?"

Skafloc did not break the flow of his voice:

Swiftly goes the sword-play.
Skald who lately chanted
gangs unto the game where
grim are stakes we play for.
Mock not at the mortal
may who is not dancing.
Better luck she brings me
by a kiss than magic.

But now a shudder of dismay went up among the weaving elves, for Leea, harking more to the words of Skafloc than to their beat, had danced into one of the yelling blades. Red was the slash across her silken shoulders. But she went on in the measures, her blood sprinkling the elves about her. Skafloc forced cheer into his voice:

Swiftly goes the sword-play.
Some must lose the gamble.
Norns alone are knowing
now who throws the dice best.
Winner in the wailing
weapon-game we know not,
but our foes will bitter
battle find in Alfheim.

But now other women, shaken by Leea's ill fortune, were

missing the hair-splitting rhythm and being slashed by the hissing swords. Imric called a halt ere someone should be slain and bring the very worst luck, and the company broke up in ill-contented silence or furtive whisperings.

Skafloc went in troubled silence with Freda to their rooms. There he excused himself for a while. He returned with a broad silver-chased girdle. On its inside was a flat metal vial.

He gave it to Freda. "Let this be my parting gift to you," he said quietly. "I got it of Imric, and I would you wore it. For though I still think we shall win, I am not so certain after that cursed sword dance."

She took it, wordlessly. Skafloc said: "In that vial is a rare and potent drug. Should evil luck befall you and our foes be nigh, drink it. You will be as one dead for many days, and any who find you will not think to molest you. Then when you awaken there may be a chance to slip free."

"What use would it be to escape, if you are dead?" asked Freda sorrowfully. "Better I should die too."

"Perhaps—but the trolls would not kill you at once, and there are many worse things than clean death." Skafloc smiled wearily. "'Tis not the most cheerful of farewell gifts, dearest one, but 'tis all I have."

"No," she whispered. "I will take it, and thank you. But we have a better gift, one we can give to each other."

"Aye, so," he laughed, and both of them were all at once merry.

15

The elf and troll fleets met off the northeastern coast soon after dark of the next night. And as Imric, standing by Skafloc in the prow of the great flagship leading his wedge of vessels, saw the size of the enemy force he drew a sharp breath of dismay.

"We English elves have nigh all the ships of Alfheim," he said, "yet is that fleet more than twice as great as ours."

"They cannot all be trolls," said Skafloc, "and I look for no great trouble from goblins and whoever else fights with them."

"Mock not the goblins. They are good warriors when they have the weapons they need." Imric's taut white face gleamed briefly out of darkness, caught in a fleeting moonbeam. A few snowflakes danced in that ray, whirled on a bitter wind. "Magic will avail neither side," he went on, "since the powers of both are in that regard equal. Thus it depends on strength of hosts alone, and there we are weaker."

He shook his silvery-locked head, eyes glittering strange and moon-blue. "I held, at the Erlking's council, that it were best all

Alfheim drew together into one place, letting the trolls have the outer provinces, even England, while we held fast and gathered ourselves for a counter-attack. But the other lords would have none of it. Now we shall see whose rede was best."

"Theirs was, lord," said Firespear boldly, "for even now we shall smite these dogs. What—let them wallow swinish in Elf-heugh? The thought was unworthy of you." He hefted his spear and strained eagerly ahead.

Skafloc too, though he felt these were heavy odds, would have naught but battle. This would not be the first time valiant men had wrested victory from a greater power. He blazed with the cold wish to meet Valgard, Freda's mad brother who had wrought her so much ill, and cleave his skull.

And yet, thought Skafloc, if Valgard had not borne Freda off to Trollheim, he, Skafloc, would never have met her. So he owed Valgard something. A quick clean slaying, rather than the slow torture he preferred, should settle the debt.

Now the great war-horns shrieked their summons on both sides. Down came the sails, and the fleets rowed to battle with ships linked together by ropes. As they neared, the arrows began their flight, a moon-darkening storm that hissed over the restless waves and struck home in wood or flesh. Three shafts rattled off Skafloc's mail, and a fourth missed his arm by a narrow distance and quivered in the ship's figurehead. But with his night-seeing eyes he discerned others aboard the vessel who were not so lucky, who sank wounded or slain under the sighing hail.

The moon showed ever less often through the flying clouds, but will-o'-the-wisps danced on the spindrift-blowing wind and the surging waves ran with cold white phosphorescence. There was light enough for seeing and killing.

Now spears and slung stones flew between the approaching ships. Skafloc cast a shaft which pinned a dark figure to the mast of the troll flagship. Back came a stone which bounced with a mighty clang off his helmet. He leaned on the rail, briefly dizzy, and the sea slapped cold salt water over his ringing head.

The horns yelled, almost into each other, and now the two lines shocked together.

Imric's ship laid alongside Illrede's, and the warriors in the bows struck at each other. Skafloc's sword screamed, and beat aside the ax of a troll and hewed off his arm. He pressed against the line of shields at the rail of the enemy vessel, his steel blade clamoring and his own shield taking the thunder of mighty blows that numbed his arm. On his left, Firespear thrust and jabbed with a pike, yelling in battle madness, reckless of the blades that rained about him. On his right, Angor of Pictland, tall and strong, fought stolidly with his long-shafted ax. For a time the two sides traded blows, and whenever a man in either line fell another pressed into his place.

Then Skafloc buried his sword in the neck of a troll. As that one fell, Firespear thrust into the breast of the one behind him. Skafloc leaped the rails, into that breach in the troll line, and cut down the man to his left. As the one on his right thrust at him, Angor's ax descended and the troll's head rolled into the sea.

"Forward!" roared Skafloc, and the nearer elves swarmed after him. They stood back to back, striking and hewing—hewing—at the trolls who snarled around them. And at this confusion, still more elves boarded the troll craft.

Swords flew in a blur that spouted blood. The shock and crash of metal drowned wind and sea. The elves stood in a ring, and around that circle was another one of corpses.

Tall and terrible, his fair locks flying in the gale and his eyes ablaze with blue hell-flames, Skafloc loomed over the struggle. Never did his sword rest, and he ducked the clumsy troll thrusts and swipes with a flickering grace from which his own glaive darted like a snake's tooth. The trolls began to fall away from him, and his band cleared the bows.

"Now forward!" he yelled.

The elves advanced sternward behind a curtain of flashing steel. Mightily did the trolls fight. Elves sank with crushed skulls or cloven bellies or transfixed hearts. But the trolls went back and back, only their trampled dead holding fast.

"Valgard!" roared Skafloc into the din. "Valgard, where are you?"

Now the changeling stood forth. Blood was streaming from his temples. "A slingstone knocked me out," he said, "but now 'tis time I went into battle."

Skafloc shouted and ran forward. The elves held the troll ship up to the mast, and now there were more of them aboard than there were trolls. From their own vessel, archers sent a steady rain of gray-feathered death.

Skafloc's sword and Valgard's ax met in a howl of steel and a shower of sparks. The madness did not come on the berserker just then; he fought with grim coldness, standing rock-firm on the rolling deck. As Skafloc's sword crashed into his shield, his own ax smote the elf-chief's byrnie-clad left shoulder.

Numbed, Skafloc's shield-arm fell to his side. Valgard hewed at his enemy's neck. Skafloc dropped to one knee and took the dreadful blow on his helmet. Even at the same moment, he was stabbing upward.

He sank half senseless from the fury that dented his helmet, but Valgard stumbled with a ripped leg. They rolled into the scuppers and the battle snarled past them.

Grum Troll-Earl led the fight for his side, and his huge stone-headed club crushed many skulls. Against him went Angor of Pictland, who struck out and hewed off the troll's right arm. Grum caught his falling club in his left hand and swung a blow that broke Angor's neck; but then the troll had to crawl under a rowing-bench so that he could carve healing-runes for his spouting wound.

Now Skafloc and Valgard came out again, found each other, and took up their fight anew in a rain of metal. Skafloc smote with a blow that bit through Valgard's byrnie and into his side. "That for Freda!" he shouted. "Ill have you done to her."

"Not so ill as I think you have," snarled Valgard, and even staggering and bleeding as he was he struck a blow that met Skafloc's descending sword in mid-air. And the sword sprang in twain.

"Ha!" cried the berserker, but ere he could follow up his chance Firespear was at him like an angry cat, and others of Alfheim besides. The elves held the ship.

"Now there is no reason for me to stay here," said Valgard, "but I hope to see you again, brotherling." And he sprang overboard.

The mast of a wrecked ship—many vessels were broken by ramming or the press of battle—swept by him and he grasped it with one hand. The other hand still held the ax Brotherslayer and for a moment he wondered if he should not let it go.

But no—accursed or not, it was a good weapon.

Others who had fled the ship, Grum among them, swam through the roaring waves to the floating mast. "Kick out, brothers," shouted Valgard, "and we will reach one of our own ships—and win this battle yet."

Aboard the troll flagship, the elves yelled their exultation. But Skafloc asked: "Where is Illrede? He should be aboard his own vessel, but I saw him not."

"Belike he is flying from ship to ship, directing his fleet, even as Imric is doing in form of a sea-mew," said Firespear. "But now let us chop a hole in this damned hulk and be back to our own boat."

There they saw Imric waiting for them. "How goes the battle, foster-father?" called Skafloc gaily.

The elf-earl's voice fell cold on his ears: "Ill goes it, for however well the elves fight, the trolls throw two to one against them. And others of the troll force are landing unopposed on the beaches."

"Ill is that indeed!" cried Golric of Cornwall, "and now we must fight like very demons or we are lost."

"I fear we are lost already," said Imric bleakly.

Skafloc could not at once comprehend this. Looking around, he saw that the flagship drifted alone. Both fleets were breaking up as the linking ropes were cut, but the troll ships held more closely together. And the trolls were laying one vessel on each side of an elf craft.

"To oars!" shouted Skafloc. "They need help. To oars!"

"Well spoke," sneered Imric bitterly.

The longship sprang forward to the closest knot of battle. Arrows began to rain on it.

"Shoot back!" cried Skafloc. "In the name of hell, why don't you shoot back?"

"Our quivers are nigh empty, lord," said an elf.

Crouching low under their shields, the elves rowed into the fight. Two of their fellow ships were at bay before three mercenary craft and one troll dragon. As Imric's vessel neared, the bat-winged black demons of Baikal came flying down on her.

The elves hewed manfully, but it was hard to fight enemies that struck from above with lances. They spent their last arrows, and still the swooping death smote.

But now they laid alongside a goblin ship, and it was from here that the arrows had come. Skafloc sprang across the rails and struck out with the elf sword he was carrying. One goblin he clove in two, another he sent reeling with a gashed belly, the head of a third he chopped leaping from its shoulders. Firespear cast a javelin that transfixed two, and turning on another he kicked in the goblin's breast. Others of the elves swarmed aboard, and the smaller goblins were hurled back.

Skafloc reached their arrow chests, and threw the heavy cases across to his own ship. As the goblins rallied and advanced again, he led a quick retreat. And now elf bows twanged anew and the hovering demons tumbled out of the sky.

The trolls came alongside. Skafloc saw that the other two elf ships at once fell on the goblins, demons, and Shen. "If they can handle those, I suppose we can take care of the trolls," he said.

The green-skinned warriors boomed their cry and came over the rail of the elf dragon. Skafloc ran to meet them, slipped on the bloody deck, and fell as a spear whizzed just where his breast had been. Golric of Cornwall toppled with the spear through his own heart.

"Thanks," muttered Skafloc, rising. The trolls were on him, their blows hailing on his dented shield. He struck out, and a foeman sank. Ere he could withdraw his sword, another troll was howling on him. He thrust up his iron shield. The troll screamed and staggered back with his face seared away.

Shock and thunder of blows sounded through the drifting snow. The ships reeled under the gale, and the fight scrambled over their decks. Skafloc's byrnie hung in rags, and he threw away his blunted sword for another. Presently his crumpled shield was also useless, and his shattered helmet fell off of itself. Almost naked he was—no longer protected by iron.

A troll traded blows with him. He sheathed his sword in the enemy's heart. Then another rushed on him, pulling him away and grappling him with terrible arms.

Cold and rock-hard was the troll's flesh. Skafloc knew grimly that the creature could break his ribs like arrow shafts. He put his feet against the troll's belly as they rolled on the deck, got his hands on the corded throat, and then braced himself against that bear hug.

Perhaps no other man could have held his back arched against the frightful drag. Skafloc felt the strength drain from him like wine from an overturned cup as he fought. He poured all muscle and will and heart into his back and legs, and into the hands he clamped on the troll's windpipe. It seemed forever that they rolled with the ship, and he knew he could not hold out much longer.

Then the troll let go and clawed at Skafloc's wrists, wild for air. The man snarled and rammed his enemy's head against the mast with a fury that sang in the wood and split open the horrible skull.

Skafloc lay over his dead foe, gasping for air, his heart nigh to breaking loose from its rib-cage and the blood roaring in his ears. Dimly he saw Firespear bending over him, heard the elf's awed voice:

"Not elf nor human was yet known to have slain a troll in barehanded combat. That deed will be unforgotten while the world stands. And now we have won."

He helped Skafloc erect. Looking over the nearby scene, the man saw that the enemy ships had all been cleared.

But at what a cost— Not a score of elves on all three craft remained whole, and the others who lived were grievously hurt. The ships drifted shoreward, manned with corpses and a few elves too weary to lift a sword.

And straining through the murk, Skafloc saw yet another troll longship, fully crewed, bearing toward them.

"I fear we have lost," he groaned, sick with exhaustion and despair. "Now there is naught left but to save what we can."

The ships rolled helplessly toward tumbling surf. And on the beaches waited a line of trolls, mounted on their great black horses and ready for any who landed.

A sea-mew flew out of the snow, shook himself, and was Imric. "We have done well," said the elf-earl grimly. "Nigh half the troll fleet is destroyed. But that half is mostly their mercenaries and allies, and we—we are all broken. Such of our ships as can still be sailed are in full flight, while others like this await their final doom." Suddenly tears glimmered in his chill strange eyes. "England is lost. And I fear me Alfheim is lost."

Firespear gripped the shaft of his lance. "We will go out fighting," he vowed. His voice was hollow with weariness.

Skafloc shook his tawny-maned head, and as he thought of Freda waiting in Elfheugh something of strength and will flowed back into him. "We will go on fighting," he answered. "But first we must save our own lives."

"'Tis a good trick if you can do it," said Firespear doubtfully.

By rowing, and reaching out with boathooks, the elves brought their ships together so that all could assemble in one. Then they raised sail. The approaching trolls were downwind, and both ships were close to the rocky shore.

Skafloc fought the steering oar and sent his ship quartering shoreward. The trolls dug in oars, seeking either to cut off the elf vessel's escape or drive it onto the rocks.

"'Twill be a tight squeeze," said Imric.

"Tighter than they think!" Skafloc grinned a mirthless skinning of teeth and squinted into the rushing snow. He saw a white spuming of surf where waves dashed themselves to death on fanged skerries—but beyond these were the shallows.

Too late, the trolls sought to veer. Skafloc rammed them with a shock at which timbers groaned. The enemy vessel was borne into the thundering surf, against the reefs—caught and smashed!

Skafloc's elves pulled like madmen, seeking to swing their own craft. He had no hope of saving it, but he was trying to hit as easily as he could. When the ship struck and began to break up, there was only a narrow spine of rock between it and the shallows.

"Now save himself who can!" cried Skafloc. He leaped out onto the slippery rock and over into neck-deep water. Seal-swift he darted for the beach, and the other elves were with him—save the wounded, who drowned there in sight of land.

They waded ashore, and they were well past the end of the troll line. But some of those saw the elves and galloped down on them.

"Scatter!" shouted Skafloc. "Some at least must escape!"

As he ran into the snowstorm he saw elves spitted on lances or trampled under hoofs, but most of his little band were getting away. High up swung the sea-mew.

And down on the bird stooped a mighty erne. Skafloc groaned, his heart going cold. Crouching behind a rock, he saw the erne bear the mew down to the ground, and there they became Illrede and Imric.

Troll clubs thudded onto the elf-earl. He lay limp in a pool of his own blood while they bound him.

If Imric was dead, Alfheim had lost one of its greatest leaders. If he lived—woe for him! Skafloc slid into the snow-covered ling. He scarcely felt his own weariness, or the cold, or his stiffening wounds. The elves were beaten, and now he had but one goal—to reach Elfheugh and Freda ahead of the trolls.

16

The trolls rested through the day, for the struggle with the elves had drained them of strength. Thereafter they set south, half by land and half by sea. The ships reached Elfheugh harbor the same night, and their crews landed and burned the ships and houses around the bay, then waited around the castle for their comrades.

The land army, with Grum and Valgard at the head, went more slowly. Horsemen scoured the country, and wherever little bands of elf warriors sought to fight they were slain—not without loss to the trolls. Outlying garths were plundered and burned, their folk chained into the long lines of captives who stumbled neck linked to neck and hands manacled, with Imric at their head. The trolls made merry, with food and drink and women of Alfheim, and took their time in reaching Elfheugh.

But that first night, looking down from the high towers to the blaze down by the bay and the black ships grimly at anchor, the folk of the castle knew Imric had lost.

As Freda stood staring out to the seaside fires, mute and pale, there came a noiseless step and the faintest rustle of silken garments. Turning, the girl saw Leea beside her, and in the elf woman's hand gleamed a knife.

Pain and malice were on Leea's beautiful face. She said in human speech: "You weep little for one whose love is now raven food."

"I will weep when I know he is dead," answered Freda tonelessly. "But there was too much life in him for me to believe that he is now lying stark."

"Where then might he be, and what use is a skulking hunted outlaw?" Leea's pale full lips curved in a smile. "See you this dagger, Freda? The trolls are camped around Elfheugh, and your law forbids you to take your own life. But if you wish to escape, I will gladly give it to you—now."

"No—I will wait for Skafloc," said Freda. "And have we not spears and arrows and engines of war? Is there not meat and drink, and are the walls not high and the gates strong? Let such as had to remain in the castle hold it for those who went forth."

Leea's knife sank. She looked long at the slim gray-eyed girl. "Good is your spirit," she said at last, "and methinks I begin to see what Skafloc found in you. But your rede is mortal—foolish and impatient. Can women hold a fort against storm when their men are fallen?"

"They can try—or fall like their men."

"Not so. There are other weapons." Brief cruel mirth flickered across Leea's white countenance. "Women's weapons—but to use them we must open the gates. Would you avenge your lover?"

"Aye—with arrow and knife, and poison if need be!"

"Then give the trolls your kisses—swift as arrows, sharp as knives, bitter and deadly as poison in the cup. Such is the way of the elf women."

"Sooner would I break the great law of Him above and be my own murderer than whore of my man's slayers!" flared the girl.

"Mortal chatter," sneered Leea. She smiled her secret cat-smile. "I will find the caresses of trolls interesting—for a time. They are something new, at least, and cruel hard it is to find something fresh and untasted after many centuries. We open the gates of Elfheugh when our new earl arrives."

Freda sank onto the bed, burying her face in her hands. Leea said fleeringly, "If you wish to follow your brainless human blood I will be glad enough to get rid of you. Tomorrow at high noon, when the trolls sleep, I will let you out of the castle with whatever you want to take. Thereafter you can do as you please—flee to lands of men, I suppose, and join your voice to the shrill whine of nuns whose heavenly groom somehow never comes for them. I wish you joy of that!"

And Leea turned and left.

For a time Freda lay on the bed, with darkness and despair whelming her. Weep could she not, and the tears were bitter in her throat. Now all was gone indeed, her kindred, her love—

No!

She sat up, clenching her fists. Skafloc was not dead. She would not believe that till she had kissed his bloodless lips—and then, if God were merciful, her heart would break and she would fall beside him. But if he lived—if he lay sorely wounded, perhaps, with foes ringing his lair and the need of her heavy on him—

She hastened to gather what she thought would be needed. His own helm and byrnie, and the clothes that went therewith (unfilled by him, they seemed strangely empty, more so than any other man's unused dress), ax and sword and shield, spear and bows and many arrows. For herself she took also a byrnie such as shield-mays among the elves were wont to use. It fitted well her slender form, and she could not but smile at the mirror as she set a gold-winged helmet on her bronze-ruddy locks. He liked to see her in such dress, tall and boyish and beautiful.

All of this had to be of elf metal, since the faerie horses would not bear iron, but she supposed he could make good use of it.

Something of food and drink she added to her pile of goods, and furs and needle and thread and whatever else might be useful. "I am becoming a housewife!" she said, smiling again. The homely word gladdened her, like the sight of an old friend. Then she added certain things whose use she did not know but which Skafloc had seemed to set much store by—skins of wolf and otter and eagle, rune-carved wands of ash and beechwood, a strangely wrought ring.

When it was assembled, she sought out Leea. The elf woman looked in surprise at the Valkyr-like figure before her. "What will you now?" she asked.

"I want four horses," replied Freda, "and help to load one of them with what I am taking. Then I want you to let me out of here."

"But 'tis still night, with trolls awake and prowling about—and elf horses cannot travel by day."

"No matter. They go more swiftly than any others, and speed is all I wish."

"Aye—you can reach a church ere dawn if you can get past the enemy lines," sneered Leea, "and the arms you take will give you some protection on the way. But you cannot hope to keep faerie gold long."

"I have no gold to speak of, nor do I go to any lands of men. It is the north gate I want you to open for me."

Leea's eyes widened, then she shrugged. "'Tis a foolish thing to do. What good is Skafloc's cold corpse? But let it be as you wish." Suddenly tears glimmered briefly in her eyes. "And—kiss him once for Leea, will you?"

Freda said naught, but she thought that alive or dead Skafloc should not get that kiss.

The snow was flying thick when she left. Noiselessly the great gate swung open, and the elf guard waved a hand in farewell as Freda rode out with her string of horses. She did not look back. Elfheugh was a place of splendor, but without Skafloc it was empty.

The wind whined around her, biting through layers of fur. She leaned over and whispered in her horse's ear: "Now quickly, quickly, best of horses, quickly gallop! North to Skafloc, swiftly—find Skafloc and you shall sleep in golden stables and walk unsaddled through summer meadows all your days."

There came a roaring, booming shout. Freda leaned low over her horse's shoulders, and despite herself she was of a sudden racked with shuddering fear. Naught was so dreadful to her as the trolls, and now they had seen her—"Oh, swiftly, my horse!"

The wind of her passage screamed about her, nigh ripping her from the saddle. She could scarce see in the raving darkness, but she heard the roar of mighty hoofs behind her.

Faster and faster—north, ever north, with the cloven air hooting its mockery and the relentless thunder of the great troll stallions. Like yelping dogs the warriors cried after her. She glanced back once and saw a deeper shadow racing through the night. Could she but send an arrow after them—! But she had not strength or skill to sit erect when the elf horses were a-gallop.

The snow swirled around her. Presently the trolls began to fall behind, but she knew they would track her unwearyingly. And as she fled north she came nearer the southward-marching land army of Trollheim.

Time seemed to roar past like the wind. She caught a far-off glimpse of fire atop a high hill—belike some burning elf garth.

The army must be near, and they would have scouts over the whole land.

As if to answer her thought, a deep mad howl rose out of the darkness to her right. She heard the roll of hoofbeats echoing between the hills—nearer, nearer! If they cut her off now—

Up ahead in her very path loomed a monstrous form, a giant shaggy horse, blacker than night but with eyes like glowing coals, and on it a rider in black ring-mail, a creature huge of thew and hideous of face—a troll! The elf horse veered aside, and he reached out a mighty arm and grasped the bridle. He pulled the horse to a rearing halt with one hand.

His laughter roared thunderous as he clutched for Freda. She screamed, and sought to draw her sword. Were she but wearing a cross—or an iron byrnie—The hand clamped monstrously on her wrist.

"Ho, ho, ho!" shouted the troll.

Out of the night, summoned through the windy dark by her far-sensed need, still gasping with the heartbreakingly long run and the fear of coming too late, Skafloc sprang. One foot he put in the troll's stirrup, and lifted himself up to hew off the rider's head.

Freda toppled from her saddle into darkness and his arms.

17

When the troll host reached Elfheugh, a horn sounded from the watch towers and the great brazen gates swung wide. Valgard reined in, narrowing his eyes. "A trick—" he muttered.

"No, I think not," said Grum. "Few except women are left in the castle, and they expect us to spare them." He shook with laughter. "As we will! Ho, ho, as we will!"

The heavy hoofs of the huge-boned shaggy horses rang hollowly on the courtyard flagstones as they rode inside. Here it was warm and calm, with a cool half-light resting blue on the mighty walls and the sky-piercing towers. Flowering gardens reached on every hand, the eternal blossoms breathing their languorous odors into the dusky air; fountains splashed, and clear streamlets ran past bowers meant for two alone.

The women of Elfheugh were gathered in the courtyard to meet the conquerers. Used as he had become since landing in Alfheim to the haunting white loveliness of the elf-mays, Valgard drew a sharp breath at sight of the glorious ladies.

One stepped forth, with thin robes clinging to every curve, and she outshone the others as the moon the stars. She curtsied low before Grum, the cool mystery of her eyes veiled by sweeping lashes. "Greeting, lord," she said in a voice that sang rather than spoke. "Elfheugh makes submission."

The earl puffed himself out. "Long has this castle stood," he said, "and many assaults has it beaten off. Yet you were wisest, who chose to recognize the might of Trollheim. Terrible are we to our foes, but our friends have good gifts of us." He sought to smile at her. "Erelong I will make you a gift. But what is your name?"

"I hight Leea, lord, sister to Imric Elf-Earl."

"Call him not that, for now I, Grum, am earl in England's faerie lands, and Imric the least of my thralls. Bring forth the prisoners!"

Slowly, heads bent and chains clanking, the captive warriors of Alfheim were led forward. Bitter were their bloody faces, and their shoulders were bowed under a weight heavier even than the links binding them. Imric, hair matted with his own crusted blood, and blood in the prints of his bare feet, led the line. Naught did the elves say, or even look at their women, as they were led down toward the dungeons.

Now Illrede came up from the ships. "Elfheugh is ours," he said, "and we leave it to you, Grum, to hold it for us while we are laying the rest of Alfheim under our feet. There are still English elfholds to be taken, and many elves skulking in the hills and forests, so you will have work enough."

He led the way into the castle. "We have but one thing to do ere leaving," he said. "Imric took captive our daughter Gora, nine hundred years ago. Let her be brought forth to freedom."

As the king's men followed him, Leea plucked at Valgard's arm to draw him aside. Her gaze was widened in astonishment.

"I took you for Skafloc at first," she breathed. "Yet I can sense you are not human—I can smell that, and see and feel it—"

"No." He smiled, a humorless twisting of thin lips. "I am Valgard Berserk of Trollheim. Yet in a way Skafloc and I are brothers. For I am a changeling, born of the troll-woman Gora by Imric, and left in place of the infant Skafloc."

"Then—" Leea's fingers tightened on his arm and her breath came in a sharp hiss. "Then you are the Valgard of whom Freda spoke—her brother—?"

"That one." His voice harshened. "Where is she now?" He shook her roughly. "Where is Skafloc?"

"I—do not know—Freda fled the castle when we knew the elves were beaten, she said she was going to him—"

"Then if she was not caught on the way, and I have heard nothing of such, she is with him." Valgard snarled. "Ill is that!"

Leea smiled, a cold and guileful smile with closed lips and hooded eyes. "Now I see what Tyr of the Aesir meant," she whispered to herself, "and why Imric kept the secret—" And to Valgard, boldly: "Why think you that is so bad? You have slain all the seed of Orm but those two, and you have been the means of bringing a yet worse disaster on them. What better revenge could you want?"

Valgard shook his head. "I had naught against Orm or his house," he muttered. And then, looking about him in sudden bewilderment, as if waking to life from a strange dream: "Yet I must have hated them, all of them, to have worked so much evil—on my own siblings—" He passed a hand over his eyes. "No—they are not my own blood, are they—were they?"

Suddenly he broke away from her and hastened after the king. Leea followed more slowly, smiling.

Illrede sat in Imric's high seat. His eyes were fixed on the door into the chamber, and he chuckled softly as he heard the tramp of his guardsmen. "They are bringing Gora," he breathed. "They are bringing my little girl, who once laughed and played about my knees—" He put a heavy hand on the changeling's shoulder. "Your mother, Valgard."

She shambled into the hall, gaunt, wrinkled, bent over from the centuries of crouching in darkness. Out of her hollow skull-face the eyes stared, empty save for little ghosts of madness swimming far behind them.

"Gora—" Illrede's voice broke.

She blinked around, almost blind. "Who calls for Gora?" she mumbled. "Who calls for Gora calls for a ghost. Gora is dead, lord, she died nine hundred years ago. They buried her under a castle, her white bones hold its towers against the stars. Can you not let the poor dead troll-woman rest?"

Valgard shrank back, lifting a hand against the monster that stumbled over the floor toward him. Illrede started out of his chair. "Gora!" he cried. "Gora—know you not me, your father? Know you not your son?"

Her voice came windy and remote through the spacious hall. "How can the dead know anyone? How can the dead give birth? The brain which once gave birth to dreams is now the womb of maggots. Ants crawl within the hollowness where once a heart beat. Oh, give me back my chain! Give me back the lover whose arm was about my neck down in the dark!" She whimpered. "Raise not the poor frightened dead, lord, and wake not the mad, for life and reason are ravening monsters which live by devouring that which gives them birth."

She cocked her head, listening. "I hear hoofbeats," she whispered. "I hear hoofs galloping out on the edge of the world. It is Time, riding forth, and snow falls from his horse's mane and lightning crashes from its hoofs, and when Time has ridden by like a wind in the night there are only withered leaves left, blowing in the gale of his passage. He rides nearer, I hear worlds crashing to ruin in his path—Give me back my death!" she shrieked. "Let me crawl back into my grave to hide from Time!"

She fell huddled on the floor. Illrede sank back into the high seat and signed to his guards. "Take her out and kill her," he whispered. Turning to Grum: "Hang Imric by the thumbs over hot coals until we have conquered Alfheim and can give some thought to his reward." Then rising, with his voice a shout: "Ho, trollsmen, make ready to fare! We sail at once!"

Though the host had been expecting a great feast in Elfheugh, none who saw the king's face dared protest, and soon the black ships were sweeping southward out of sight.

"So much the more for us," laughed Grum. He saw Valgard's white visage and said: "Methinks you would do well to drink deep tonight."

"So I will," answered the berserker, "and ride to battle as soon as I can ready a host."

Now the troll chiefs gathered the women of the castle and took whom they wanted before turning the rest over to the men. Grum laid his remaining arm about Leea's waist. "You were wise to submit," he laughed, "so I can scarce see you degraded in rank. Earl's lady shall you still be."

She followed him meekly, but as she went by Valgard she smiled at the changeling. The berserker's eyes could not but follow her. Never had he seen such a woman—aye, with her he might forget the dark-haired witch who haunted his dreams.

The trolls held riotous feast for a while, then Valgard gathered men and rode against another castle which still held out. It was of no great size, but its walls were high and massive, and the defenders" arrows kept the trolls at a respectful distance.

Valgard waited through daylight, then near sunset sneaked through cover of forest and rocky outcrop until he was almost under the walls without the drowsy sun-dazzled elves seeing him. At dusk the horns blew to battle and the trolls rushed forth. Valgard stood up and with a mighty cast sent a grappling hook over the wall. Up the rope tied to it he swarmed, up to the top, and blew his horn.

The elf sentries stormed at him, and despite the iron he wore he had a desperate fight. But then the trolls had found the rope and come up after him. Erelong he had a large enough force atop the wall to hew his way to the gates and open them for his host.

There was a great slaughter of elves, with still more being taken captive and led in chains back to Elfheugh. Valgard plundered and burned in the castle and the elf-hill towns around it and came back with a huge booty.

Grum gave him sullen greeting, for he thought Valgard was getting too good a name among the trolls. "You could have stayed there," he said. "There is scarce room in this place for both of us."

"Perhaps not," murmured Valgard, measuring the earl with his chill pale eyes.

Grum could not do less than hold a great feast for his chief and place him in the high seat at his right. The elf women served the trolls, and Leea came to Valgard with horn after horn of the strong wine.

"To our great hero, mightiest of warriors in lands of men or faerie," she toasted him, smiling. The silvery light gleamed through her thin silks to the supple wonder of her body, and Valgard's head spun with her nearness.

"You can give me better thanks than that," he cried, and pulled her onto his lap. Fiercely he kissed her, and she responded no less eagerly.

Grum, slumped back in his seat and draining the horns without a word, now stirred in anger. "Get back to your work, faithless bitch," he snarled, and to Valgard: "Best you leave my woman alone. You have enough of your own."

"Perhaps," said Valgard. "But I like this one. I will give you three others for her."

"Ha, I can take your three if I like—I, your earl. What I choose is mine—and leave her be."

"The loot should go to him who can best use it," taunted Leea, not moving from Valgard's lap. "And you have only one hand."

The troll sprang from his seat, blind with rage and clawing for his sword. "Help me!" cried Leea.

Valgard's ax seemed to leap of itself into his grasp. Ere Grum, awkward with his left hand, could draw blade, the changeling's weapon sank into his neck.

He fell at Valgard's feet with blood spurting and looked tip into the twisted white face. "You are an evil man," said Grum, "but she is worse." And he died.

Now a great uproar rose in the hall, weapons flashed forth and the trolls surged for the high seat. Some cried for Valgard's instant death, others swore they would defend him. For a moment it was about to become a battle.

Then Valgard snatched the blood-smeared coronet, which had been Imric's, from Grum's head and set it on his own locks. He stood forth in front of the high seat and his great voice shouted out, calling for silence.

Slowly that silence came, until only a heavy breathing was heard in the hall. The bared weapons gleamed, and every eye was on Valgard where he stood tall and prideful in his strength.

He spoke at last, quietly but with metal in his cold tones: "This came somewhat sooner than I looked for, but it was bound to come. For what use to Trollheim was a cripple like Grum, unfit for battle, useful only for drinking wine and sleeping with women that might have gone to better men? I, who come of blood as good as any in Trollheim, and who have shown I can win victory, am more fit to be your earl. Better will it be for all trolls, particularly those of England, if I lead. I promise you victory, rich booty and high living and a glory in faerie, will you but belt me earl."

He pulled the ax out of Grum and lifted it. "Whoever disputes my right must argue it with me—now," he said. "But whoever shall stand true to me now will be repaid a thousand fold."

At this, the men who had followed him to the siege let forth a mighty cheer. Others, who wished not to fight, joined them, so it ended with Valgard's taking the high seat and the feast's going on.

Later, alone with Leea, the changeling sat looking darkly at her. "This is the second time a woman has driven me to murder," he said bleakly. "Were I wise, I would chop your body in three."

"I cannot stop you, lord," she smiled, and laid her white arms about his neck.

"You know I cannot do it," he said hoarsely. "'Tis idle talk—my life is black enough without such peace as I can find in a woman's love."

Still later he asked her: "Were you thus with the elves—with Skafloc?"

She lifted her head over his so that the fragrant net of her hair covered both. "Let it suffice that I am thus with you, lord," she whispered, and kissed him.

Now Valgard ruled Elfheugh for some time. Even in the ever deepening winter he was afield, breaking down elf strongholds and hunting the fugitives and outlaws with hounds and men through the snow. Scarce a garth in all the land remained unburned, and when the elves sought to make a stand he led his army roaring over them. Some of the men he took captive he threw into dungeons or put to slave work, but most of them he killed, and divided their women among his trolls. He himself took none, having eyes for none but Leea.

Word came from the south that Illrede's armies were driving the elves before them. All elf lands in Valland were now held by the trolls, and in the north only the elves of Scania still were free—and the burning and plundering went apace there. Erelong the trolls would be entering the central lands where the Erlking lay.

Men had some glimpse of these doings—distant fires, galloping shadows through the land, storm-winds bearing the remote clangor of battle. And the loosed magic often wrought havoc on the farms, with sickening livestock and spoiling grain and evil luck in the family. Now and again a hunter would come on a trampled, bloody field and see ravens tearing at corpses which had not the look of men. Folk huddled in lonely houses and hung iron before the door and called on their various gods for help.

Thus the winter wore on. And Valgard came to sit more and more in Elfheugh. For he had now been to all castles and hill-towns and garths he could find, he had harried from Orkney to Cornwall, and such elves as had escaped him were now hidden—striking out of cover at his men, so that not a few trolls never came home; sneaking poison into the food; hamstringing horses; rusting armor; raising howling blizzards as if the very land rose against the invader.

The trolls held England—no doubt of that, and ever their grip tightened. But never had Valgard longed for spring as now he did.

18

Skafloc and Freda took shelter in a cave. It was a deep hole in a cliff slanting back from the sea, well north of the elf-hills. Behind it was a forest of ice-sheathed trees which grew thicker toward the south and faded into moor and highland toward the north. Dark and desolate was the land, unpeopled, and on that account about as safe as any place.

They could not use much magic, for fear of being sensed by the trolls, but Skafloc did a good deal of hunting and fishing in guise of the wolf or otter or eagle whose skins Freda had brought, and he conjured ale from sea water. It was hard work simply staying alive in that wintry world, and he was ranging for game most of the time.

Dank and chill was the cave, with winds screaming in its mouth and an angry gray sea snarling on the rocks below. But when Skafloc returned from his first long hunt, he could scarce recognize it.

Now a fire blazed cheerily on a hearthstone, with smoke let out a rude chimney of branches, clay, and green hides. Other skins were a warm covering on floor and walls, and one hung in the cave mouth against the bitter wind. The extra horses stood in a corner chewing hay Skafloc had magicked from sea-weed, and the spare weapons were polished and hung on the wall as if this were a chief's feasting-hall. And behind the bright crossed arms was a little spray of red winter berries.

Crouched over the fire and turning meat on a spit was Freda. Skafloc paused in the entrance, his heart beating faster at sight of her. She wore only a brief tunic, and her slim-legged boyish body, with its sweet curves of thigh and waist and young breasts, seemed poised in the gloom like a white bird ready for flight.

She turned a flushed, smoke-smudged face, and from under tousled ruddy hair her great gray eyes lit with gladness. Wordlessly she came to him, in a run that had all of her dear coltlike awkwardness and grace, and they held each other close for a while.

Then he asked wonderingly: "But how did you ever do all this, sweet?"

She laughed softly. "I am no bear, or man, to make a pile of leaves and be content to sleep in that for the winter," she said. "Some of these skins and so on we had, the rest I got for myself. Oh, I am a good housewife." Then pressing against him, shivering: "You were gone so long, and time was so empty. I had to pass the days, and make myself weary enough to sleep at night."

His own hands shook as he fondled her. "This is no place for you," he murmured. "Hard and dangerous is the outlaw life. I should take you to a human garth, to await our victory or else to forget our defeat."

"No—no, never shall you do that!" She grasped his ears and pulled his face down to hers, laughing and sobbing. "I have said I will not leave you. No, Skafloc, 'twill be harder than that to get rid of me."

"Truth to say," he admitted after a while, "I do not know what I would do without you. Naught would seem worth the trouble any more."

"Then do not leave me—do not leave me, ever again."

"I must hunt, dearest one."

"Then I will hunt with you." She gestured at the hides and the cooking meat. "I am good at that."

"As well as other things," he laughed. Then grimly: "But it is not alone game I hunt, Freda, but trolls."

"There too will I be," she said. Her soft young face was all at once as hard as his own. "Think you I have no vengeance to take?"

His head lifted in pride, and he kissed her with a fierce quick movement. "Then so be it!" he said. "And Orm the warrior could be glad of such a daughter."

Her fingers traced the taut bony lines of his face, and a distant wonder was in her eyes. "Know you not who your father was?" she asked.

"No." He grew uneasy, remembering Tyr's words. "No, I never knew."

"No matter," she smiled, "save that he too could be proud. I think Orm the Strong would have given all his wealth for such a son as you—not that Ketil and Asmund were weaklings. And failing that, he must be glad indeed to see you joined with his daughter."

As the winter strengthened its cold, life grew harder. There was often hunger in the cave, and the relentless chill crept in past the hide door and the fire until only huddled together in a great bearskin could Skafloc and Freda find warmth. But they ceased not their ranging. For days at a time they would be afield riding the swift elf horses which sank not into the snow, hunting for game in a vast white emptiness.

Now and again they would come on the smoldering ruins of an elf garth, and at such times Skafloc grew white about the nostrils and said nothing for many hours. Once in awhile a living elf, gaunt and ragged, would appear, but the man did not try to build up a band. It would only draw the enemy's heed without being able to stand before him.

Always he was on the lookout for trolls. If he found their tracks, he and the girl would be off at a wild gallop. If it was a large group, they would fire arrows from a distance, then wheel and race away; or Skafloc might wait for daylight, then creep into the cave or other shelter in which the trolls slept and cut some throats. Were there no more than two or three, he would be on them with a sword whose song of vengeance, with Freda's arrow-whine, was the last sound they heard.

Relentless was that hunt, and desperately dangerous. Often they crouched in cave or brush with the troll pursuit galloping by their faces, and naught but a thin screen of sorcery wrought by the rune staves, scarce hiding them from a direct glance, to throw off the spoor. Spears and arrows and slung stones hissed after them when they fled from shooting down two or three of a company. From their home cave they saw troll longships sweep grimly along the shore, near enough for them to count the rivets in the warrior's shields.

And it was cold, cold.

Yet in that bleak life they found each other. Skafloc wondered how he could have had the heart to wage his fight without the slim beautiful shield-maiden who rode beside him. Her arrows had brought down many trolls, and her daring schemes of ambush still more—but perhaps the kisses she gave him in their brief dear moments of peace were the power driving him to his own deeds. And to her, he was the greatest and bravest and kindest of men, her sword and shield at once, lover and comrade.

Grim and bitter was the outlaw life, but she felt her body responding, in keenness of sense and tautness of sinew and unending endurance of spirit. The freezing wind whipped the blood in her veins, the icy stars seemed to lend some of their brilliance to her eyes. When life hung on a wavering sword-edge, she learned to savor each moment of it with a passion and clarity she had not dreamed before.

Strange, she once thought, how even when hungry and cold and afraid they had no hard words between them. They seemed to think and act like one, as if they had come from the same mold. Their only differences were those in which each filled the need of the other.

"I bragged once to Imric that I had never known fear, or defeat, or love-sickness," said Skafloc once. He lay in the cave with his head on her lap, letting her comb out his wind-tangled hair. "He said those were the three ends and beginnings of human life. At that time I understood him not, but now I see he was wise."

"How should he know?" she asked.

"I cannot say, for elves know defeat only sometimes, fear rarely, and love never at all. But since meeting you, dear, I have found all three in myself. I was becoming more elf than man—now you are making me human, and elfdom fades within me."

"And somewhat of elf has entered my blood, I fear less and less do I think of what is right and holy, more and more of what is good and pleasant. My sins grow heavy—"

Skafloc pulled her face down to his. "In that you do right," he said. "This muttering of duty and law and sin brings no good."

"You speak profanely—" she began. He stopped her words with a kiss. She sought to pull free, and it ended in a laughing, tumbling wrestling match. By the time they were done she had forgotten her forebodings.

◆ ◆ ◆

But now as the trolls finished wasting the elf lands, they withdrew into their forts, venturing out only in bands too strong to attack. Skafloc grew moody in inaction, his gay banter dropped off and he spent days at a time slumped sullen and unspeaking in the cave.

Freda sought to cheer him. "Now we are in less danger of death or capture," she said.

"What good is that, when we have no chance to fight?" he answered glumly. "Now we can only sit and wait for the end. Alfheim is dying, soon all lands of faerie will belong to the trolls, and I—I sit here!"

Another day he went out and saw a raven beating upwind under the lowering sky. The gray cold sea dashed in endless thunder on rocks at his feet and rattled and roared back for another leap, and the flying spindrift froze as it struck.

"What news?" called Skafloc in the raven tongue. It was not in such words that he spoke or was answered, for beasts and birds have different sorts of language from men, but the meaning is near enough.

"I come from south beyond the channel to fetch my kindred," replied the raven. "Valland and Vendland have fallen to the trolls, Scania is harried and plundered, and battle rages about the Erlking's last strongholds. Good is the feasting, but ravens had best hurry there for the war cannot last much longer."

At this such a blaze of anger flamed in Skafloc that he put an arrow to his bow and shot the bird. But when it lay dead at his feet the wrath drained from his breast, leaving a great empty darkness which sorrow slowly rose to fill.

"It was evil to slay you, brother," he muttered, "who have done no harm—and do much good by clearing the stinking clutter of a dead past from the world. Friendly you were to me, and defenceless, yet I slew you and let my foes sit in peace."

He turned back into the cave, and of a sudden he was weeping. The huge racking sobs nigh shook his body apart. Freda held him, murmuring to him as to a child, and he wept himself out on her breast.

That night he could not sleep. "Alfheim is falling," he mumbled. "Ere the snows melt, Alfheim will be a memory. Now there is naught for me but to ride against the troll army and take as many with me down hell-road as may be."

"Say not that," she answered. "It would be a stupid betrayal of your trust—and of me too. Better and braver to live, fighting."

"Fighting with what?" he asked bitterly. "The elf ships are sunken, the warriors dead or in chains or scattered and hunted. The proud castles lie in ruin, and the foe sits in the high seat of our old rulers. Alone are we, naked, hungry, weaponless—"

She kissed him. As it were a lightning bolt, he seemed to see a blinding flash before his eyes, the bright gleam of a sword lifted high against darkness.

For a long moment she felt his hard body lying stiff as an iron bar but trembling, shivering with a rising vibrant excitement, and then he breathed into the gloom: "The sword—the naming-gift of the Aesir—aye, *the sword—*"

A sudden fear, formless and ominous, sprang up cold in her breast. "What do you mean?" she cried. "What sword is this?"

Then as they lay there in the dark, close together against the frost, he whispered it to her, soft in her ear as if afraid the monstrously crouching night would listen. He told her of Skirnir's bringing the broken glaive, of Imric's hiding it in the wall of Elfheugh's dungeons, and of Tyr's warning that the time was nigh when he would have sore need of it.

In the end he felt her tremble in his arms, she who had hunted armed trolls. Her voice was small and quivering: "I like it not, Skafloc. It is not a good thing."

"Not good?" he cried. "Why, it is the one last great chance we have left. Odin, who reads the future, must have known of this day of Alfheim's need—must have given us the sword against it. Weaponless? Ha, we shall show them otherwise!"

"It is not good to deal with heathen things, least of all when the heathen gods offer them," she pleaded. "No good can come of it, Skafloc. Forget the sword!"

"It is true that the gods must have their own purposes in this," he admitted, "but it need not be one which is contrary to ours. I think all faerie is a chessboard on which Aesir and Jötuns move their pieces, elves and trolls, in some game beyond our understanding. Yet the good chess player takes care of his men."

"But the sword is buried in Elfheugh and the trolls are there—"

"I will get in somehow. I think I know a way already."

"The sword is broken. How shall you—we—find that giant whom it was said could mend it? How make him forge it anew to be used against his own kin, the trolls?"

"There will be a way." Skafloc's voice was like metal. "Even now I know a way to find out, though it is difficult and dangerous. We may well fail, aye, but the god-gift is our last chance."

"The god-gift." She began to cry. "I tell you, naught but ill can come of this. I feel it in me, cold and heavy. If you embark on this quest, Skafloc, our days together are numbered."

"Would you leave me on that account?" he asked unbelievingly.

"No—no, Skafloc—" She clung to him, blind with darkness and tears. "It is but a whisper in my soul, yet—I know—"

He drew her into his arms with hard eager strength. All the mirth and bravery and will dammed up in him now burst their bonds. Wildly he kissed her, until her head swam, and he laughed and was joyous—finally, she could do no more than drive the fears from her mind, for they seemed unworthy of Skafloc's bride, and be glad with him.

But there was a fierceness and yearning in her love which had not been there before. Far down in the darkness of her soul, she felt that they would not have many more nights together.

19

It was the next night when they reined in their horses after a blinding gallop from the cave. Skafloc could not wait, not when Alfheim was dying day by day. There was a half moon riding in a cloudy sky, its dim light filtering through bare icicle-gleaming trees and shimmering eerily on the deep snow. The night was still and cold, so cold that breathing was pain, and their breaths steamed out of the shadowed ravine in which they hid and up to glimmer in the moonlight like ghosts escaping the lips of dying men. Now and again through the great cold silence came ringing the sharp cry of trees splitting open.

"We dare go no nearer Elfheugh." Skafloc's whisper sounded unnaturally loud in the frost-choked quiet. "But I can make it alone, on wolf-foot, ere dawn."

"Why can you not wait?" Freda clung to his arm and he saw her eyes tear-bright under the moon. "Why not, at least, go by day, when *they* will be asleep?"

"The were-beast guise cannot be used by day," he answered. "And once inside the castle walls, day or night are the same, the most of the trolls are as likely to be sleeping as wakeful. When I am in, there are those who can help me; I think chiefly of Leea."

"Leea—" Freda bit her lip so that sharp pain came. "I like it not, this whole mad scheme. Is there no other way?"

"None I can think of. But you, my sweet, have the hardest task—that I admit—waiting here, alone in the dark and cold, until I return." He looked at her shadowed face as if to learn every least line of it. "Be not foolish, princess. If trolls come near, or if I am gone longer than three days, be off. Fly to the world of men and sunlight!"

"I can endure waiting," she said tonelessly, "but to abandon this place, not knowing whether you lived or—" she choked "—or died, that may be past my strength."

Skafloc swung from his horse into the snow. Quickly he stripped off furs, helm and byrnie, all garments until at last he stood naked, shivering in the silent gnawing cold. Then he wrapped the otter skin about his waist, the eagle skin about his shoulders, and flung the great gray wolfskin cloak-like over both.

Freda dismounted and stood in the snow. Fiercely, hungrily, he kissed her. "Now goodbye, dearest one," he whispered. "Until I return with the sword, goodbye."

He turned away, not daring to linger by the quietly crying girl, and drew the wolfskin tighter about him. He dropped to all fours, feeling his body shift and mold itself, feeling his senses in a blur of change. And Freda saw him, swiftly as if he melted, alter, until a great wolf stood beside her with eyes glowing green in the dark.

Briefly the cold nose nuzzled her hand, and she rumpled the rough gray coat. Then he turned and padded noiselessly away.

Over the snow he went, weaving between trees and slipping lithely under tangled bushes, loping swifter and more tireless than a man. It was strange, being a wolf. He could feel the alien interplay of nerve and sinew, the air ruffling his fur. His sight was dim, flat, and colorless, but he heard every faintest sound, every sigh and whisper, the night's huge silence was now alive and murmurous for him—many of those tones too high for men to hear at all; and he smelled the air as if it were a living thing, the uncounted subtle odors, the hints and traces swirling in his nostrils. And there were other sensations for which men had no words whatever.

It was like being in another world, a world which in every way *felt* different. And he himself was changed, not alone in this new taut body but in brain and nerve. His mind moved in wolfish tracks, narrower but in a way keener. He was not able in beast body to think all the thoughts he did as a man, nor, on becoming man again, to remember all he had sensed and thought as a beast.

On and on! The night and the miles fled under his racing feet. The forest stirred with its secret life. He caught the scent of hare—frightened hare, crouched nearby with big eyes watching him—and his wolf mouth drooled with desire. But his man soul drove the gaunt gray body ahead, relentlessly ahead. An owl hooted far away in frost and silence. Forest and hills and ice-scabbarded rivers went by in a blur, the moon sank low, and still he ran.

And at last, looming against the moon-swallowing horizon, its towers seeming crusted with frosty winter stars, he saw Elfheugh. Elfheugh, Elfheugh, the lovely and fallen, now a crouched menace bulking black across the sky!

He flattened himself on his hairy belly and slid up the hill toward the rearing walls. Every quivering wolf-sense reached out, feeling around him—were enemies at hand?

Trolls! He caught the cold snaky smell and bunched his lean form, snarling in rage and hate. The castle reeked of troll. And of subtler, even worse smells, fear and pain and throttled wrath.

With his dim wolf-eyes he could not see the top of the mighty wall under which he crouched. But he heard the troll guardsmen pace above him, and smelled them, and his gray moon-silvered body trembled with the longing to rip out their throats.

But easy—easy! There they went, they were well past him—now to turn his skin again.

He writhed, felt the shifting and shrinking, his brain swam with the change. But then he beat the mighty wings of the eagle and rose regally heavenward.

His sight was keen now, inhumanly so, and the pulsing joy of flight, the mastery of air and skyey space, tingled in every feather of him. But the cold sharp eagle brain had will to refuse that magnificent drunkenness. His eyes were almost blind in the dark, and in flight he was a target for troll arrows.

Over the wall he went and soared across the courtyard, braking his flight with the wind whistling in his pinions. He landed against the castle, under the shadow of a thickly ivied tower, and again he shuddered with change. Then as otter he crouched and waited.

He could not smell in this shape quite so well as a wolf, though better than a man, but his eyes were somewhat sharper and his ears as good. Also, his body had a wiry alertness where every fur-hair and whisker tip quivered with awareness, with subtlest sensations indescribable to man; and his litheness and swiftness and grace, the deep luster of his pelt and the supple slimness of his body, were a joy to the vain, cocky, frolicsome otter brain.

Now he lay tense and still, straining every sense. He heard startled halloos from the wall—someone must have had a fleeting glimpse of the eagle, and it was not well for him to stay here.

He slipped lithely along the wall, keeping to the shadows. An otter was too big to be safe—better had he been a weasel or a rat—but it was the best he could do. It would have to serve, and glad he was that Freda had brought those three magic skins. A great tenderness welled up in him at thought of her, but he could not stop, not now.

A door stood open, and into this he sneaked. It was in the back of the castle, but he knew every hole and corner of that mysterious labyrinth. His whiskers twitched as he snuffed the air. The place was stinking with troll, but it was also heavy with the smell of sleep. In that much he was lucky. He could sense some few moving about, but they were easy to avoid.

He padded by the great feasting hall. Trolls sprawled there, snoring drunkenly. The tapestries hung in rags, the cunningly carved furnishings were scarred and stained, and the ornaments of gold and silver and jewels, the work of many centuries, had been looted. It would have been better, thought Skafloc, to be conquered by goblins. They were at least a mannered people. But these filthy troll savages—

Up the stairs toward Imric's tower chambers he wound. Whoever was now earl would most likely sleep there—and have Leea beside him.

The otter flattened against the wall, a soundless snarl showing needle teeth. His yellow eyes blazed as around the curve he smelled troll. The earl had mounted a guard and—

Like a gray thunderbolt the wolf was on the troll. Sleepy, he could not know what had struck until the terrible fangs closed in his throat. He fell in a clatter of armor, clawing at the beast on his chest, and thus he died.

Skafloc stood taut, with blood dripping from his jaws. It had been a loud racket—no, no sound of alarm or awareness in all the great castle—He would have to chance the troll's body being found before he was away. It would surely be found soon—no, wait—

Briefly, as a man, Skafloc used the dead troll's sword to chop face and throat until it could not be seen that teeth rather than blade had torn out life. They might think the guard had been murdered in some drunken quarrel. They had better! The thought was grim in him as he wiped and spat the blood from his mouth.

Then as otter he raced on his way again. At the head of the stairs, the great door to Imric's chambers stood closed, but he knew the secret hiss and whistle which would open the lock. Softly he gave them, and nosed the door open a crack.

Two slept in Imric's bed. If now the earl awoke, that would be the end of Skafloc's quest. He crawled on his lissome otter stomach toward the bed, and every movement seemed loud as thunder in the room.

He stood up on his hind legs. Leea's pale lovely features lay in a cloud of her silvery-blonde hair on the pillow. Beyond her he discerned a tawny-maned head with a countenance gaunt and grim even in slumber—but in every blunt, strong, muscled line it was his own.

Valgard—so Valgard the evil-worker was now earl. Barely could Skafloc hold himself back from sinking wolf teeth in that corded throat, tearing with eagle beak at the closed eyes, nuzzling and licking with otter tongue among the ripped-out guts.

But the sword—

He touched Leea's smooth white cheek with his nose. Her eyes fluttered open, and though she made no move remembrance flared in them.

Slowly, slowly, with infinite care, Leea sat up. Valgard stirred and groaned in his sleep and she froze. The berserker mumbled to himself, Skafloc caught broken fragments: "—changeling—the ax— O Mother, Mother!—"

Leea slid one leg to the floor. Poised on that slender foot, she eased her whole body out. Its whiteness gleamed through the swirling cloudy veil of her hair. Like a drifting shadow, she slipped out of the room, through another, and into a third, with Skafloc padding after. Noiselessly she closed the door.

"Now we can talk, Skafloc," she breathed.

He stood forth, man again, and she fell into his arms with a half laugh, half sob. She had never kissed him thus before, and despite Freda he was hotly aware of what a fair woman it was he held.

"Skafloc," she whispered. Her voice shook. "Skafloc."

"I have no time," he said harshly. "I am come for the broken sword which was the Aesir's naming-gift to me."

"You are tired." Her hands touched the haggard lines of his face. "You have been cold and weary and hungry. Let me rest you now—come, there is a secret room—"

"No time, no time," he fairly snarled. "Freda waits for me in the very heart of the troll holdings. Quickly, lead me to the sword."

"Freda—" Leea's ivory cheeks went a shade whiter. "So the mortal girl is still with you."

"Aye, and a valiant warrior for Alfheim has she been."

"I have not done too badly myself." Leea smiled with her old malicious humor. "Already Valgard has slain Grum Troll-Earl for my sake. He is strong, but I am bending him." She swayed closer. "He is better than a troll, he is almost like you—but he is not you, Skafloc, and I weary of pretending."

"Oh, hurry!" He shook her. "If we are caught it is the end of Alfheim, and every moment strengthens the chance."

She stood very quiet for a long moment. Then she looked away, out the broad window through which a bitter breeze blew and over a world silent and frozen in the moonless dark before dawn. "Indeed," she whispered. "You are right, of course. And what is better or more natural than that you should hasten back to your love—to Freda?"

She swung on him, shaking with noiseless terrible mirth, hair blowing wild about her. "Do you want to know who your father was, Skafloc? Shall I tell you who you really are?"

He clamped a hand over her mouth, the old ghastly fear choking him: "No! No, never—you know what Tyr said!"

She stood trembling in the cold air. "Seal my lips," she said. "Seal them with a kiss."

"I cannot wait—" He kissed her. "Come!"

"Cold was that kiss," she murmured desolately. "Cold as duty ever is. Well, let us be on our way. But you are naked and unarmed. Since you cannot carry the iron sword away as a were-beast, you had best have some clothes." She opened a chest. "Here is tunic, breeches, shoon, cape, whatever else you like."

He tumbled into the garments—his own, and richly fur-trimmed—with feverish swiftness. Leea threw a flame-red cloak over her own nakedness. Then she led the way out and down another stair.

Down they wound and down. It was cold and silent here, a death-like silence but stretched near the breaking point, quivering with its own tautness. Once they passed a troll soldier, and Skafloc's hackles rose and he reached for the sax at his belt. But the guard saluted, taking the man for the changeling.

Now the dank gloom of the dungeons hid them, only the widely spaced, flaring torches lighting the eternal night. Skafloc's steps boomed in hollow echoes down corridors which seemed to fill their emptiness with thronging, watchful shadows. Leea flitted ahead, ghost-silent.

They came at last to a place, where the ancient stone showed a lighter splash of cement in which were scratched mighty runes. Not far beyond was a great closed door. Leea pointed to it. "In the cell there Imric kept the changeling-mother," she said. "Now he is in there himself, hung by his thumbs over an undying fire. It is often Valgard's pleasure when drunk to lash him senseless."

Skafloc's knuckles were white on his sword haft. He said naught, but with the tip of the sax he dug fiercely at the wall.

Dimly a sound drifted down to them, shouting of voices and hurrying of feet. "There is an alarm," hissed Leea.

"Belike they found the guard I had to kill." Skafloc dug frantically. The cement scraped slowly from the stone.

"Were you seen entering?" she asked sharply.

"I may have been glimpsed in eagle guise." Skafloc cursed as his tool snapped. He dug with the broken blade.

"Valgard is shrewd enough, if he hears about that eagle, to think this may be no ordinary killing. If he sets men to search the castle, and they find us—Hurry!"

The clamor above beat faintly on their ears, less loud than the scrape of metal on stone or a centuries-old dripping of water.

Skafloc got the blade into a crack and heaved, heaved with every surging muscle. Once—twice—thrice, and the stone crashed out!

He reached into the niche beyond. His hands shook as he brought forth the sword.

It was old—old. Rust and damp and ancient earth clung to the halves of the mighty iron blade. It had been two-edged, and so huge and heavy that only the strongest of men could swing it. The black haft was of some strange iron-like wood, carved in the shape of a coiling dragon whose tail made the guard and whose gape-jawed head the pommel, and great rivets held it to the snapped blade. There were runes, half hidden by rust and mold, running down the dark iron length.

"The weapon of the gods." Skafloc held it with an almost holy awe. "The hope of Alfheim—"

"Hope?" Leea shrank back. "I wonder! Now that I see the old sword, I wonder!"

"What mean you?"

"Can you not feel it? The monstrous slumbering power locked in that iron, held by those runes so ancient even I cannot read them—the power ravenous and resistless and—evil! There is a curse on that weapon, Skafloc. It will bring the bane of all within its might." Her eyes were wide and frightened. She shivered with a cold not that of the dungeon. "I think—Skafloc, I think it were best for you if you walled up that sword again."

"What other hope have we?" he asked grimly. He wrapped the sword in his cloak and took the bundle under one arm. "Come, let us away."

Leea shuddered, but led him to a stair. "This will be hard and perilous," she said. "We can scarce avoid being seen by the trolls. Let me speak for both of us."

"It would be too dangerous for you—" he began. She swung around. Her eyes were alight. "You fear for me?" she breathed.

"Why, of course—as I fear for all Alfheim."

"And for—Freda?"

"For her I fear more than for all the rest of the world, gods and men and faerie together. I love her."

Leea turned forward again, her face hidden from him and her voice colorless: "I will be able to save myself. I can always tell Valgard you forced or tricked me."

They came out on the first floor. It was a bustle of hurrying guards, uproar, clamor, confusion. "Hold!" roared a troll as he saw them.

Leea's face flared cold arrogance. "Dare you halt the earl?" she cried.

"Pardon—your pardon, lord," mumbled the troll. "'Twas just that—I saw you but a moment ago, lord—"

They went out into the courtyard. Every nerve in Skafloc shrieked that he should run, every muscle was knotted in expectancy of the cry that would mean they were found out. Run—run! He shook with the effort of walking slowly.

But few trolls were outside. The first chill silvery streaks of the hated dawn were in the east. It was very cold.

Leea stopped at the great outer gate and signed that it should be opened. Then she looked into Skafloc's eyes with an inscrutable blind gaze.

"Now you must make your own way," she said softly. "Know you what to do?"

"Somehow," he answered, "I must find the giant Bölverk who forged the sword and make him bring it forth anew for me."

"Bölverk—evil worker—his very name is a warning." Leea shook her head. "But I know that stubborn set to your jaw, Skafloc. Not all the powers of hell shall stop you—only death or the loss of your will to fight. But what of your dear Freda on this quest?" She sneered the last words.

"She will come along, though I will try to persuade her to shelter." Skafloc smiled in pride and love. The dim dawn-light touched his hair with frosty gold. "We are not to be parted."

"No." A strange and secret smile stole over Leea's mouth. "But as to finding the giant—who can tell you the way?"

Skafloc's face grew bleak. "It is not a good thing to do," he said, "but I can raise a dead man. The dead know all things, and Imric taught me the charms to compel speech from them."

"Yet is it a desperate deed," she said, "for the dead hate most of all that breaking of their timeless sleep, and they wreak vengeance for it. Can you fight a ghost?"

"I must try. I think my magic will be too strong for it to strike at me."

"Perhaps not at you, but—" Leea paused, and her smile was cruel. "That would not be as terrible a revenge anyway as one it could work through—say—Freda."

She watched the blood drain from his face. Her own went white with his. "Love you the girl that much?" she whispered.

"Aye. More," he said thickly. "You are right, Leea. I cannot risk it. Better Alfheim should fall than—than—"

"No, wait! I was going to give you a plan. But I would ask one thing first."

"Hurry, Leea, hurry!"

"Only one thing. If Freda should leave you—no, no, do not stop to tell me she won't, I only ask—if she should, what would you do?"

"I know not. I cannot dream of that."

"Perhaps—come back here? Become elf again—?"

"Perhaps. I know not. Hurry, Leea!"

She smiled again, a cat-smile cold as the bitter dawn-wind which stirred her glorious hair. Her eyes rested dreamy and remote on him. "I was simply going to say this," quoth she, "that instead of raising just any dead man, call on those who would be glad to help you and whose own revenge you would be working. Has not Freda a whole family, all slain by Valgard? Raise *them*, Skafloc!"

For a moment Skafloc stood moveless. Then he dropped the sword-bundle, swept Leea into his arms, and kissed her with numbing force. Seizing anew the burden, he sprang through the gate and rushed into the forest.

Leea stared after him. Once her fingers came up to her still tingling lips. Then she began to laugh.

◆ ◆ ◆

Valgard learned that his own likeness had been seen within the castle. His leman, looking dazed and a-tremble, could only say that something had cast a spell on her as she slept, so that she remembered naught. But there were tracks in the snow, and the hounds of the trolls could follow colder trails than this.

At sunset, the earl led his trolls on horseback, in pursuit.

Freda stood in the shadow of a tree, looking through the bare moon-ghostly forest toward Elfheugh.

She was cold on this second night of her waiting, so cold that it had long since passed feeling and was now like a part of herself. She had huddled between the horses, but they were cool and elfly, not the warm sweet-smelling beasts of home. Strangely, it was the thought of Orm's horse that brought her loneliness back to her. She felt now as if she were the last living creature in a frozen dead world of moonlight and snow and desolation.

She dared not weep, but—*Skafloc, Skafloc! Lived he yet?*

A rising wind blew snow-heavy clouds ever thicker over the sky, so that the wan moon seemed to be fleeing great black dragons which swallowed it and smothered the dead world in darkness. The wind alone lived, it wailed in the trees, it roared through the sky, it snarled around her where she stood in a blind fury of bitter noise. Hoo, hoo, it sang, blowing a sudden sheet of snow before it, eldritch white in the moon, hoo, halloo, hunting you!

Hoo, hoo! echoed the troll horns. Freda stiffened with a fear like a dagger. *They* hunted now—hunted, and what game could it be save—

Now she heard the yelp of their hounds, the huge black monsters with eyes like red coals, baying on the trail, nearer, nearer. Oh, Skafloc! Freda stumbled forward, scarce hearing her own screams. Skafloc!

Raving darkness closed on her. She crashed into a tree. Wildly she beat at it, get out of my way, you thing, step aside, Skafloc is calling me— Oh!

In the suddenly streaming moonlight she saw the stranger. Tall he was, with a cloak tossing like great dark wings around his shadowy form. He was old, with long hair and beard blowing frosty gray in the eerie hurrying light, but the unearthly flashing spear he carried could have been wielded by no mortal man. A wide-brimmed hat threw his face into shadow, but she saw the cold terrible gleam of a single eye fixed on her.

She stumbled backward, gasping in fear, seeking to call on Heaven's help. The voice stopped her, deep and strong, seeming a part of the berserk roar of the storm, but chill and calm: "I bring help, not harm. Would you see your man again?"

She sank dumbly to her knees. For a moment, in the blurring, wavering moonlight, she seemed to see—past flying snow, past frozen miles, to the hill up which Skafloc stumbled. Weaponless he was, spent and reeling from weariness, and the hounds were springing toward him. Their howling seemed to shake the moon.

The vision faded. She looked up to the figure of night and storm and mystery looming over her. "You are Odin," she whispered. "You are Odin, and it is not for me to have dealings with you."

"Nevertheless I can save your lover—and only I, for he is heathen." The god's blazing eye held her as if she were speared. "But you must pay the price. Now quickly, woman, quickly!"

"What do you want?" she gasped.

"Hurry, the hounds are about to rend him!"

"I will give it to you—I will give it—"

He nodded slowly. His grim deep voice rolled over her: "Then you must swear by your own soul and all which is holy to you, that when I come for it you must give me what is behind your girdle."

"I swear!" she cried, and now tears blinded her, wild weeping of relief. Odin could not be the cruel implacable being of whom they spoke, not when he only wanted the drug Skafloc had given her. "I swear it, lord, and may all the earth and Heaven forsake me if I do not keep the vow."

"It is well," he said. "Now the trolls are off on a false trail, and Skafloc is here. Woman, remember your oath!"

Darkness came as a cloud swallowed the moon. When light returned, the As was gone.

But Freda scarce noticed that, not when she was laughing and sobbing in the arms of Skafloc. And he, bewildered at being of a sudden removed from the very jaws of the troll dogs to his goal, was not too mazed to answer her kisses.

20

They spent no more than two days resting in the cave, and then Skafloc busked himself to go.

Freda did not weep, but she could feel the unshed tears thick and bitter in her throat. "You think this is dawn for us," she said once, the second day. "I say it is night."

He looked at her, puzzled. "What mean you?"

"The sword is evil. The deed we now go to do is evil. No good can come of it."

He laid his hands on her shoulders. "I know you do not like making your own kin travel the troublous road," he said gravely. "Nor do I. Yet who else of all the dead will help and not harm us? Stay here, Freda, if you cannot bear it."

"No—no, I will be at your side even at the mouth of the grave. It is not that I fear my folk. Living or dead, there is love between them and me—and the love is yours too, now." Freda lowered her eyes and bit her lip to halt its trembling. "Had you or I thought of this, I would not be so frightened. But Leea meant no good with her rede."

"Why should she wish ill on us?"

Freda shook her head and would not answer. Skafloc said slowly: "I must say, I like not altogether your meeting with Odin. It is not his way to ask a small price. But what the Wanderer really meant I cannot imagine."

"And the sword—Skafloc, if that broken sword is made whole again, a terrible power will be loose in the world. It will work unending woe."

"For the trolls." Skafloc straightened until his fair head touched the smoky cave roof. His eyes flashed lightning-blue in the gloom. "There is no other road than the one we take, hard though it be. And no man outlives his weird. Best to meet it bravely, face to face."

"And side by side." Freda bowed her shining bronze head on his breast, and now the tears flowed heavily. "One thing only do I ask of you, my dearest of all."

"What is that?"

"Ride not out tonight. Wait one night more, only one, and then we will go." Her fingers dug into the muscles of his arms. "Only that, Skafloc—"

He nodded reluctantly. "Why is that?" he asked.

She would not say, and in the sweet riot of their love he forgot the question. But Freda remembered. Even when she held him most closely and felt his heart beating against hers, she remembered, and it gave a terrible yearning to her kisses.

Blindly, reasonlessly, she knew this was their last such night.

The sun rose, glimmered palely at noon, and sank behind heavy storm-clouds scudding in from the sea. A wolf-fanged wind howled over the breakers dashing themselves to thunderous death. Once there seemed to come the remote sound of hoofs galloping through the sky, swift as the storm, and a frightful baying and yelping. Even Skafloc shivered—the Wild Hunt was out.

They mounted their elf horses, leading the other two with all their goods, for they did not expect to return. Lashed to his back, Skafloc had the broken sword wrapped in a wolfskin. His own elf blade was sheathed at his side, one hand carried a spear, and both of them wore helm and byrnie under their furs.

Freda looked back at the black cave mouth as they rode away. Cold and gloomy and barren it was, but they had had happiness there. Then, resolutely, she turned her eyes forward.

"Now ride!" shouted Skafloc, and away they went at full elf-gallop.

The wind roared and bit at them as they raced along the coast. Sleet and spindrift blew in stinging sheets, white under the flying fitful moon. The sea bellowed on the rocks, its dark heaving wastes reaching out to a wild horizon. When the breakers foamed back, the rattle of stones was like some ice-bound monster stirring and groaning. The night was a chaos of wind and sleet and surging waters, its angry roar ringing to the cloud-flying heavens. The moon seemed to keep pace with the tearing, hoof-clattering gallop along the cliffs.

Now swiftly, swiftly, best of horses, swiftly southward by the sea, spurn ice under your hoofs, strike sparks from naked rocks, gallop, gallop! Ride with the wind roaring in your ears, ride through a moon-white curtain of hissing sleet and through screaming darkness, rush through the foeman's land ere he can tell you are abroad. Swiftly, ride swiftly, south to greet a dead man in his howe!

A troll horn screamed once as they raced past Elfheugh harbor. They could not see the castle in the rushing dark, but they heard a thunder of hoofs behind them. A thunder that dwindled into the storm—the trolls rode not so fast, nor would they follow where their quarry went tonight.

Swiftly, swiftly, through forests where the wind skirls in icy branches, weaving between trees that claw with naked twigs—gallop past frozen bog and darkling lake, rush out on open fields—gallop, gallop!

Now Freda began to know the way. The wind still drove sleet before it but the clouds were thinning, the moon cast its cold pale glitter over fields and dales locked in snow and slumber. She had been here before. She remembered this river and that darkened croft, here she had gone hunting with Ketil, there she and Asmund had fished all one lazy summer day, in that meadow had Asgerd woven chains of daisies for them—how long ago, how many centuries ago?

The tears froze on her cheeks. She felt Skafloc reach out to touch her arm, and she smiled back into his moonlit, shadowy face. Her heart could scarce endure this return, but he was with her—and when they were together there was nothing they could not stand.

And now the speed-blurred countryside became the remembered fields of Orm, and her breath sobbed in her throat as she reined in.

They rode slowly on their panting, trembling horses, not saying a word but riding close together. They came into what had been the garth of Orm. There were great snowdrifts, white in the racing moonlight, out of which the charred ends of timbers stuck like fangs. And huge at the head of the bay rose the dark bulk of the howe.

A cold fire wavered over it, roaring and blazing its terrible blue-tinged white—heatless, cheerless, leaping up into the sleeting night. Freda crossed herself, shuddering. Thus had the grave-fires of the old heathen heroes burned, each night after sunset.

It could not be holy ground in which Orm lay—but however far into the nameless lands of death he had wandered, he was still her father.

She could not fear the man who had ridden her on his knee and sung songs for her till the hall rang. But she was racked with trembling.

Skafloc rode up and dismounted. He felt his own body cold with sweat. He had never used the spells he must make tonight.

He went forward—and stopped, breath hissing between his teeth as he snatched for his sword. Black in the light of moon and fire, a figure sat motionless as if graven atop the barrow, under the howling flames. If now he had to fight a drow—

Freda's voice whimpered in the dark, the voice of a little lonely child: "Mother."

Skafloc took her hand. Together they walked up on the barrow.

The woman who sat there might almost have been Freda, thought Skafloc bewilderedly. She had the same pert beauty of thin-chiseled features, the same great gray eyes, the same red-sparked brown glory of hair. But no, no—she was older, she was ravaged by sorrow, her cheeks were sunken in and her eyes hollow, staring emptily out to sea, and her hair streamed unbound, unkempt, in the gale. She wore a thick fur cloak, with rags under that, over her gaunt unmoving body.

She turned slowly around as they came into the shuddering light. Her eyes sought Skafloc's tall form.

"Welcome back, Valgard," she said tonelessly. "Here I am. But you can do me no more harm, I am beyond all hurting now. You can only give me death, which is a boon."

"Mother—" Freda sank to her knees before the woman.

Aelfrida stared at her. "I do not understand," she whispered. "It seems to be my girl, my little Freda—but you are dead. Valgard took you away, and you cannot have lived long." She shook her head, smiling, and held out her arms. "It was good of you to leave your quiet grave and come to me. I have been so lonely. Come, my little dead girl, come lie in my arms and I will sing you to sleep as I did when you were but a baby."

"I live, Mother, I live—and you live—" Freda choked on her tears. "See, feel, I am warm, I am alive. And this is not Valgard, it is Skafloc who saved me from him. It is Skafloc, my lord, a son for you—"

Aelfrida stood slowly up, leaning heavily on her daughter's arm. "I have waited," she said. "I have waited here, and they thought I was mad. They bring me food and clothing, but they fear the mad woman who will not leave her dead." She laughed, softly, softly. "Why, what is mad about that? The mad are those who leave their beloved ones."

She scanned the man's face. "You are like to Valgard," she said quietly, "you have the height and strength and much of the face of Orm—but your eyes are kinder than Valgard's." She laughed again, tenderly. "Why, now let them say I am mad! I waited, that is all, I waited, and now out of the night and mystery of death two of my children have returned to me."

"We may return more ere dawn," said Skafloc. He and Freda led the stumbling woman down the icy mound.

"Mother lived," whispered the girl. "I thought her dead too, but she lived, and she sat shivering alone in the winter— What have I done?"

She wept, and Aelfrida comforted her.

Now Skafloc staked out his rune wands, one at each corner of the howe. He stood in its shadow with his arms raised. The sea raged at its foot and the moon fled through ragged monstrous clouds. Sleet blew in on the keening wind.

Skafloc spoke the spell, and it racked his body and seared his throat with a blinding pain. Shuddering with the unearthly might surging up in him, he made the rune signs with his lifted hands.

The grave-fire roared higher. The storm screamed like a wild beast and clouds swallowed the moon. Darkness fell on the world, a living darkness in which tremendous presences stirred.

Skafloc called out above the wind and sea and coldly leaping fire:

Waken, chieftains,
fallen warriors!
Skafloc calls ye,
sings ye wakeful.
I conjure ye,
come on hell-road.
Rune-bound dead men,
rise and answer!

The barrow groaned. Higher and ever higher raged the icy flame above it. Skafloc chanted:

Grave shall open.
Gang forth, deathlings!
Fallen heroes,
fare to earth now.
Stand forth, bearing
swords all rusty,
broken shields, and
bloody lances.

Then the howe opened with leaping fires, and Orm and his sons stood in the grave-mouth. The chieftain called:

Who dares sunder
howe, and bid me
rise from death, by
runes and song-spells?
Flee the dead man's
fury, stranger!
Let the deathling
lie in darkness.

Orm stood leaning on his spear. Earth still clung to him, and he was bloodless and covered with rime. His eyes glared frightfully in the flames that roared and whirled around him. On his right hand stood Ketil, stiff and pale, with the gash in his skull black against his blood-clotted hair. On his left was Asmund, wrapped in shadow, arms folded over the spear wound in his breast. Dimly behind them, Skafloc could see the buried ship and the dead crew stirring awake within it.

He bit back the fear that came out of the grave-mouth and quoth:

Terror shall not
turn my purpose.
Runes shall bind thee.
Rise and answer!
In thy ribs may
rats build nests, if
thou will give not
that I call for!

Orm's voice rolled out, far and windy and strange:

Deep is dreamless
death-sleep, warlock.

Wakened dead are
wild with anger.
Ghosts will take a
gruesome vengeance
when their bones are
hailed from barrow.

Now Freda stood forth. "Father!" she cried. "Father, know you not your daughter?"

Orm's terrible dead eyes flamed on her, and the cold wrath died in them. He bowed his head and stood in the whirling, hissing sleet of fire. Ketil quoth:

Gladly see we
gold-decked woman.
Sun-bright maiden,
sister, welcome!
Ashy, frozen,
are our hollow
breasts with grave cold.
But you warm us.

Aelfrida came slowly up to Orm. They looked at each other, standing there in the dreadful roar of heatless fire. She took his hands, they were cold as the frozen earth in which they had lain. He quoth:

Dreamless was not
death, but frightful!
Tears of thine, dear,
tore my heart out.
Vipers dripped their

venom on me,
when in death I
heard thee weeping.

This I ask of
thee, beloved:
live in gladness,
laughing, singing.
Death is then the
dearest slumber,
wrapped in peace, with
roses round me.

"That I have not strength to do, Orm," she said. She touched his dead face. "There is frost in your hair. There is mold in your mouth. You are cold, Orm."

"I am dead. The grave lies between us."

"Then let it be so no longer. Take me with you, Orm. Take me with you!"

His lips were cold on hers.

Skafloc said to Ketil:

Speak forth, deathling.
Say me whither
Bölverk giant
bides, the swordsmith.
Tell me farther,
truly, warrior,
what will make him
hammer for me.

Ketil quoth:

Ill thy questing
is, thou warlock!
Worst of evil
will it bring thee.
Seek not Bölverk.
Sorrow brings he.
Leave us now, while
life is left thee.

Skafloc shook his head, wordless and grim. Then Ketil leaned on his sword and chanted:

North in Jötunheim,
nigh to Utgard,
dwells the giant,
deep in mountain.
Sidhe will give thee
ship to find him.
Tell him Loki
talks of sword-play.

Now Asmund spoke from where he stood with his face in shadow, and there was sorrow in his voice:

Bitter, cruel—
brother, sister—
fate the Norns let
fall upon ye.
Wakened dead men

wish ye had not
wrought the spell that
wrings the truth out.

Of a sudden terror came on Freda, the black knowledge that now—now!—was the end of a world for her. She could not speak, she crept close to Skafloc and they stood facing the sorrowful wise eyes of Asmund. He said slowly, while the fires flamed white around his dark form:

Law of men is
laid on deathlings.
Hard it is to
hold unto it.
But the words must
bitter leave me:
Skafloc, Freda
is your sister.
Welcome, brother,
valiant warrior.
All unwitting
are you, sister.
But your love has
broken kinship.
Farewell, children,
fey and luckless!

The howe closed with a shattering groan. The flames sank and the moon gleamed wanly forth, low on the dark horizon.

Freda shrank from Skafloc with horror in her eyes. Like a blind man, he stumbled toward her. A strange little dry sob rattled in her throat. She turned and fled from him.

"Mother," she whispered, "Mother."

But the howe was bare under the moon. Nor did men ever see Aelfrida again.

Dawn came, a bleak and cheerless gray light stealing over the snow. The sky was low and heavy, clouds frozen over the empty white land. A few snowflakes drifted down through the silent bitter air.

Freda sat on the barrow, staring empty-eyed before her. She was not weeping. It seemed to her that she had wept out all her tears and could never cry again. Her breast felt cold and hollow.

She did not look at Skafloc when he sat down beside her. His face was white and haggard in the dull dawn. His voice came low and hopeless: "I love you, Freda."

She said no word. After a while he went on: "I can never do other than love you. What matters the chance which made us of the same blood? It means naught. Come—Freda, come, forget the damned law—"

"It is God's law," she said tonelessly. "I cannot disobey it, my sins are too heavy already."

"I say that a god who would come between two that love is an evil creature, a demon—I would smite such a god with my sword if he should come near. Surely I would not follow him."

"Aye—a heathen you are!" she flared. "Fosterling of soulless elves, for whom you would even raise the dead from their great sleep." A faint color tinged her pale cheeks as her eyes flamed at him. "Then go back to your elves! Go back to Leea!"

He stood up as she did. He tried to take her hands, but she wrenched away. His wide shoulders sagged then.

"There is no hope?" he whispered.

"No." She half turned. "I will go to a neighbor garth now. It may be I can still atone for my sins." Suddenly she swung around to face him. "Come with me, Skafloc! Come, forget your heathen life, become Christian and make your peace with God."

He shook his head, and his eyes were angry. "Not with that god."

"But—I love you, Skafloc, I love you too much to wish your soul anywhere than in Heaven."

"If you love me," he said softly, "come with me. I will lay no hand on you, save as—as a brother. But come."

"No," she breathed, shudderingly. "Goodbye."

And she turned about and ran.

He ran after her. The snow crunched under their feet. When he caught her, his face was twisted as if a knife were being turned within him.

"Will you not even kiss me goodbye, Freda?" he asked.

"No." He could barely hear her voice, and she looked away from him. "No. I dare not."

And again she fled.

He stood watching her lovely young form. His own body seemed frozen. The light struck coppery sparks from her hair, the only color in the gray and white dawn. He watched her until she rounded a clump of trees and was lost to sight. Then he walked slowly the other way, out of the empty garth.

21

Within the next few days, that long and cruel winter began to die. And one evening at sunset Gulban Glas Mac Grici stood atop a snowy hill and on the south wind caught the first supernaturally faint breath of spring.

He leaned on his spear and stood looking over the twilit whiteness that sloped down to the sea. A sullen ember of sunset still smoldered in the west. Darkness and stars rose out of the east, and he saw a little fishing boat coming thence. It was a plain mortal craft, bought or stolen from some English seaman, and the tall warrior at the steering oar was flesh-and-blood human. But a strangeness brooded over him, and his sea-stained garments were of elf cut.

As he landed and sprang ashore, Gulban recognized him. The Irish Sidhe held aloof from the rest of faerie, but they had had some traffic with Alfheim in past years and Gulban remembered the merry youth Skafloc who had been with Imric. But he had become gaunt and grim, more even than the fortunes of his people seemed to warrant.

Skafloc walked up the hill toward the tall warrior-chief etched black against a sky of red and cold greenish-blue. As he approached, he recognized Gulban Glas, one of the five guardians of Ulster, and hailed him.

The chief returned grave greetings, inclining his gold-helmed head till the long black locks hid his fine strong features. But he could not keep from shrinking a little away as he sensed the incalculable power of the evil sleeping in a wolfskin bundle on Skafloc's back.

"I was told to await you," he said.

Skafloc looked at him out of weary eyes. "Have the Sidhe that many ears?" he asked.

"No," said Gulban, "but they know when something of great portent nears—and what could it concern this time save the war of the elves and the trolls? So we looked for an elf to come bearing strange tidings, and I suppose you are that one."

"Elf—yes!" said Skafloc with searing bitterness. There were deep lines drawn in his lean face, and dark hollows of sleeplessness about his eyes. Sea-salt streaked his war-gear—which was odd, thought Gulban, since the elves were careful of their appearance even in the most desperate times.

"Come," he said. "Lugh of the Long Hand must think this a great matter, for he has called all the Tuatha De Danaan to council in the Cave of Cruachan, and the chiefs of all other people of the Sidhe as well. But you are tired and hungry, Skafloc. First must you come to my abode."

"No," said the man with a rude bluntness equally strange to elves. "It cannot wait, nor do I care for more rest and food than I need to keep going. Take me to the council."

The chieftain shrugged and turned away, with his great night-blue cloak swirling about him. He whistled, and two of the lovely light-footed horses of the Sidhe came galloping up. But they snorted and shied away from Skafloc.

"They like not your burden," said Gulban.

"Nor I," answered Skafloc shortly. He caught a long silky mane and sprang onto the horse. "Now swiftly!"

Away they went, nigh as quickly as elf steeds, soaring over hills and dales, fields and forests, tarns and frozen rivers. In the dusk Skafloc saw some of the Sidhe glimpse-wise: a tall flashing-mailed horseman with a spear of bright terror, a gnarly little leprechaun at the door of his tree house, a strangely beak-like face on a gaunt cloak-wrapped man with gray feathers for hair, a flitting shadow and a faint skirl of pipes in secret forests. The keen wintry air held a faint mist in it, the shifting mysterious Irish fog glimmering above the crusted snow.

Now they neared the Cave of Cruachan, and their hoof-beats rang between the wooded hills in the softly gathering night. Stars blinked forth overhead, bright and clear as Freda's eyes—No! Skafloc wrenched his mind from such thoughts.

Four tall warriors stood outside the cave, and they lifted their spears in grave salutation. They took the curvetting horses, and Gulban Glas led Skafloc inside.

It was vast and dim within, an eerie sea-green light filling the rugged vaulting of the cave. Flashing stalactites hung from the groined roof, and the shields hung on the walls gave back the clear glow of tapers. Rushes had been spread on the floor, and the soft rustle of them beneath his feet was all the sound Skafloc heard as he neared the great council table.

At its foot were the chiefs of the people of Lupra, small and strong and roughly clad: Udan Mac Audain, king of the leprechauns, and Beg Mac Beg his tanist; Glomhar O'Glomrach, mighty of girth and muscled arm; the chiefs Conan Mac Rihid, Gaerku Mac Gaird, Mether Mac Mintan, and Esirt Mac Beg, clad in hides and raw gold. With such folk even a mortal could feel at home.

But up at the head of the table were the Tuatha De Danaan, the Children of the earth-mother Dana, come from Tir-nam-Og, the Golden, to hold council in the Cave of Cruachan. Silent and awesome they sat, beautiful and splendid to look on, and the very air seemed to crackle with the power that was in them. For they had been gods in Ireland ere Patrick brought the White Christ thither, and though they had had to flee the cross, still they wielded great powers and lived in a splendor like that of old.

Lugh of the Long Hand sat in the great throne at the very head, and on his right he had the warrior Angus Og and on his left the sea king Mananaan Mac Lir. Others of the Tuatha De Danaan were there, Eochy Mac Elathan the Dagda Mor, Dove Berg the Fiery, Credh Mac Aedh, Cas Corrach, Coll the Sun, Cecht the Plow, Mac Greina the Hazel, and many other names great of fame; and with the chiefs were their wives and children, and harpers and warriors who followed in their train. Wondrous it was to see that assemblage, and the sight was one to strike awe in any heart.

Save perhaps that of Skafloc, who was beyond caring for power or magnificence or danger of death. He walked up to the council with his gold-maned head held high, and his eyes met the dark brilliance of Lugh's as he gave greeting.

The deep voice of he of the Long Hand rolled out of the stern god-like face: "Be welcome, Skafloc of Alfheim, and drink with the chiefs of the Sidhe."

He signed that the man should sit in an empty seat near his own left, with Mananaan and his wife Fand all there were between. The cup bearers brought great golden bowls of the wondrous wine from Tir-nam-Og, and the harps of the bards rippled a luring melody as they drank.

Strong and fiery sweet was that wine, it seemed to Skafloc to be a flame burning out the weariness that dragged at him. But it left the grimness and desolation all the plainer.

Angus Og, the fair-locked warrior, spoke: "How goes the fight in Alfheim?"

"Ill goes it, as you know," said Skafloc bitterly. "The elves fight alone, and fall—even as one by one all the divided people of faerie will be swallowed by Trollheim."

Lugh's voice was steady and implacable: "The Children of Dana have no fear of trolls. We who won over the dark Fomorians, and who even defeated by the Miletians, became their gods, what have we to fear? Glad would we have been to battle beside Alfheim—"

"Glad indeed!" Dove Berg rattled his sword in its sheath. His hair was like a red flame in the cool green twilight of the cave, and his shout woke echoes rolling between its hollow walls. "Why, there has not been so glorious a fight for a hundred years! Why, could we not go?"

"Well you know the answer," said Eochy Mac Elathan, the Father of Stars. He sat wrapped in a cloak like blue dusk, and bright points of light winked and glittered on it and in his hair and deep within his eyes. When he spread his hands, a little shower of star-sparks spread out and danced on the hushed air. "This is more than a simple hosting in faerie. This is a chess game played by Aesir and Jötuns and we will not risk our freedom to become pieces on the board of the world. Ill have such chessmen fared."

Skafloc's hands gripped the chair arms till the knuckles stood whitely forth, and his voice wavered a little: "I come not for help in war, however sorely 'tis needed. I want only the loan of a ship."

"And may we ask why?" It was Coll who spoke. Bright was his face, and little flames wavered over his gleaming hauberk and the sun-rayed golden brooch at his muscled throat.

Skafloc told briefly of the Aesir's gift, and finished: "I made shift to steal the sword from Elfheugh, and by magic found out that I could get a ship from the Sidhe which would bear me to Jötunheim. So I came hither to ask for it." He bent his head a little. "Aye, as a beggar I come. To this has Alfheim fallen. But if we win, you shall have goodly gifts of us."

"I were fain to see this glaive," quoth Mananaan Mac Lir. Tall and strong and lithe he was, white of skin and silvery-gold of hair, the faintest greenish tinge in them. His eyes were slumbrous, a shifting green and gray and blue, his voice soft though it could rise to a roar. Richly clad he was, with gold and silver and jewels on the hilt and scabbard of his sword, but he wore a great leather cloak over his shoulders.

Skafloc unwrapped the broken sword, and the Sidhe, who could handle iron, crowded around it—and shrank back as they felt the cold sorcerous powers locked in its ancient rusty blade. A low ominous murmuring rose among them.

Lugh lifted his crowned head and looked darkly at Skafloc. "You deal in evil things," he said. "There is a demon sleeping in this sword."

"What would you expect?" shrugged Skafloc. "A Jötun forged it. But its powers are great."

"Great for ill. This glaive carries victory, aye, but it also carries death. It will be your bane if you use it."

"And what of that?" Skafloc gathered his bundle together. The iron rang, loud in the taut silence, as the two pieces clashed together, and something in that harsh belling note sent chills along the nerves of those who heard.

"I come asking for a ship," went on Skafloc. "I ask in the name of what friendship there has been between Sidhe and elves, in the name of knightly honor, and in the name of mercy. Will you give it to me?"

There was a long silence. At last Lugh said: "It goes hard not to help you—"

"And why not help?" cried Dove Berg. His sword gleamed high in the air, he threw it up and let it twirl glittering back to his hand. "Why not call up all the hosts of the Sidhe and fare against barbarous Trollheim?"

Lugh stood towering forth. "You are our guest, Skafloc Elf's-Foster," he said. "You have sat at our board and drunk our wine. We cannot refuse this boon. Also," his head lifted arrogantly, "I am Lugh of the Long Hand, and the Tuatha De Danaan do as they please without asking Aesir or Jötuns."

At this, a great shout went up in the council, weapons blazed forth, swords, dinned on shields, and the bards swept out wild ancient war-chants on their shuddering strings. But cool and soft-spoken in the surging tumult, Mananaan Mac Lir said to Skafloc:

"I will lend my own best boat to your faring. And as she is tricky to handle, and the perilous journey will be of interest, I will come along myself."

At this, Skafloc was glad, for the sea god would make the best of shipmates on a hard and desperate trip. "Then tomorrow—" he began.

"Not so swiftly, hot-head," smiled Mananaan. His sleepy-seeming eyes were inscrutable as he studied Skafloc. "We will rest and hold feast for a while. I see you need some mirth, and a voyage to Giant Land is not to be lightly undertaken."

Skafloc turned away. He could not say aught against it, but inwardly he raged at waiting. He would have no joy of the feast, wine simply made him remember—

He felt a light touch on his arm, and turned to face Fand, the wife of Mananaan.

Tall and stately and utterly beautiful were the women of the Tuatha De Danaan, for they were goddesses born. There were no words to tell of their radiant loveliness. Yet even in that company Fand stood out.

Her silken hair, golden as sunlight at evening, swept from her coronet to her feet. She wore a shimmering robe that clung to the curves of her body, and her white round arms blazed with jeweled rings, yet she herself outshone all her gorgeous apparel.

Her wise violet eyes seemed to look past Skafloc's tormented blue gaze, into the emptiness of his heart. She smiled, and her low voice was music.

"Would you have fared to Jötunheim alone?"

"Of course, my lady," said Skafloc.

"No living human ever went there and returned, save Tjalfi and Roska, and they went in company with Thor. You are either very brave or very reckless."

"What difference?" he shrugged. "If I die in Jötunheim, it is the same as anywhere else."

"And if you live—" She shivered. "If you live, you will bring back the unleashed demon which is the sword—a demon that must turn on you?"

He nodded, nor did he care.

"I think you look on death as your friend," she murmured. "It is a strange friend for a young man to have."

"The only faithful friend in all the world," he said bitterly. "Death is the only one sure to be at your side."

"I think you are fey, Skafloc Elf's-Foster, and that is a great sorrow. Not since Cu Chulain—" for a moment pain flickered in her eyes—"not since him has so great a warrior as you might become lived among mortals. Also, it grieves me to see the merry mad boy I remember grown so dark and lonely. A worm gnaws in your breast, and the pain drives you to seek death."

He said naught, but folded his arms and looked beyond her.

"But even sorrow dies," she said. "You can outlive your grief. And I will seek by my arts to shield you, Skafloc."

"That is fine!" he snarled, unable to stand more. "You magicking for my body and *she* praying for my soul!"

He swung away toward the wine bowls. Tears glimmered in Fand's eyes as she watched him.

"You sail with sorrow, Mananaan," she said to her husband.

The sea king shrugged. "Let him mope as he wishes. I will enjoy the trip."

22

It was some three days later that Skafloc stood on the beach under tall gray crags and saw Mananaan's boat sculled forth by a leprechaun from the sea-cave where she was berthed. She was a small slender craft, her thin silvery hull seeming all too frail for the angry seas of winter. The mast was inlaid with ivory, and the sails and cordage were broidered with silk. Proud and gallant and beautiful, the golden image of Fand seemed to leap from the prow.

The goddess herself saw them off. There was no one else about in the cool gray mists of morning. The fog glittered in little dewdrops in her braided hair, and her eyes were brighter and deeper than before, violet depths of mystery, as she bade Mananaan farewell.

"Luck be with you in your faring," she said to him, "and may you soon return to the green hills of Erin and the golden streets of Tirnam-Og. My eyes shall be bent seaward by day and my ears shall listen to the wild song of the waves by night for news of Mananaan's homecoming."

Skafloc stood aside, looking seaward. He thought dully how he might have been bade such a goodbye by Freda, and he quoth to himself:

Luckless is the lad who
leaves without his dearest
sweetheart farewell saying
softly, in the morning.
Colder than her kisses
comes the blowing spindrift.
Heavy is my heart—but
how could I forget her?

"Now let us away," said Mananaan. He and Skafloc sprang into the boat and raised the bright sail. The man took the steering oar, and the god struck a wailing, rippling melody from his carven harp and sang:

Wind, I call thee, thou unresting,
from the deeps of sea and sky.
Blow me outward on my questing,
answer me with eager cry.
From the hills of home behind me,
out through restless leagues of sea,
blow, wind, blow! My song shall bind thee.
South wind, sea wind, come to me.
Come to set my vessel free.

At his music, a strong breeze came as he willed, and the boat sprang from the snowy hills out into running waves, cold and green, with salty spindrift blowing keen in the face. Swift were the ships of Mananaan, even elf craft lagged behind them, and erelong the gray land was not to be told from gray clouds on the horizon.

"It seems to me finding Jötunheim will mean more than simply sailing north," said Skafloc.

"That is true," replied Mananaan. "It will need certain spells. Still more will it need a brave heart and a stout arm."

He looked ahead into the cloudy north. The chill wintry wind tossed his hair about his face that was at once majestic and merry, keen and slumbrous. "The first faint breath of spring is on the lands of men," he said. "It has been a cruel long and hard winter, and I think the reason is that Jötun powers have been abroad. We sail into the everlasting ice of their own home."

His eyes turned back to Skafloc. "It is past time that I should make this voyage to the edge of creation. Am I not a king of the sea? Yet I should not have waited so long, but gone when the Tuatha De Danaan were still full gods and had all their powers. Now we are only half-gods at best." He shook his head. "Even the Aesir, who are still gods, came not unscathed back from their few voyages to Jötunheim. As for us two—I know not. I know not."

Then recklessly: "But I sail where I will! There shall be no sea in all the nine worlds which has not been plowed by the keels of Mananaan Mac Lir."

Skafloc stood at the steering oar and made no answer, wrapped as he was in his own thoughts. The boat handled wondrous easy, like a live thing. The steady south wind harped in the rigging, and spray sheeted in a rainbowed veil about the beautiful figurehead of Fand. The sea shouted around them, under a cold blue sky filled with wind and scudding clouds. Despite himself, Skafloc felt the freshness of the morning touch his heart. He quoth softly:

Clear the day is, coldly
calling with a wind-voice
to the sea, where tumbles
titan play of billows.
Stood you by my side now,
sweetheart, on the deck-planks,
life were full of laughter.
(Long you for me, Freda?)

Mananaan looked strangely at him. "This is a voyage which will need all a man's heart," he said. "Sometimes, though, a woman can tear a heart out and leave only emptiness behind."

Skafloc flushed angrily. "It was not I who first set out on this venture," he replied curtly.

"The man who has naught to live for is not the most dangerous to his foes," quoth Mananaan. And then quickly he took his harp and sang one of the wild old war-songs of the Sidhe. Strangely did it ring in the empty vastness of sea and sky and rushing wind. For a moment Skafloc thought he saw cloudy hosts galloping to battle, the sun ablaze on plumed helmets and ranked forests of spears, banners flying and horns shouting and the dreadful scything wheels of the war-chariots booming over the sky.

Now they sailed steadily for three days and nights. Ever the wind blew behind them, and the boat rode the waves like a soaring bird. They took turns to steer, neither sleeping much, and lived on stockfish and cheese and whatever else of supply was aboard. There were few words between them, for Skafloc was of no heart for idle chatter and Mananaan had all an immortal's satisfaction in his own thoughts. But they had each a respect for the other that grew with the long weary work, and they sang certain powerful spells together to get through the sorcerous barriers of Jötunheim.

Swiftly went the boat, swift as the crying gale behind her, for even more than with elf vessels had the skill of her builders removed all sea-drag from her. They could feel the cold and gloom deepen almost hour by hour as they sped tirelessly north into the heart of winter.

The sun lowered until it was a far pale disc on a sullen horizon, briefly seen through hurrying storm-clouds. The gathering cold was a relentless, searing presence, the soul of those grim waters; it gnawed through clothes and flesh and bone into the very soul. Sea-spray hung in icicles on the rigging, and the golden beauty of Fand on the prow was veiled in rime. To touch metal was to peel the skin from the fingers, and breath froze in the mustache.

More and more did it become a world of night, where they sailed over darkened silver-sparked seas between the drifting moon-ghostly mountains of the icebergs. The sky was a tremendous vault of utter blackness, frosted with uncounted bitter-brilliant stars, and between the constellations leaped the silent spectral flames of the northern lights. Only the drone of wind and the rush of sea had voice in that stupendous frozen stillness, only they had life in the darkened world.

They did not cross the borders of Jötunheim all at once. It was just that they sailed farther than mortal ship would have gone ere sighting land, into seas that grew ever more chill and dead and gloomy, until at last they had only stars and moon and the shuddering aurora for light. Skafloc thought that the lands of the ice giants, like those of gods and demons, must not lie on earth at all, but in strange dimensions reached only by spells, out near the edge of all things where creation plunged into primal chaos. He had the eerie notion that it was the Sea of Death on which he now sailed, outward bound from the world of life to the realm of ancient night.

Now, after those three days where they saw the sun, they lost track of time. There was no time in the unending immensity of wheeling stars and running seas. There was only the wind and the moon and the frightful, deepening cold. But presently Mananaan's spells began to fail as he reached the edge of seas where his power held good. Contrary winds came, against which few craft other than his own could have sailed. Snow and sleet blew blindingly on crazy gales, and the boat pitched and rolled and shipped water of numbing chill. The icebergs loomed monstrously out of snow or death-silent fog, towering beyond sight and breathing forth cold, and barely did they save themselves from shipwreck.

Perhaps it was the fog which was most terrible—windless, sound-choking, dripping and freezing gray damp, blinding vision half an arm away, creeping its still, steady way through clothes to shivering skin. It was like a malignant ghost. The boat lay moveless, rocking ever so faintly to unseen waves, and the only sound was their muffled slap and the fog dripping from ice-sheathed ropes. Skafloc and Mananaan, stumbling and cursing, teeth clapping in their heads, sought to break such weather with spells—to little avail. They had the feeling that monstrous and watchful powers crept through the grayness, just outside of vision, and stared hungrily inboard.

Then the screaming fury of a storm might come, like as not from the wrong direction, and there would be unending eons of struggle. Ice-slick lines and rudder fought demoniacally, the dark white-frothed combers roared over the rails, and the boat mounted one wave toward the raving sky only to slide down its trough as if into hell.

Skafloc quoth:

Black and cold, the breakers
bellow, thunder inboard.
Ropes are snapped, and rudders.
Roaring winds are sleet-cloaked.
Seamen weary stumble,
sick with cold and hunger.
Bitter is the brew here:
beer of waves is salty.

Then he threw himself back into the work. Mananaan, who thought a plaint about evil weather better than one about a lost love—for one could fight a storm—smiled into the galing sky.

But there came a time at last when they raised land. Skafloc saw a grim and desolate coast under the mighty sky, lit by unwinking stars and a noiseless cold flame of bitter-blue aurora leaping and flickering over gaunt mountains and greenly flashing glaciers. The sea roared on looming cliffs behind which the land climbed steeply to the stars, a lifeless gigantic world of crags and ice-fields and wind screaming over ancient snow.

Mananaan nodded slowly as the boat neared. "'Tis Jötunheim," he said, his voice almost lost in the sullen crashing of distant surf and the booming of wind under the hollow sky. "Utgard, nigh which you say the giant bides, should by my reckoning lie to the east of here."

"As you say," muttered Skafloc. He had long since lost his way, nor did any elf know much more than frightened rumors about these coasts.

He felt weariness no longer, he was past that. It was as if he went on like a ship with lashed rudder, because there was naught else to do and no one to care if it foundered. His breast seemed dark and void, with a deep smoldering pain its only light, but his mind was cold and keen and steady.

It came to him, as he stood there looking at the terrible face of Giant Land, that Freda could not be less unhappy than he. More so, perhaps, since he could lose himself in the quest of the sword and know *she* was safe, while she only knew he was on a hopeless and deadly journey, and had little to do save think about it.

"That thought had not come to me before," he whispered in surprise, and he felt, of a sudden, tears freezing on his cheeks. He quoth:

Late will I the lovely
lost one be forgetting.
Ways that I must wander
will be cold and lonely.
Heavy is my heart now,
where she sang aforetime.
Greatest of the griefs she
gave me is her sorrow.

And he fell again to brooding. Mananaan let him be, having learned it was no use trying to hasten his rousing from such fits, and the boat ran eastward on a harrying wind.

Naught seemed to stir in this waste of rock and ice, naught save the tumbling breakers and the snow-devils whirling on the mountains and the leaping auroral fires. But he could feel the nearness of vast and ancient presences, looming up toward the stars and watching the little intruders with eyes of night.

By the time Skafloc had shaken off his gloom, the boat had sailed a long way, and Mananaan was steering close to every fjord in search of sign of their goal. The sea king was growing uneasy, for he could almost smell the evil lairs of Utgard now, and even the reckless Sidhe did not care to near that dark city.

"Bölverk dwells in a mountain, I was told," said the man. "That would mean a cave."

"Aye, but this cursed land is riddled with caverns."

"A big one, I should think," went on Skafloc thoughtfully. "And with signs of smithery about."

Mananaan nodded, and steered for the next inlet. As they neared the sheer cliffs rising out of the sea, Skafloc began to understand the size of them. Up they towered, up, up, storming the stars in such a cataract of height that he grew dizzy trying to see their tops. A few aurora-lit clouds sailed over them, and he had the feeling that those walls of rock were toppling on him—now the sides of the world were sundering as it sank into the sea!

Ant-like, the boat crawled under the foot of the cliffs and peered into the fjord. It ran past sight, a maze of holms and skerries and jutting rock faces high enough to block out the stars. But Skafloc's nostrils tingled to a faint scent blown on the cruel wind—smoke, hot iron, and he heard the remote banging of a hammer.

There was no need for words, and Mananaan steered into the fjord. The boat had not gone far ere the cliffs had shouldered all wind aside, so that the seamen had to scull. They went right swiftly, but so huge was the fjord that they scarce seemed to move.

The vast and ominous stillness seemed even deeper here, as if sound had frozen to death and the aurora danced on its grave. A few noiseless snowflakes circled down out of the great starry sky. The cold ate and ate at living flesh. It seemed to Skafloc that the moveless quiet was that of some great beast of prey crouched for a spring, taut and still, with hungrily glittering eyes and a lashing auroral tail. He knew with blind certainty that eyes were on him.

Slowly, slowly, the boat won around the many twists and bends in the fjord. Deeper into the stark land it crept. Once Skafloc heard a slithering over ice and ancient crusted snow, keeping pace. The wind yowled, far above the cliffs, so high that it might almost have been blowing between the great white stars.

Strangely out of place was the lovely golden image of Fand, dancing ever farther into that bleak realm.

Now at last the boat came to a place where a broad rough slope cut down from a mountain so vast its top seemed crowned with stars. A glacier ran along that slope, glimmering in the weird uneasy light, down to the water. "This seems to be our only landing spot," quoth Mananaan.

Something hissed from the great tumbled blocks of ice at the glacier's foot.

"Methinks there is a guard to get by," said Skafloc. He and his companion busked themselves, putting on helm and byrnie, with furs above against the tearing fangs of cold. Each took a shield on his arm, and girded a sword at his waist. Skafloc had yet another sword in his hand, while Mananaan bore his great spear whose bright head gave back the light in a gleam of rippling lightnings.

Now the boat grounded gently on the ice and shale. Skafloc drew her ashore and made fast while Mananaan stood guard, peering into the gloom between the huge ice-boulders heaped just beyond. Thence came a grinding, rustling sound as of something monstrous in weight dragging slowly over the rough ground.

"It is dark ahead of us," said Mananaan, "and there is an evil smell. But come, the peril grows no less by our waiting."

He led the way between and over the enormous chunks of ice and stone. The darkness thickened until the warriors groped their way, only a few ragged patches of stars showing above the misshapen crags. A foul stink assailed them, with something of utter cold about it, and the hungry stirring and hissing grew louder.

Now they came into a narrow ravine leading up toward the glacier. Dimly Skafloc saw the great white form that waited, and his hand tightened on his sword haft.

The thing swayed toward them. Mananaan shouted a war-cry that rang glassily between the ice cliffs, and drove his spear into the looming shape. "Out of the way, white worm!" he shouted.

The beast hissed and struck at him, its coils scraping over rock and snow. He darted aside, and as the evil head smote near, Skafloc hewed mightily. The shock of the blow rammed up into his shoulders, and the worm turned gape-jawed on him. Barely could he see the creature in the dark, but he knew the mouth was wide enough to swallow him whole.

Mananaan thrust his spear into the white neck, and Skafloc smote again at the nose. The snaky smell made his head whirl, he gasped for air and struck a rain of blows. A drop of blood or venom splashed on him, ate through his furs, and seared his arm.

He cursed, and hewed again at the weaving head. Even as his sword sank in, he felt it crumple, consumed by the icy blood. He heard Mananaan's spear-shaft break as it went in.

Drawing their scabbarded blades, he and the sea king pressed forward anew. The worm withdrew before them, and they came out on the glacier.

Terrible to see was the thing. Its writhing coils reached halfway up the mountainside, white as snow and thicker than a horse. The flat serpent head swayed high above them, dripping blood and poison. Mananaan's broken spear was in one eye, the other glittered balefully down. Its tongue flickered in and out, faster than vision could follow, and it hissed like a sleeting gale.

Skafloc slipped on the ice. Blinding swift, the worm struck down at him. Even swifter was Mananaan, holding his shield above the fallen man and smiting mightily with his sword. The screaming blade gashed open the puffed throat. Skafloc scrambled to his feet and swung likewise.

The worm brought its huge coils lashing around. Skafloc rolled aside into a snowdrift. Mananaan was swept off his feet and enclosed in a loop, but ere it could smash him his glaive had flayed open the pulsing side.

The worm fled then, plunging past them like a snowslide into the bitter sea. Gasping and trembling, the two warriors sat for a long while under the aurora ere taking up their journey anew.

"Its blood has pitted our swords," said Skafloc. "We had best go back for new weapons."

"Nay—the worm may be waiting for us by the shore, or if not that then sight of us may waken its wrath again," answered Mananaan. "These blades will serve for a while, till we have the rune sword."

They climbed slowly up the slick, mysteriously shimmering glacier. The mountain loomed blackly ahead, blotting out half the sky. Dimly, the keening wind brought sounds of a beating hammer. It was cruelly cold and lonely.

Up and up they climbed, until their hearts fluttered and their lungs gasped. Often they had to rest, even sleep, there on the enormous back of the glacier, and it was well they had brought some little food along. Slowly went the climb over the treacherous ice, a struggle into heights of darkness such as might have daunted even the stoutest heart.

Naught stirred, naught seemed to live in the tremendous desolation, but nearer and louder came the ringing of the hammer.

Until at last Skafloc and Mananaan stood at the head of the glacier, halfway up the mountain crowned with stars. A narrow trail, broken and icy, scarce to be seen in the murk, led off to one side. Sheer cliffs dropped from it to depths of windy gloom dizzyingly far down. The warriors roped themselves together and made their creeping way along it.

They came at last, after many falls where one saved the other by clawing himself to the rock, out on a ledge fronting a huge black cave-mouth. From the deeps of the cavern rolled the sounds of hammering.

A great dog was chained at the entrance. It howled and flung itself at them with slaverous jaws agape. Skafloc half raised his sword to kill it.

"No," said Mananaan. "I have the feeling that seeking to slay this beast would bring the worst of luck. We had best try to slip by it."

They held their shields close together and their backs to the rock as they entered. The hound's mighty weight slammed against them and its teeth sought to rip them open. Its howling rang up to the coldly seething sky. Barely could they press off that furious attack and win past the reach of the chain.

Now they came into utter lightlessness. They held hands and groped along the downward-slanting tunnel, feeling ahead for pits and often crashing into fanged stalagmites. The air was dank and bitter cold. They heard the noise of mighty waters rushing through the dark, and they thought that this must be one of the sounding rivers that flow through hell. Louder and nearer clamored the beat of the hammer.

Twice there came a howling, and they stood braced for battle. Once they were set upon by something huge and heavy, with teeth that bit chunks out of the iron shields. Blind in the dark, they yet made shift to slay the thing. But they never knew what shape it had had.

In the end they saw a red glow far ahead, and when they hastened forward they came, more slowly than they would have thought, to a vast frosty chamber. And into this they stepped.

Dimly was it lit by the sullen coals of a low fire, but by that light, the color of clotting blood, they could discern vague gigantic shapes which might have belonged in a smithy, and at the anvil was a Jötun.

Huge he was, so tall they could scarce see his head in the gloom, and so broad that even with his height he seemed squat. He wore only a dragon-skin apron on his hairy dark body, which was muscled and gnarled like a tree bole, and his matted black hair and beard hung to his waist. His legs were short and bowed, one of them lame, and he was hunchbacked, bent over so that his monstrously long arms touched the stony ground.

As the warriors entered, he turned a terrible face on them, broad-nosed, wide-mouthed, scarred and seamed, with black hollows under the heavy eyebrow ridges. Skafloc saw that his eyes had been plucked from the sockets.

His voice roared out with sound of the rushing underground rivers that flow through the hollow caves of hell. "Oho, oho!" he cried. "Someone comes, light-foot in the dark. For three hundred years has Bölverk worked alone in the night of his eyes. Now the blade must be hammered out." And he took the huge sword on which he had been working and flung it across the room. The metal roar when it struck flew in jeering echoes around the frosty walls.

Skafloc stood boldly forth, meeting the empty glare of the sightless giant, and said: "I bring an old, broken work of yours to be forged again."

"Who are you?" cried Bölverk. "Mortal man I can smell, but there is more than a little of faerie about him. Another I can smell who is more than half god, but he is not of Aesir or Vanir." He groped around him. "I am not easy about either of you. Come closer so I can tear you apart."

"We come on a mission you will not dare hinder," said Mananaan.

"What is it?" Bölverk's somber voice rolled between the walls and down the tunnel.

Skafloc quoth:

Asa-Loki,
angry, weary
with his prison,
wishes sword-play.
Here is weapon
which gives victory.
Bölverk, take the
bane of heroes.

And he opened his wolfskin bundle and flung the broken sword clanging at the giant's feet.

Bölverk's hands fumbled over it. "Aye," he breathed. "Aye, well I remember this blade. I forged the powers of ice and death and storm into it, mighty runes and spells, a living will to work evil." He grinned. "Many heroes have owned this sword, because it brings victory to the wielder. There is naught on which it does not bite, nor does it ever grow dull of edge. Venom is in the steel, and the wounds it gives cannot be healed by leechcraft or magic or prayer. Yet this is the curse on it: that every time it is drawn it must drink blood, and that in the end, somehow, it brings the bane of him who uses it."

He leaned forward. "For that reason," he said slowly, "Thor broke it, long ago, and it has lain forgotten in the earth ever since. But now—now, if as you say Loki calls to arms, there will be need of it."

"I did not say that," muttered Skafloc, "but I meant you to think I did."

Bölverk did not hear him. The Jötun was staring sightlessly ahead of him, rapt in his thoughts. "So it is to end," he whispered. "Now comes the last evening of the world, when gods and giants meet in sundering battle and lay waste the earth, as they slay each other, when Surt scatters flame which leaps up to the cracking walls of heaven, when earth sinks in the sea and the hot stars fall and the sun turns black. It ends—my long and weary thralldom, blind beneath the mountain, ends in a blaze of fire! Aye—aye, well will I forge the sword, mortal!"

Now he went mightily to work, the clamor of it filling the cave, sparks flying and bellows roaring, and as he worked he sang spells which made the walls shudder. Skafloc and Mananaan took shelter in the tunnel outside.

"I like this not, and now I am sorry I came," said the sea king. "There is a frightful evil being awakened to life again. None have called me coward, yet I will not touch that sword—nor will you, if you are wise. It will bring your weird on you."

"What of that?" asked Skafloc moodily.

They heard the hissing as the blade was quenched in venom. The fumes stung where they touched bare skin. Bölverk's doom-song roared through the cave.

"Throw not your life away for a lost love," pleaded Mananaan. "You are young yet."

"All men are born fey," quoth Skafloc, and there the matter ended.

Time dragged its slow way. At last came Bölverk's shout: "Enter, warriors!"

They came into the bloody light. The giant held forth the sword. Brightly gleamed the blade, a blue tongue about whose edges little flames seemed to waver. The eyes of the dragon carved on the haft glittered.

"Take it!" cried the giant.

Skafloc seized the sword two-handed. Heavy it was, but strength to swing it seemed to flow into him. So wondrous was the balance that the weapon was like a part of his own body.

He swept the glaive in a yelling arc, down on a rock. The stone split asunder. He shouted and whirled the hissing blade about his head. It shone like a baleful lightning bolt, flickering in the gloom. Cold blue fire seemed to stream from it.

"Ha, halloo!" Skafloc's fierce war-cry rang triumphant through the cave. He shouted forth:

Swiftly goes the sword-play!
Soon the foe shall hear the
wailing song of weapons.
Warlock blade is thirsty!
Howling in its hunger,
hews it through the iron,
sings in cloven skull-bones,
slakes itself in blood-streams.

Bölverk's laughter bellowed forth. "Aye, wield it, wield it, warrior!" he roared. "Smite your foemen—gods, giants, mortals, it matters not. The sword is loose and the end of the world draws nigh!"

He gave the man a scabbard. "Best you sheathed it now," he said. "And draw it not save when you wish to slay." He grinned. "But the sword has a habit of getting drawn at evil moments—and in the end, fear not, it will turn on you."

"Let it but hew down my foes first," replied Skafloc. "Then I care not overly much what it does."

"You may—then," muttered Mananaan. And aloud: "Now let us be away. This is an ill place to bide."

They left, with Bölverk's eyeless face staring after them.

When they had won out—this time the hound shrank whimpering aside—they set swiftly down the glacier. But as they neared the bottom they heard a rumble as of thunder, and turned about to look.

Black against the sky, towering up higher than the mountains, loomed three monstrous forms striding down on them. Mananaan said, as he scrambled for the boat: "I think Utgard-Loki has somehow learned of our trick and wishes not that we should carry out whatever plans the Aesir have. Hard will it be to escape this land alive."

23

The war which Mananaan Mac Lir and Skafloc Elf's-Foster waged on Jötunheim was well worth the telling. One should sing of the long cruel struggle with windless mist and berserk gale, with skerry and surf and looming iceberg, of the weariness which grew so great that only the image of Fand, bright and lovely against the undying night, gave cheer. That best of boats should have been honored with golden trim and a song.

Many were the enchantments with which the Jötuns sought to destroy their visitors, and evil luck did the two warriors suffer on that account. But they wrought mightily in return, not alone warding off the worst of the giant magic but also turning storms loose to scourge the land and singing mountainsides down on Jötun garths.

They could hardly hope to stand in open fight against the giants, though twice when one giant alone fell on them they killed him, but they fought monsters of land and sea raised against them, and they outran or hid from enemy pursuit. Often were their escapes narrow, especially when they went foraging inland during the long time of contrary winds, and each would make a story in itself.

It should be told of their raid on one of the greatest garths, to steal horses. In the end they left the place ablaze and made off with a good booty of which the animals were not all. The beasts they took were the smallest of ponies in that land, but huge and heavy, shaggy big-boned monsters with fiery eyes and devil hearts, in the outer world—and they feared not iron, or bearing Skafloc's dreadful sword, nor did they ever weary.

Not all the Jötuns were hideous giants. Some of the women, in particular, were of human size and well favored. Mananaan found the outlaw life not all a grim struggle. But Skafloc did not look twice at any woman.

There is much else to tell, of the dragon and his gold hoard, of the burning mountain and the bottomless chasm and the quern of the elemental giantesses. It should be told of their fishing in the river that ran from hell, and of what they caught there. The story of the everlasting battle and of the witch in Iron Forest and of the song they once heard the aurora hissing to itself in the secret night—all were worth telling, and each would almost make a saga in itself. But since they do not concern the main thread of the story, they must be left among the annals of faerie.

Thus suffice it to say that Skafloc and Mananaan won out of Jötunheim and sailed south to the lands of men and faerie.

"How long have we been gone?" wondered the man.

"I know not." The sea god smelled the fresh breeze and looked up into a clear blue sky. "But it is spring."

Presently he went on: "Now that you have the sword—and have already blooded it well in Jötunheim—what will you do?"

"I will seek to join the Erlking, if he still lives." Skafloc looked grimly ahead, over the racing waves to the dim line of horizon.

"Set me on shore south of the channel and I will find him. And let the trolls dare try to stop me! When we have cleared southern Alfheim of them, we will land in England and regain that—finally, we will go to their homelands and make an end of their cursed race."

"*If* you can." Mananaan scowled. "I wonder if a weary remnant of a beaten people can ever throw off their conquerors. But you must try, of course."

"And will the Sidhe not help at all?"

"That is a matter for the great council. Certainly we cannot help ere the elves are in England, lest our own home be ravaged while its warriors are away. But it may well be we will strike then, for the battle and glory as well as to clear a menace from our flank." The sea god's proud head lifted. "But however that may be—for the sake of blood shed together, toil and suffering and peril in common, and lives often owed each to the other, Mananaan Mac Lir and all his hosts will be with you when you enter England!"

They clasped hands, wordlessly. And presently Mananaan set Skafloc and his Jötun horse off, and sailed for Ireland and Fand.

Skafloc rode his black stallion toward the distant Erlking. The horse was gaunt and shaggy, still stepping proudly but with hunger in his belly. Skafloc did not look rich himself, his clothes were ragged and faded, his helm and byrnie and shield battered and rust-streaked, the cloak he wrapped around himself worn thin. He had lost weight in the winter, the great muscles lay just under the skin and the skin was drawn tightly over the big bones. But he was still arrogantly erect, leonine in litheness and power, the swift steely mind flashing in the metallic blue of his eyes. There were lines graven deeply in his face, it had lost its youth and grown harsh and remote and grim, the face of an outlaw god—its only emotion a faint one of mockery, its strength solitary and aloof. Only the fair wind-tossed hair was young. So might Loki look, riding to Vigrid plain on the last evening of the world.

He rode over hills, the young spring around him. It had rained in the morning and the ground was still muddy, pools and rivulets glittering in the sunlight. But the grass had grown, its first cool, light viridescence reached to the horizon. The trees were budding forth, the new green life shaded the world with its delicate tint, the vanguard of summer.

It was still chilly, a strong wind gusted over the hills and whipped Skafloc's cloak about him; but it was a wind of spring, its rough boisterous shout in trees and over the earth was a call to the summer, its raw damp lash stirred blood to tingling life. The sky was high and blue and light, the sun struck through white and gray clouds that still raced over the greater part of the heavens, shafts of luminance stabbing down to gleam on the new wet grass. Thunder rolled from the still darkened southern horizon, but against that smoky cloud-mass a rainbow was shining.

The honking of geese came from overhead, the migratory birds were coming home. A thrush was trying out his song in a wind-dancing grove, and two squirrels chased each other in the grass.

Before long now came full spring and summer, warm days and light nights, green forests and nodding flowers, love and life and hope. Something stirred within Skafloc as he rode over the hills, a dim unfolding of old forgotten instincts, a bright blossom of memory.

O Freda, if you were with me—

The day smoldered toward the west. Skafloc rode straight forward on his tireless horse, taking no great pains to be inconspicuous. He went at an easy pace for the Jötun breed, but the land slipped by in the dusk, quivering under the black stallion's mighty hoofs. He was entering faerie realms, the central province of Alfheim, riding toward the mountain fastnesses where the Erlking must be if he still held out. He found signs of war—burned garths, clean-picked bones, broken weapons. Now and again a fresh troll spoor showed, and Skafloc licked his lips hungrily.

Night rose, strangely warm and light after the bitter dark whence he had come. He rode on, at times dozing in the saddle but never ceasing to listen. Long ere the troll horsemen crossed his path he heard them and was alert.

There were six, dark powerful forms in the half-lit gloom. They were puzzled by him—a mortal, in clothes and armor half elf and half Sidhe, riding a horse akin to their own but even huger and stronger. They barred his path, and one shouted forth: "In the name of Illrede Troll-King, halt!"

Skafloc struck spurs in his stallion and drew the giant's sword as he shot forward. The blade seemed to flame hell-blue in the night. He rode full tilt into the company, and the screaming thundering sword clove one helm and skull, and lopped another head off, ere the trolls were aware of it.

Then one struck at Skafloc with an ax. His sword roared to meet it, tearing through the weapon and the breast behind it. Swinging the glaive about, Skafloc split the troll on his other side from shoulder to waist. He reined in his monster horse, so that it stood on its hind feet and pawed with its fore hoofs. A troll skull crunched.

The last soldier screamed and turned to flee. Skafloc threw the sword in a flaming bolt that went through the troll's back and out his breast.

Thereafter he rode on, seeking the beleaguered Erlking. Near dawn he stopped by a river for a brief sleep.

He woke at once when he heard the rustle of leaves and the faint quiver of the ground. Two trolls were stealing on him. He sprang to his feet, drawing the sword as they rushed. Through the shield and face and heart of the first he hewed. He raised his dripping blade at once and the second troll, unable to halt his lunge, spitted himself on it. Even against that frightful shock Skafloc stood braced, the chill unearthly strength of the sword stiffening him to iron hardness.

"This is nigh too easy," quoth he, "but 'twill soon grow hard enough to suit the most exacting."

He rode on through the day. Near noon he came to a cave in which several trolls were asleep. He killed them and ate their food. It mattered little to him that he was leaving a trail of slain foes for anyone to follow. Let them—if they dared!

Near dusk he began to come into mountains. High and beautiful they reared, their remote snowy heads seeming to float serene in the sunset sky. He heard the singing of waterfalls and the soughing of pines. Strange, he thought, strange that so much peace and loveliness was but a place for murder. By rights, he should have been here with Freda and their love, not with a grim black horse and a sword of horror.

But so it went, so it went. And how went it for her—?

Skafloc rode up the slopes and across a glacier on which his steed's hoofs rang. Night spread across the sky, clear and cold at these snowy heights, with a rising moon to turn the peaks into dreaming ghosts. Presently Skafloc heard, far and weird in the great skyey spaces, the bray of a lur horn. His heart leaped with a fierce gladness and he spurred the horse to a gallop, leaping from crag to crag and over windy abysses. The cloven air hooted in his ears and the echoes of the mighty hoofbeats rolled like rising thunder between the silent mountains.

Someone still fought!

The harsh bray of a troll horn came to him, and then the distance-muted shout of warriors and clang of weapons. An arrow zipped past his face. He snarled and crouched low in the saddle—no time to deal with one archer, bigger game was at hand.

He burst over a snowy ridge and looked across moonlit chasms to the scene of battle. Men might only have seen a single high mountain on which blew whirling snow-devils, and heard only a strange roar and boom about the craggy peak. But Skafloc's witch-sight discerned more—he saw the top of the mountain as a high-walled, frost-covered castle whose towers climbed for the distant stars. Ringed about it on the upper slopes of the mountain, on snow-field and glacier, were the black tents of a great troll army. One in particular was of more than ordinary size and had a dark ensign over it—and flying from the highest tower of the castle was the banner of the Erlking. The monarchs had met.

The trolls were storming the fortress. Like mad dogs they yelped about the walls, they set up ladders and sought to climb, they hid its base with their numbers. Many engines of war did they have, mangonels throwing balls of fire over the walls, huge wheeled towers trundling ever closer, rams clamoring at the gates, ballistae hurling their mighty stones against shuddering masonry. The shouts of the men, the trampling of feet and hoofs, the clash of metal, the roar of drums and horns, filled the night with a storm of sound that started landslides grinding down and made the ice-fields ring an answer.

The elves stood atop the walls and fought the trolls off. Swords gleamed, spears and arrows darkened the moon, blazing oil poured from great cauldrons, ladders were upset—but still the trolls came on, and the elves were few, few. It was near the end of the siege.

Skafloc pulled out his sword, the blade snarling hungrily through the scabbard and flaring icy-blue under the moon. "Hai-ah!" His shout woke flying echoes as he spurred his horse down the slope in a cloud of moon-eerie snow.

At the brink of the chasm he felt the stallion's huge muscles bunch, and then he was soaring through the middle of the sky with stars swirling around him. He struck the mountainside with a shock that slammed his teeth together, but at once he was rushing up the slope with his blade a whirling frozen hell-flame.

The troll camp was almost empty. Skafloc reined in, his horse pawing the sky, and leaned over to snatch a brand from a fire. The speed of his gallop whipped it to a bright blaze as he rode through the camp, setting tents afire. In a short time many were burning and the sparks were spreading to others. Skafloc rode swiftly on toward the castle gates.

He wore his shield on his back, steered the horse with his knees and voice, and swung the great sword two-handed. Ere the trolls about the gates were aware of him he had struck down three and his horse had trampled as many.

The foemen turned on him then. His sword leaped and whirred and shrieked, clove with a shout of metal through helm or hauberk, flesh and bone, to rise streaming—never did its death-dance halt, and Skafloc mowed trolls like ripe wheat.

They surged around him, but none could touch the iron he wore and few of their blows landed. Those that did, he scarce felt—not when the sword was in his hands!

He swung sideways and a head rolled off its shoulders. Another swing, and he had opened a horseman's belly. A third blow shore through helm and skull and brain down to the neck. A warrior on foot stabbed at him with a spear, scraping his arm—he leaned down and hewed the troll to earth. But most of the foot soldiers went down under the kicks and bites of the huge black horse.

Clamor and clang of outraged metal rose under the moon. Blood steamed in the trampled snow, corpses wallowing in its pools. The Jötun horse and his rider and the blade of terror rose high over the battle, carving a road of death.

Hew, sword, hew!

Now the trolls veered away in panic. Skafloc's voice lifted ringingly: "Hai, Alfheim! Victory rides with us tonight! Sally forth, elves, come out and kill your foes!"

A ring of fire, the burning troll camp, surrounded the battlefield. The trolls grew aware of it and felt dismay. Also, they knew a Jötun horse and a demon glaive when they met them—what manner of being fought against them tonight?

Skafloc rode his curvetting stallion before the gates, his blood-splashed helm and byrnie agleam in the light of moon and fire. His eyes blazed with a bitter blue no less terrible and remorseless than the sword dripping in his hand, and he taunted the trolls hoarsely and bitingly, and called on the elves to rally.

The frightened whisper ran about the milling troll army: "*—It is Odin, come to fight—no, he has two eyes, it is Thor—it is Loki, risen from his chains, now the end of the world is nigh—it is a mortal, possessed by a demon—it is Death—*"

Now lur horns blew and the gates swung wide, and the elves of the castle rode forth. Fewer by far than the trolls were they, but a new hope lit their haggard faces and a light of battle gleamed in their strange eyes. At their head, on a milk-white stallion, with his crown aglitter in the moonlight and his hair and beard flowing white over byrnie and the dusk-blue cloak that wrapped him in magic and mystery, came the Erlking.

"We looked not to see you alive again, Skafloc," he called.

"But you have, and well it is for Alfheim," replied the man, with not a trace of his old awe—for nothing, he thought, was left to frighten him who had sailed to the edge of the world and had naught to lose anyway.

The Erlking's weird eyes rested on the wizard sword. "I wonder how well it is even for Alfheim," he murmured, "and I think it is all ill for you." Then his voice rose in a shout: "Forward, elves!"

Now the elves charged upon the trolls, and bloody was that battle. Swords and axes rose and fell and rose streaming again, metal cried out and sundered, a rain of spears and arrows clouded the sky—horses screamed and trampled the rolling corpses under their hoofs—warriors shouted and fought and sank to earth.

"Hola, Trollheim! Forward, trolls!" The shout boomed forth as Illrede rode into battle. His black stallion snorted fire, his ax never rested and never missed, and he clove a frightful way from which elves began to flee. Above his black byrnie, his face gleamed icy green under the moon—hideous, a mask of rage, the tendrils of his beard writhing, his eyes boiling pits of black horror and death. No one could stand before his blows, and the trolls rallied around him and drove back the elves.

Skafloc saw him and howled, a berserker's wolf-cry. He swung his Jötun horse about and pressed toward the troll-king. His sword screamed and thundered, hewing trolls as a woodman hews saplings, a blur of blue flame in the night. Shock and clang of battle rose about him, heralding his passage.

"Ha!" roared Illrede. "Make way, trolls, make way—he is mine!"

They rode at each other through a suddenly cleared path. Skafloc's eyes were like icy blue moonlight, Illrede's like the night itself, as they glared at each other. But as the troll-king saw the rune sword, he shuddered in sudden horror.

Skafloc's laughter rang harsh and pitiless between the nighted mountains. "Aye, your weird is upon you," he shouted. "Darkness comes for you and all your evil race."

"The evil done in the world was never all troll work," said Illrede quietly. "It seems to me you have done a deed more wicked than any of mine in bringing that sword back to the world. Whatever his nature, which the Norns and not himself gave, no troll would do such a thing."

"No troll would dare!" sneered Skafloc, and rode in upon him.

Illrede struck valiantly out. The ax smote the Jötun horse in the shoulder. It did not go deep, but the stallion screamed and reared, and while Skafloc fought to stay in the saddle Illrede hewed at his side.

The byrnie gave, but held long enough to stop the edge of the ax. Skafloc rocked in his seat from the blow. Illrede pressed closer, smashing at the man's helmet. It crumpled, and only the uncanny strength lent by the sword kept Skafloc conscious.

Illrede raised his ax again, shouting. Dizzily Skafloc struck at him. Sword and ax met in a shower of sparks, and with a mighty sound the ax burst asunder. Skafloc shook his head to clear it, then laughed as a hunting wolf yelps. He cut off Illrede's left arm.

The troll-king sagged in the saddle. Skafloc's blade whined about his head and carved off his other arm. "It ill becomes a warrior to play with a helpless foe," quoth Illrede. "It is the devil in the sword doing this, not you."

Skafloc killed him.

Now a great dismay fell on the trolls and they began to retreat. The elves pressed furiously on them, and the din of battle rang beneath the mountains. In the van of the elves, the Erlking wielded his sword and shouted encouragement. But it was Skafloc, riding everywhere, reaping the foe with a blade that screamed and bellowed, who struck the deepest terror.

And the trolls broke and fled. Hotly did the elves pursue, cutting them down, driving them into the blazing camp. Not many escaped alive.

The Erlking sat his horse in the first thin dawn-light, looking over the death heaped about the castle walls. A cold breeze blew his hair and the white mane and tail of his horse about. Skafloc rode up to him, gaunt and weary, painted with blood and brains, but eyes still smoldering revengefully.

"This was a great victory," quoth the Erlking. "But we were one of the last elf strongholds. The trolls are everywhere in Alfheim."

"Not for long," replied Skafloc. "We will ride forth against them. They are scattered thinly, and every free elf now skulking as an outlaw will join us. We can get weapons for them from the trolls we kill, if nowhere else. Hard will the war be, but—my sword carries victory.

"Also," he added slowly, "I have a new standard which we will bear in the forefront of our army, a banner to strike fear into all enemies." And he held up a spearshaft, on the top of which was impaled the head of Illrede. The dead eyes still seemed to watch and the mouth to grin with menace.

The Erlking shuddered. "Grim is your heart, Skafloc," he said. "You have changed since last I saw you. But let it be as you wish."

24

In the desolation of a winter's dawn, Freda stumbled into Thorkel Erlendsson's garth.

The landholder was just arisen and had come out into the snowy yard to look at the weather. For a moment he scarce believed his eyes—a shield maiden, with arms and armor of a strange coppery metal and clothes of utterly foreign cut, groping forward blind with her own tearless grief and horror—it could not be.

He reached for a spear he kept just inside the door. But his hand dropped as he saw the girl more closely. Freda—Freda Orms-daughter, worn out with sorrow and weariness, her eyes dry and hollow and emptily staring, Freda was back.

Thorkel said no word, but led her inside. Aasa his wife hastened to them.

"You have been gone long, Freda," she said. "But welcome—welcome home!"

The girl sought to reply, but no words would come out. "Poor child," murmured Aasa. "Poor lost child. Come, I will help you to bed."

Freda followed slowly, her shining head bent.

Audun, Thorkel's next oldest son after the slain Erlend, came into the house. "'Tis colder outside than a proud maiden's heart," said he, and then: "But who is this—"

"Freda Ormsdaughter," answered Thorkel. "Freda Ormsdaughter, come back somehow."

Audun stepped over to her with his voice a glad cry: "Freda! Freda, come home again!" He laid his arms about her waist, but ere he could kiss her the mute woe of her gaze fell chill on his heart. He stood aside. "What is the matter?" he asked.

"Matter?" Aasa snapped. "Why, ask what is not the matter with the poor sorrow-burdened girl. Now get out, you heavy-footed goggle-eyed men, get out and let me put her to bed."

Freda lay awake for a long time, staring at the wall. But when at last Aasa brought her food and murmured to her and stroked her bright hair, as a mother to a babe, she began to weep. Long and long she wept, a terrible unending flow of tears, noiseless and with all her grief to make them bitter, and Aasa held her and let her cry it out. Thereafter Freda fell asleep.

Now at Thorkel's bidding she made her dwelling there. It did not take her long to recover herself, but she was not the glad girl folk remembered.

Thorkel asked her what had happened. When she lowered a suddenly whitening face, he added quickly: "No, no, you need not say it if you wish not to do so."

"No reason to hide the truth," she said in so low a voice he could scarce hear it. "Valgard bore Asgerd and myself east over the sea, but he troubled us not. Scarce had he landed when—another viking fell on him and slew his men. But Valgard escaped, and Asgerd was killed in the fight. This other chief took me with him, but at last he set me ashore near my father's garth."

"That was a strange outfit you wore."

"The viking gave it to me, he had it from somewhere else. I often fought by his side. He was a good man." Freda looked up, into the heart of the fire. "Aye, he was the best and bravest and kindest of men." Bitterness twisted her face. "Why should he not be? He came of good folk."

And she turned swiftly away. Thorkel looked after her, tugging thoughtfully at his beard. "Not all the truth has she told," he muttered to himself, "but I think it is all we will ever hear."

Even to the priest by whom she was shriven, Freda said no more than that. Afterward she went off alone and stood on a high hill looking skyward.

It was a bright day, warm for winter. The snow lay clean and white and glistening on the silent earth, and overhead the sky was high and blue.

Freda said quietly: "Now I have done a mortal sin, in not confessing what Skafloc and I did, yet I put the burden thereof on my own soul and will bear it to the grave. All-Father, You know our sin was too sweet and wonderful to be defiled by the eyes of men and the ugliest of names. Lay what penance You will on me, but spare him, who knew no better." She flushed, alone under the great sky. "Also, I think I feel beneath my heart the same dear stirring which you, Mary, must remember—and he shall not bear an evil name for the sake of what his parents did. Father and Mother and Son—do what You will with me, but spare the child."

Presently she came down, feeling somewhat eased at heart. The cool air kissed the blood into her cheeks, the sunlight flamed in bronze and copper and soft-silken waves from her hair, and her gray eyes were bright. There was a smile on her lips when she met Audun Thorkelsson.

The boy was scarce older than she, but already tall and strong, a promising warrior and a good husbandman. His curly fair hair gleamed about a face blushing and shyly smiling like a girl's, as he ran toward her.

"I—was looking for you—Freda," he said when he was beside her.

"Why, was I wanted?" she asked.

"No, save—well—yes, I wanted—to see you," he mumbled. He walked by her side, now and then stealing a glance from downcast eyes.

"What will you do now?" he blurted presently.

The smile faded from her mouth. She cast one woeful look up into the sky, and then almost wildly around the snowy horizon. She could not see the ocean here, but its unending voice came faintly to her ears, tireless, relentless.

"I know not," she said. "I have no one left—"

"But you have!" he cried. And then his tongue seemed locked and he could say no more, however he cursed himself for it.

Winter died slowly into spring, and still Freda dwelt in Thorkel's house. She worked endlessly, and when there was no more work to do she went for long walks, alone by choice though Audun often came along. Aasa was glad enough of help and of someone to talk to, having no daughters and few bond-women. But she did nigh all the talking. Freda said almost nothing save when she was spoken to, and even then she was apt not to hear.

For her, time was the most cruel torment, not alone in the weight of her sin and the death of her folk—those she could bear, and the new life within her was some cheer for them—but in the loss of Skafloc.

No sign, no word, no sight since that last stricken gaze by Orm's howe with the winter morning bleak about him. He was alone, ringed in by his deadly foemen, starting out on a quest into the grimmest of lands for a prize that would bring doom on him. Where was he now? Did he live yet, or was his tall form stiff on the ground with ravens tearing out the empty eyes which once had shone alone for her? What hopeless misery drowned his laughter and made him long for death as once he had longed for Freda? Or had he forgotten what he could not endure to remember, abandoned his humanness altogether for the cool oblivion of Leea's kisses—? No, that could not be, he would not forget his love while he lived.

But lived he yet—and how, and for how long?

"Skafloc," she whispered. "Skafloc, I love you. I will always love you."

Now and again she dreamed of him, as if he stood living before her, their hearts throbbed together and his arms were strong and tender about her. His voice murmured in her ear or rang with the old wild laughter or spoke his gay love verses— She awoke in a black and pitiless night, alone in a strange bed, and lay waiting for the hopeless gray dawn.

She was changed. The life of men seemed a dull and petty round after the eerie glamor of the elf court and the mad glad days of their troll-hunt in a winter world. Thorkel having been christened only so the English would leave him in peace, she rarely saw a priest—and, knowing her heart sinned, was glad of that. Dark and dreary was a church after the forests and hills and sounding sea. She still loved God—and were not the open lands His work, and a church only man's?—but she could not bring herself to call very often on Him.

Now and then she could not keep from slipping out in the middle of the night, taking a horse, and riding northward. With her witch-sight she might catch a few glimpses of the faerie world—a scuttering gnome, a fleeting shadow, a black longship coasting by. But those she dared hail fled her, and she could get no word of how the war went.

But even so, the briefly seen world, weird and moonstruck, was Skafloc's. And for a short wonderful while it had been hers.

She kept herself too hard at work for overmuch brooding, and her young healthy body bloomed. As spring came, she could almost feel the same stirring within her that brought back the birds and called forth buds like clenched baby fists. She saw herself in a polished shield and knew she was now more woman than girl—the slim figure becoming stronger and fuller, the breasts rising and swelling, the blood coursing steadier in the smooth lovely cheeks. She was becoming a mother.

Could he who loved her but see her now, in this full glorious bloom— *No, no, it is sin. But I love him, I love him so—*

The winter went in a fury of rain and pealing thunder. The first light soft green spread over the dark rain-washed trees and fields. The birds came home. Freda saw a remembered pair of storks wheeling puzzledly over Orm's lands. They had built their nest on his roof. She wept, quietly and gently as the rains of late spring. Her heart felt empty.

No—no, it was filling again, not with the old boundless joy, but with a stiller gladness deepened by sorrow. Her child was growing to life within her. In him—or her, it mattered not—all her ashen hopes rose anew.

She stood alone in twilight with the blossoms of an apple tree over her head, drifting down in a rain of petals with every gentle wind. The winter was gone and spring had come to a haunted land. Skafloc lived in it, in every cloud and shadow, in the dawn and sunset and the high-riding moon, he spoke in the wind and his laughter was in the sea's voice. There would be winter, and winter again, in the great unending wheel of years. But she bore the summer beneath her heart, and all summers to come.

Now Thorkel made ready for a trading and viking voyage to the east which he and his sons had long planned. But Audun seemed not overly happy about it, and finally one day he said to his father: "I cannot go."

"What is that?" cried the landholder. "You, who have worked for this and dreamed of it more than any of us, cannot go?"

"No, I—well, someone is needed about the place."

"We have good housecarles. Be not a fool."

"But—" Audun looked uneasily away. "Well I remember what happened to Orm's folk when all the men were gone—"

"We have plenty of people quickly summoned, as well as near neighbors, which Orm's garth did not have after his death." Thorkel's shrewd eyes impaled his son. "What ails you, lad? Speak the truth. Are you afraid of fighting?"

"You know I am not," flared Audun, "and I will kill anyone who says I am. But it is not my will to go this year, and there is an end of that."

Thorkel nodded slowly. "It is the woman Freda, then," he said. "I thought as much. But she is without folk or wealth."

"What of that? Our house is rich. I myself will have no little money when I have sailed out next summer.

"She is with child by this viking of whom she will not speak but always seems to think."

Audun looked angrily at the ground. "Again, what of it?" he mumbled. "It was not her fault—nor the child's, for that matter. She needs someone to help her—yes, and to help her forget that other man who cruelly cast her off. Could I but find him, you would see whether I fear weapon-play!"

"Well—" Thorkel shrugged. "I cannot do much about your will. Stay behind, then, if you feel you must." After a while he added: "It is true she has no living kin in England save the evil berserker Valgard, God smite him, but she is of good stock as any in the land. Nor is she without wealth, since I suppose Orm's fields are hers now—and it were shame they lay fallow. And also, she is a good lass."

He smiled, but his eyes were troubled. "Woo her if you will, then," he said, "but I hope your luck is better than Erlend's."

Some days later, Thorkel sailed. Audun stood on the shore looking after the ship, with longing bitter in his eyes. But when he turned and saw Freda beside him, he felt he had been well repaid.

"Why do you stay?" she asked.

His face was hot, but he answered boldly: "I think you know."

She looked away and said naught.

The days grew longer and the trees and ground burst into green life. Warm winds, shouting rains, bird songs and leaping deer and fish silvery in the rivers—flowers, light nights, and the growth of new life—Freda felt the child stirring within her.

Audun was ever oftener by her side. Now and again, in a rush of loneliness and woe, she bade him begone. But his sorrowful eyes brought remorse to her.

He sought to woo her with awkward, lame words she scarcely listened to. But she buried her face in the cool fresh fragrance of the great flower-bunches he gathered for her, and she saw his smile, timid and friendly as a puppy—strange, that so strong and sure a youth was weaker than she.

If she wed him, it would be he that was given to her. He was not Skafloc, who took her and guarded her and gave her of his boundless strength and laughter. He was only Audun.

O Skafloc, Skafloc, unforgotten beloved.

But his memory was becoming a wistful caress, a summer that was past, recalled in the new springtime. He warmed her heart without searing it, the vision was no longer a blinding pain but a deep quiet sorrow on which danced the sun-glints of a lost joy. Lived he or died he, he was forever lost to her, and grief was no way to end such a love as had been theirs. That love lay too deep for tears.

Audun was kind and glad. She liked the boy. And he would be a strong shield for the child, Skafloc's child.

There came an evening when the two stood on the beach, the sea murmurous at their feet and the sunset all red and gold behind them. Audun took her hands and said with a steadiness new to him: "You know I have long loved you, Freda, even before you came here. I have wooed you, and at first you would not listen and then you would not reply. But I ask for an honest answer now, and if it is your wish then I will trouble you no longer. But I love you, Freda. Will you wed me?"

She looked into his eyes and her voice was low and clear: "Yes."

25

In late summer it began to rain, and for days on end the wind scourged the elf-hills and veiled them in a lightning-blinking gray. The trolls in Elfheugh, ever more held near the castle for fear of the outlaw elves, finally could not even leave its walls. They slumped in their rooms or in the halls, drinking and gaming and quarreling and drinking again. Sullen and fearful they were, on edge so that the lightest word might lead to a death battle. And their elf mistresses grew more and more wanton, so that not a day went by without friendships broken and often lives lost over a woman.

Evil rumors muttered along the dim corridors. Illrede—aye, he had fallen, and his grinning head was the new elf standard. Earl Guro could not hold the troll armies together as the king had done, and each time he rallied for a stand he was driven back. A demon, a fiend with a sword of evil and a heart of murder, led the elves to victory over twice their number.

Vendland had fallen, whispered someone, and the elves" terrible general had ringed in all trolls there and spared not a one. It was said one could walk on troll corpses from end to end of the battlefield.

The troll strongholds in the Northlands were stormed, said another, and—somehow, though they were elf castles and built to stand off any assault—they fell, one after the other, and every troll who lived was put to the sword. A fleet was captured in a Jutish bay and used for raids into Trollheim itself.

The trolls" allies, or such of them as still survived, were falling away. A company of Shen was said to have turned on its troll companions in Gardariki and slaughtered them. A goblin uprising wiped out three towns—or five or a dozen, the rumors were growing—in Trollheim.

The elves were driving into Valland with the trolls retreating before them—a retreat that became a rout and finally, caught against the sea, a butchery. Whispers went around the castle of the dreadful horse that trod out warriors" lives, of the hungrily screaming devil in the form of a sword.

Valgard, growing gaunter and grimmer and shorter of speech as the summer wore on, sought to raise his folk's flagging spirits. "The elves have rallied," he said. "They fight well, and have new sorcerous powers. But it is their last gasp, soon their might will be broken forever."

But this the trolls knew: that fewer and fewer ships came from across the channel or the eastern sea, and the news they brought got worse and worse until Valgard forbade his folk to speak with the crews; that the outlaw elves under Flam and Firespear grew ever bolder, until a whole army was not safe from their arrows or their swiftly raiding ships and horsemen; that the Irish Sidhe were arming as if for war; that a growing weariness and dull despair and savage hatred of one's fellow spread poisonously through the castles, fed by the elf women's bold eyes and their subtle hints.

Valgard raged like a prowling beast. Up and down the great castle he went, from its highest windy towers to its deepest night-black dungeons, snarling, often killing in a burst of blind rage. He felt caged, hemmed in by the misty walls, by the outlaws lurking beyond, by the great and growing elf army whose strength he knew—by his whole life. And naught could he do about it.

No use leading men out against the elves. It was like fighting shadows. They would be gone, but from somewhere an arrow would sing into a troll's back, a noose tighten about a troll's neck, a pit open beneath a troll's horse. Even at the table one was never sure—now and again someone died, belike of poison sneaked into his food by some underhanded trick.

Cunning and patient were the elves, turning their weaknesses into strengths, biding their time. The trolls could not understand them and came more and more to fear the race they thought they had beaten.

Who were now beating them, thought Valgard grimly. But this he kept from his men as much as possible, though he could not stop the frightened whispers and the sullen mutinous anger.

There was naught he could do, save sit in Imric's high seat draining horn after horn of fiery wine. Leea tended to him, and his horn never seemed to be empty. He slumped in silence, sunken eyes smouldering toward blindness as he drank, until at last he slid senseless to the floor.

Often, though, when he was not yet too drunk to walk, he would slowly lift his great body. Reeling a little, he made his way down the gutted hall where embered fires showed the troll chiefs sprawled like corpses. He took a torch and fumbled down a rough-hewn stair. Leaning on the cold slippery wall, he groped to a certain dungeon door and opened it.

Imric's white body, now streaked and blackened with clotted blood, showed red against the gloom by the light of the coals just below his feet. The imp tending the fire kept it ever dull and hot, and the earl hung by his thumbs without food or drink. His belly was sunken in and his skin taut over the arching ribs, his tongue was black, but the terrible vitality of the immortal would not let him die.

His slant, cloudy-blue eyes rested on Valgard with the unreadable elf-stare that, somehow, always turned the changeling's heart cold. The berserker snarled to overcome that fear. Then he grinned.

"You know why I am here," he said. His voice was thick and he swayed on his feet.

No word spoke Imric, but hung like one dead. Valgard struck him in the face, a dull heavy blow that seemed unnaturally loud in the dungeon silence. The little imp shrank aside, his eyes and fangs agleam in the dark.

"You know, if your brain has not yet shriveled in your skull," said Valgard. "I have been here often enough. I will be here again."

He took the great whip from its place on the wall and slowly ran the thongs through his hands. His eyes were fever-bright and he licked his lips.

"I hate you," he mouthed. He brought his face close to Imric's. "I hate you for bringing me into the world. I hate you for stealing my heritage. I hate you for being all I can never be—nor would, cursed elf! I hate you because of your evil works. I hate you because your damned fosterling is not at hand for my vengeance and you must suffice—now!"

He lifted the whip. The imp huddled as far into a corner as he could get. Imric made no sound or movement.

When Valgard's one arm tired, he used the other. And after it was also weary, he turned suddenly, threw down the whip, and left.

The wine was working out of him, but only a great coldness remained where it had been. As he came by a window he heard the roar of the rain.

The troll-hated summer for which he had longed, thinking to lie out in green vales and beside murmuring rivers, and which he had spent in futile sallies against the elves or sitting in the gloom of the castle—the summer was waning at last. But so was Troll-heim. There was silence from Valland, but the last word thence had been of a field stark with slaughter.

Would the rain never cease? He shuddered at the cold wet breath through the windows. Lightning glared blinding blue-white outside and the whole building shook to the bellow of thunder.

He stumbled up the long winding stair to his chambers. The troll guard sprawled in sottish sleep—ha, were they all drunks and murderers of their own kin? Where in all this brawling, fear-ridden horde was one to whom he could open his heart?

He entered his chambers and stood huge and stoop-shouldered in the door. Leea sat up in the bed. She at least, he thought dully, she had not played wanton like the other elf women—and she comforted him in times like these when he trembled for fear of himself.

Lightning blazed around the tower. The bawling thunder rattled its ancient floors and rafters. The wind screamed, dashing a solid gray sheet of rain against the walls. Tapestries blew wildly in the cold, gusts that whirled around the room. Tapers were snuffed out and only the incessant lightning gave a lurid vision.

Valgard sat heavily down on the edge of the bed. His eyes stared emptily before him. Leea slid up by his side and laid white arms about his neck.

Her slumbrous gaze rested on him, cool and remote and mysterious. Her smile was luring but somehow had no warmth. He heard her voice, sweet under the crashing thunder: "What have you been doing, my lord?"

"That you know," he muttered. "And I wonder why you hate me not for it."

"Victory goes to the strong, in might or guile," she said. "That is the law of life, even in faerie."

"Aye." He clenched his teeth. "And now it seems they, the elves—are the strongest. Everywhere the trolls flee. It is sorcery—it must be! I have heard some story of a sword whose wielder ever has the victory—"

He looked grimly at her. "But what I cannot understand is the fall of the great strongholds," he said. "Even an elf army victorious in the field should have dashed itself to bits against those walls. Many of them surrendered to us without a fight, the rest were starved—why, some few have never been out of elf hands in spite of all we could bring against them. But those we held, fully manned, well supplied—they were lost as soon as the Erlking's men rode against them." He shook his unkempt head. "Why?"

Then seizing her slim shoulders in rough hands: "But this castle shall not fall. It cannot! I will hold Elfheugh though the gods themselves take the field against me. Ha, I long for battle—naught else would so cheer me and my weary men. And we will smash them, you hear? We will fling them back and I will raise Skafloc's head on a pike above the walls."

"Aye, my lord," she breathed, still smiling, still cool and secret.

"I am strong," he growled, deep in his throat. "When I was a viking, I broke men with my bare hands. And I have no fear in battle, and I am cunning. Many victories have I won, and I will win many more."

His hands fell slackly to his lap and his eyes darkened with horror. "But what of that?" he whispered. "What of that? Why am

I so? Because Imric made me thus. He molded me into the image of Orm's son. I am alive for no other reason, and all my strength and looks and brain are—Skafloc's!"

He stumbled to his feet. Blindly he stared before him, and his voice rose to a scream: "*What am I but the shadow of Skafloc?*"

The thunder roared and raged. The wind ran wild, shouting its ancient power, hooting its ancient mockery. Lightning leaped and flamed, white, livid, hell-fire loose in the sky. The rain flung itself against the streaming walls.

Valgard swayed and groped through the lightning-raddled gloom. "I will kill him," he muttered between his teeth. "I will bury him deep under the sea. I will kill Imric and Freda and you, Leea—all who know I am not really alive, that I am a ghost conjured into flesh molded after another man's—cold flesh, my hands are cold—"

The thunder crashed and boomed. "Aye, throw your hammer up there!" howled Valgard. "Make your noise while you can! I will put my hands around the pillars of the sky and pull them down. I will tread the world under my feet. I will raise storm and darkness and glaciers grinding down from the north, and dust shall whirl in my footsteps. I am Death!"

Someone beat on the door, a frantic tattoo scarce heard above the banging thunder and the shrieking wind. Valgard snarled and opened. His hands sought the throat of the troll who stood swaying with weariness before him.

"I will begin with you," he mumbled. Foam flecked his lips. With all the monster troll strength, the struggling messenger could not break the hold.

But when he sprawled dead on the floor, the berserkergang left Valgard. Weak and trembling, he leaned against the door. "That was unwise," he muttered.

“Perhaps there were others with him,” said Leea. She stepped out onto the landing and called: “Hai, down there! The earl wishes to speak with any others who just arrived.”

A troll, spent and reeling, with a bloody gash in one cheek, stumbled to the foot of the stairs. “Fifteen of us set out,” he said, gasping. “Gru and I alone are left. The outlaws dogged us all the way.”

“But what is the word?” called Valgard. “What is your message?”

“The elves have landed in England, lord. And we got word that the Irish Sidhe, led by Lugh of the Long Hand himself, are already in Scotland.”

Valgard nodded his gaunt head.

26

Under cover of a wild autumn storm, Skafloc led the best of the elf warriors across the channel to England. He was chief of that host, for the Erlking stayed behind to drive the last remnants of the trolls from continental Alfheim. But to take England, he warned, would be no light matter—and if the trolls should be able to repulse the elves, they could use the island as a rallying point for new attacks.

Skafloc shrugged. “Victory goes with my sword,” he said.

The Erlking studied him for some time ere saying: “Have a care about that weapon. Well has it worked for us up to now, but it is treacherous. Sooner or later it is fated to turn on its wielder, perhaps when he is most cruelly needed.”

Skafloc paid no great heed to this, but gathered men, horses, and ships in hidden Breton bays. He also got word to the elf chiefs in England, that they should start hosting their scattered warriors. And on a night when gales cloaked all the northern world, he took his fleet across the channel.

Dark and savage was that night, with sleet-mingled rain driving in solid sheets out of a black sky split open with lightning. Thunder rolled and roared between crazed heaven and groaning earth. The wind filled the sky with its lashing clamor. Black was the sea, whitened with foam and fury, mighty waters running out of the west and snarling far up the shore. Even the elves put no sail on their pitching ships, but rowed across the channel to southeast England. The rain and sea dashed in their faces and blue fire crawled over the reeling masts.

Out of the galing dark, black against the livid lightning, reared the shores of England. The elves rowed until it seemed their muscles must burst. Surf roared on beach and skerry, and the wind caught at the ships and sought to hurl them onto darkly gleaming rocks or against each other. Fierce was the struggle to round the ness, and one ship was swamped and lost under the galloping white-maned waves. Skafloc laughed harshly and said aloud:

Cold and lustful
are the kisses
which Ran's daughters,
white-armed, give us.
Laughing, shouting,
shake they tresses
white and salt-sweet,
high breasts heaving.

He stood braced in the bow of his rolling longship, staring ahead into the storm, and when he saw the streaming rain-lashed land a mighty longing rose in his breast and nigh choked him. He quoth:

Home again the howling,
hail-streaked wind has borne me.
Now I stand here, nearing
ness of lovely England.
She dwells on these shores, but
shall I ever see her?
Woe, the fair young woman
will not leave my thinking.

But when the fleet had gotten around the cape they found waters sheltered enough for landing. The elves ran their ships up to the shore and drew them onto the beach.

Swiftly now they busked themselves for fighting. One of Skafloc's captains asked him: "Who will remain to guard the ships?"

"No one," he replied. "We will need all our men inland."

"But the trolls might come on the fleet and burn it—then we would have no way of retreat."

Skafloc looked about the lightning-lit countryside. "For me, at least," he said, "there will be no retreat. I will not leave England again, alive or dead, till the trolls are driven out."

The elves looked at him in more than a little awe. He hardly seemed a mortal, standing there tall and iron-clad, the demon sword clanking at his waist. He had grown gaunt and haggard, curt of speech and pitiless in war. Strange wolf-greenish lights flickered far back in his chill blue eyes, and he fought with berserker recklessness and cold calm at once. The elves thought he was fey.

He swung into the saddle of his grim black horse. His voice came above the wind: "Sound the lur horns. We ride on troll hunt tonight!"

The army got under way. Rain beat in their faces and lightning blazed overhead. When they rode by woods the fallen leaves scrunched soddenly under hoofs and feet. The night was cold with the first breath of a new winter.

Presently they heard the remote brassy bellow of horns, troll battle-horns. The elves hefted their gleaming weapons and smiled savagely in the flimmering lightning-glare. Rain-streaming shields flashed forth in the night and the lur horns brayed again.

Skafloc rode at the head of the elf wedge. He felt no great joy at the thought of battle, he was sick and weary with the slaughter of the last months. When he drew the sword a wild murder lust ran like a flame from it into him, and he fought tirelessly, ruthlessly, few weapons biting on him. But—was he not becoming the mere vessel of the demon power in the sword?

What did it matter? Freda had left him.

Now the trolls came out of the night toward the elves. They must have come from a nearby castle, belike Alfarhöi, and their force was strong though not so great as that of the elves. About half of it was archers and pikemen and other foot soldiers. Many of the elves were mounted, but some got down on the ground ere battle.

"We outnumber them, but not by much," said the chief on Skafloc's right. "This would not be the first time brave warriors have overthrown stronger hosts."

"I do not fear they will defeat us," replied Skafloc, "but it would be ill if they killed any great number of us, for then the next fight might indeed be our last." He scowled into the rainy night. "Curse it, England's elves knew we were to be here at this time. Where are they—? Unless the messengers were caught on the way, or the outlaws have been trapped and killed—"

The troll horns sounded to battle. Skafloc drew his sword and swung it above his head. In the glare of lightning, the blade flamed blindly and seemed to be wreathed in blue fire.

"Forward!" Skafloc spurred his mighty horse. The icy rage of murder blazed through him, he cared not whether it rose from the sword or the darknesses of his own soul—forward, kill, hew, hew!

Spears and arrows whistled overhead, unseen against the lightning-crawling heavens. But the ripping wind made it hard to aim, and so the clatter of swords was swiftly heard.

Skafloc leaned forward in his stirrups and hewed with both hands. A troll struck at him, and his sword bit through those arms. Another rode close, ax raised, and the blade screamed around into that one's neck. A foot soldier jabbed with his pike—it glanced off Skafloc's helmet, and the man leaned over to smite the troll to earth.

Ax and sword! Clang and spark-flash! Cloven metal, rent flesh, warriors sinking to the rain-running ground under the devil-dance of lightning!

Through the mighty clangor rode Skafloc, hewing, hewing. His blows shuddered through metal and bone, the shock slamming back into his own shoulders. Weapons lashed at him, striking with suddenly deadened edges he hardly felt. The hawk-scream of his blade rose high, wailing death-songs. None could stand against him, and he led his men through the troll lines and turned on the foe from behind.

But the trolls fought stubbornly. Elves sank under mighty blows. Arrows veiled the bunched archers. Charging horses ran into braced spears. Where was help, where was help?

As if in answer, a horn blew under the rolling thunder. A horn, and another, and yet another—a wild war-cry, a storm of spears and arrows, a sweeping of ragged hell-raging figures out of the night!

"Ha, Alfheim!" Firespear rode forward with blood streaming from his lance like the rain from his helmet. His face blazed with joy of victory. By his side, grim and blood-smeared, battle-dinted ax dripping red, rode Flam of Orkney. And other great elf chiefs were in the fight, rising as if out of the gory earth to strike down the trolls.

With such numbers, it was no great task to clear away the foe, and erelong only corpses held the field. Skafloc held saddle-council with Firespear, Flam, and the other elf lords.

"We came as swiftly as we could," said Firespear, "but we had to stop at Runehill to take it since the gates stood open for us and few trolls inside it lived—well did the women do their work! Alfarhöi must await us too."

"It is well," nodded Skafloc. Now that the battle was past and the sword sheathed, he felt only a great weariness. The storm was dying overhead in wink of lightning and grumble of thunder, the wind sank and the rain washed heavily out of a lightening sky.

"The Sidhe of Erin go to war too," said Flam. "Lugh has landed in Scotland, and Mananaan is driving the trolls from Orkney and Shetland."

"Ah—he held his word." Skafloc's eyes brightened. "A good friend is Mananaan. He is the only god I would ever trust."

"And that only because he is a half-god stripped of his old powers and reduced to faerie," muttered Firespear. "Ill is it to have any dealings with gods—or giants."

"Well, we had best get inside ere dawn," said Flam. "Today we sleep in Alfarhöi—oh, it has been long since I slept in an elf burh or beside an elf woman!"

Skafloc's face twisted, but he said naught.

Through the autumn the elves fought, and their blood flowing was no redder than the leaves which flamed bronze and gold under a hazy blue sky and were whirled whispering away by a cool vagrant wind. Squirrels scuttled about, hiding nuts against the winter, and the far lonely cry of southward-winging geese rang over the dreamy misty hills. At night the stars were frosty-cold, twinkling by their thousands in the deep crystal black of the sky.

Skafloc rode alone through the evening. The trolls had been cleared from the lands about, north and south their broken armies were streaming to Elfheugh for a last stand, so he had naught to fear. But his heart beat and beat, blood thundered in his ears, his hands were cold and his lips dry.

The huge black stallion went at a walk, no faster than a mortal steed. The thickly strewn leaves crackled under his great hoofs and danced before him on a breath of cool rustling wind. The forest blazed around him, seeming to crown his rider with an aureole of gold and bronze and copper. The hazy twilight closed softly in as they went through remembered woods.

Skafloc sat tall and straight in the saddle. His broad shoulders were unbowed by the weight of his battle-worn byrnie or the huge dragon-hilted sword. His hair blew long and light and fair under his winged helm. His face, strong straight lines of it standing out in bone and muscle under the weather-darkened skin, was set in unbending mold. But his eyes, huge and deep blue in the gaunt worn countenance, were bright with suffering. Godlike he might look—or demon-like—but the dreadful wounded longing burned from his eyes.

He was afraid. Death he could laugh at, but the resistless yearning which drew him forth shook his being with fear of opening old wounds.

An elf had spoken of seeing a woman who looked like Freda Ormsdaughter in the garth of Thorkel Erlendsson—a woman young and fair, with sorrow in her gray eyes, and great with child.

Skafloc rode into the rustling dark. He splashed over a murmurous brook, clear and icy cold, on which dead leaves floated seaward like little brown boats. He heard an owl hooting in the frosty twilight, and the dry voices of the trees whispered to him—but under it all was a great singing silence in which only his heart lived, fluttering in his ribbed breast like a caged bird.

O Freda, Freda, are you really so near?

The first stars began to twinkle out as Skafloc rode into Thorkel's yard. It was dark save for the house, where firelight glowed from under the door.

He dismounted. His knees wavered, and it took a surge of will for him to walk over to the house. He tried the door, and it was not latched.

Audun's eyes were warmer than the merry leaping flames as he came into the room where Freda sat alone. "All others are asleep," he said. "We can be together."

He sat down on the bench beside her. "Scarce can I believe it," he breathed. "Any day now, my father comes home and we can be wed."

Freda smiled. The light sheened ruddily from her long braided hair. "First I must have my child," she said, "but that time is also nigh."

Her eyes were grave on his. "And have you in truth naught against me for that—or against him?" she asked, slowly and softly.

"How could I?" replied Audun. "It is your child, dearest of all, that is enough. It will be like my own."

He drew her into his arms.

The door opened and the night wind blew in. Freda saw the tall form standing redly limned against the dark. She could not speak, but she shrank against the wall with something like horror whitening her face.

"Freda," croaked Skafloc above the hiss and crackle of the fire. "Freda."

She stood slowly up, leaning against the wall behind her. There seemed to be an iron band around her throat, choking off her breath.

Like a sleepwalker, Skafloc came toward her. And she took a slow step toward him, and another. The old hunger filled their eyes—*he lived, she lived, they were together again.*

"Hold!"

Audun's voice crashed across the shuddering silence. His shadow bulked huge before him as he surged to his feet. He snatched a spear from the wall, and he thrust between them.

"Hold!" His voice wobbled. A dreadful fear throttled him—who was the man at whom Freda stared as she had never looked at him? "Who are you? What will you?"

"Freda—" Skafloc looked over the boy's shoulder, scarce seeing him. "Freda, come with me."

She shook her head, slowly, wrenchingly, but her arms were held out to him.

"I love you, Freda," whispered Skafloc. "I love you. What are law and gods and all the world to us? Come with me, most dearly loved, come—"

She bent her head. Her soft young face was twisted all out of shape with pain. She trembled, sobs rattling in her throat, and the tears ran down her fair cheeks.

"You hurt her!" screamed Audun. "You hurt Freda—my betrothed!"

He stabbed with the spear. It glanced off the broad byrnied chest and furrowed up Skafloc's cheek. The elf lord snarled like an angry cat and reached for his sword.

Audun stabbed again. Skafloc leaped aside, elf-swift, the sword screaming out of its scabbard. Like a lightning bolt it clove the shaft over. "Out of the way!" gasped Skafloc.

"Not while my bride lives!" Audun, beside himself with rage and fear, feeling tears bitter in his eyes, snatched forth his dagger. He lunged at Skafloc. The sword flamed high, whistled down, and sang in bone and brain. Audun skidded across the floor and crashed into a wall, where he lay hideously limp.

With a dawning horror, Skafloc stared at the reddened glaive in his hands. "I did not mean that," he whispered. "I did not mean to kill him. But I forgot that the sword must drink blood each time it is drawn—"

His eyes lifted slowly to Freda, She was staring white and shaking at him, mouth drawn open as if for a scream.

"I meant it not!" he shouted. "And what does it matter? Come with me, now!"

She fought for a voice. It came at last, low and quivering: "Go. Go at once. Do not come again."

"But—" He stumbled toward her.

She stooped and picked up Audun's dagger. It gleamed bright in her hand. "Get out," she said. "Get out. Come any closer and I drive this into your throat."

"I wish you would," he said bitterly. He stood swaying a little. The blood coursed slowly down his gashed cheek and dripped on the floor.

"I will slay myself if I must. Touch me, murderer, heathen, incestuous, and I will sheath the knife in my own heart. God will forgive me the lesser sin if I escape the greater."

Skafloc blazed with a sudden rage. "Aye, call on your god, whine your prayers!" he said. "Is that all you are good for? You were ready to sell yourself for a meal and a roof, it is whoredom no matter how many priests snivel over it." He lifted the sword. "Better my son die unborn than he be given to that cursed god of yours."

Freda stood erect before him. "Strike if you will," she jeered. "Boys and women and unborn babes—are they your foes now?"

He lowered the great blade, and then suddenly clashed it into the sheath. As he did, he felt the demon fury drain from him and a strange weakness and grief rise in its place.

His shoulders sagged and his head sank. "Will you not come?" he asked brokenly. "The sword is accursed—'twas not I who said those evil things or slew that poor boy. I love you, Freda, I love you so that all the world is bright with my love when you are near. I—like a beggar, I ask you to come."

Her eyes were stony, but her breast rose and fell with gasping. "No—now leave, go away." Her voice rose to a scream: "I do not ever want to see you again—go!"

He turned toward the door. His mouth trembled. "Once I asked you for a farewell kiss," he said very quietly, "and you would not give it to me. Will you now?"

She looked away from him. Then she knelt down beside Audun's huddled form and kissed his dead lips. "Poor boy," she murmured, stroking his bloody hair. "Poor dear Audun—"

"Then goodbye," said Skafloc. "There may come a third time when I ask you for a kiss, but that will be the last. I do not think I have long to live, nor do I care. But I love you."

He went out, closing the door behind him against the restless night wind. The frightened folk of the garth, roused by the late noise, heard his hoofbeats like dull thunder drumming away over the world.

But in the darkness ere morning Freda's time came upon her. The child was big and her hips were narrow. Long and hard was her pain.

Aasa sent a thrall on horseback after a priest. But Thorkel had built his house as far from a church as he could, and they could not look for the clerk to arrive before the next day. Meanwhile the woman helped Freda where she could, but her face was grim.

"First Erlend, now Audun," she muttered once to herself. "Orm's daughters bring no great luck."

At last the child was brought forth, a fine, lustily screaming man-child whose mouth was soon hungrily at Freda's breast. In the cool early evening she lay, still weak and atremble, with her son in her arms.

She smiled down at the little figure. "You are a pretty baby," she said softly. "You are still red and wrinkled, but to me you are the most beautiful of all things. And you would also be so to your father."

Tears flowed down her cheeks. She held the baby close to her. "I love him," she whispered. "God forgive me, I will always love him. And you are all that is left of our love."

The sun burned bloodily to darkness. A thin moon swept through gathering clouds blown by a harrying wind. There would be storm again tonight, winter was drawing nigh.

The garth huddled under rushing heavens. Trees groaned around it and the sea was loud on the beach. The moon-guttering dark was vast and lonely about the few buildings.

Night deepened and the wind rose to a gale, driving armies of dead leaves before it. Hail drummed briefly on the roof like night-gangers thumping their heels on the ridgepole as they went by overhead. The house lay in darkness and noise.

Far away, Freda heard a horn blowing. Something in its scream ran cold through her. The child cried out at her side and she gathered him into her arms.

The horn sounded again, louder, nearer, through the hooting wind and the roar of sea. She heard the clamor of dogs, barking and baying, the earth ringing an echo. Hoofbeats rushed thunderous through the night, high, near, filling the sky with their haste. The house shook.

The Asgard's-Ride, the Wild Hunt—Freda lay in a shroud of fear and darkness. Her babe screamed at her breast. The wind rattled around the house.

There came a mighty tramping of hoofs in the yard. The horn sounded again, a windy blast to which the house trembled. The frightful clamor of hounds rolled and echoed about the walls, filling the rooms with terror.

Someone knocked on the door leading into Freda's chamber from the yard. The bolt crashed up and the door flew open. The storm-wind galed around the little room, blowing the cloak of the one who entered like huge bat wings.

He had to stoop under the roof. He bore a spear in one hand that flashed with cold unearthly light, the same steely blaze that lit his one eye. His long wolf-gray hair and beard streamed down from under the hat that shadowed his face.

His voice was the voice of wind and sea and the vast hollow spaces of the sky: "Freda Ormsdaughter, I have come for the price you swore to pay."

"My—" She shrank back into her bed, tiny and alone under that baleful stare. If Skafloc were by her side—"My girdle is in that chest, lord."

"Ha—ha, ha, ha!" The laughter of Odin was like thunder in the howling night "Think you I wanted that little flask? No, you swore to give me what you bore behind your belt—and even then you carried the child!"

"*No!*" She hardly heard her own scream. She thrust the crying baby behind her. "No, no, no!" She lifted the crucifix at her throat. "In the name of God and of Christ I command you to flee!"

"I need not run from their powers this time," snarled Odin, "for you swore away all their help in this matter. Now give me the child!"

Ruthlessly he swept her aside and took the babe in one arm. Freda huddled at his feet. "What will you do with him?" she moaned. "What do you want him for?"

The Huntsman loomed huge and shadowy over her. "His destiny is high and terrible," quoth he. "Not yet is this game of Aesir and Jötuns and the new gods played out. The devil-sword still gleams on the chessboard of the world. I gave it to Skafloc because Bölverk would on no account have made it anew for an As. Skafloc and the sword were needed to drive back the trolls—whom Utgard-Loki had been secretly helping to gain power—lest faerie be held by a race friendly to the enemies of the gods. But Skafloc cannot be let keep the sword, or he will seek to wipe out the trolls altogether—and this the Jötuns would not stand for, so that they would move against Alfheim, then the gods would have to move against them, and the end of the world would be at hand. Skafloc must die, and this child whom I wove my web to have begotten and given to me must inherit the sword and finish its destiny."

"Skafloc—die—" The girl looked wildly up into the Wanderer's hidden face. "Die—no—"

"What has he to live for?" asked Odin coldly. "If you should go to him and end his despair, you could persuade him not to fare into Trollheim. Then there would be no reason for his death, and he could be spared. But as it is, he is fey. The sword will kill him."

With a swirl of his cloak, the Wild Huntsman was gone. The horn blew outside, the hounds yelped and barked and howled, the hoofs thundered into distance and night. Then the only sounds were the piping of the wind and the shouting of the sea and the weeping of Freda.

27

Valgard stood on the highest tower of Elfheugh and watched the gathering of his foes. His arms were folded on his great breast, his huge-thewed, black-byrnied body was rock-still, and his face was as if carved in stone. Only his eyes lived, with a weird wolfish flicker far down in their chill depths. Beside him were the other chiefs of the castle and of the broken armies which now hid in this last and most powerful stronghold. Weary and despairing were they, wounded from cruel battles, staring with hollow fearful eyes at the hosting of Alfheim.

On Valgard's right stood Leea, tall and slender, shimmering whitely mysterious under the sinking moon. The wind blew her thin silken dress and the cloudy silvery veil of her hair about her. She was half smiling, her remote enigmatic smile that promised all and told naught. Her eyes shone twilight blue in the dark.

Below the frowning walls of Elfheugh, the hill-slope was white with rime and moonlight. On that glistening ground moved the elf army. Byrnies clanked and chimed, lur horns blew, horses stamped ringingly on the frosty earth. Shields flung back the moonlight, and the heads of spears and axes gleamed cold under the winking stars. The elves were setting up their camp, tents ringing the castle and fires blossoming to ruddy life. To and fro, inhuman in their swift grace, flitted the shadowy forms of the warriors.

A booming thunderous rumble rolled through the frost-silent hills. Into sight came a war chariot, bright almost as a sun, with flames flickering about the swords on the hubs. Four huge white horses drew it, arching their great moon-maned heads and snorting like storm winds. The warrior-king standing in it with his shining and terrible spear towered over all others. The dark locks blew about a face god-like in its majesty and grimness, the eyes seemed to flash with a light of their own.

The voice of a troll captain rose trembling: "That is Lugh of the Long Hand. He led the Tuatha De Danaan against us. He reaped us like wheat. The Scottish ravens darkened the earth, too gorged to fly, and not a hundred trolls escaped."

Still Valgard said no word, but stood brooding over the scene.

Red-cloaked, silver-byrnied, Firespear rode his prancing horse around the castle walls. Bright and handsome was his face, cruel in its mockery, and his lance seemed to impale the wheeling stars. "He led the outlaws," muttered someone else. "Their arrows came from everywhere. They rose out of the night against us, and left fire and death in their wake."

Valgard remained moveless.

Outside in the moon-rippling bay, the hulks of troll vessels still smouldered or lay driven onto the beach and broken. Long-ships lay at anchor, gleaming with shields and weapons. "Flam of Orkney captains those, which Mananaan Mac Lir captured back from us," said a troll chief harshly. "The seas are empty of our ships. One boat got through, to tell us that all the coasts of Troll-heim are plundered and ablaze."

Valgard might have been graven in dark stone. His eyes gleamed in the moonlight.

The elves ashore began to set up a tent bigger than the others. A man rode up on a horse of monster size with eyes like glowing coals, and planted his standard before the tent—a spearshaft atop which grinned the shriveling head of Illrede. The dead eyes stared up at the trolls.

A chieftain's voice broke in a sob. "That is their general, Skafloc," he said shakenly. "Naught can stand before him. He drove us up from the south like a flock of sheep, slaughtering, slaughtering. He leaves no troll alive, and his sword cuts through stone and metal as through cloth. He is a fiend out of hell."

Valgard stirred. "I know him," he said softly. "And I mean to slay him."

"Lord, you cannot—no one can stand before that weapon—"

"Be still!" Valgard turned to face his chiefs. His eyes raked them, and his low voice was a biting lash: "Fools, cowards, knaves! Let any who fear to fight go out to that butcher. He will not spare you on that account. But for my part, I mean to break him, here at Elfheugh."

His words rumbled like angry thunder: "This is the last troll fort in England. How the others fell I know not, but we have seen elf banners flying over them as we retreated hither. But this castle, which never yet fell to storm, and is now packed with warriors to a number greater than that outside, will stand. It is bastioned alike against magic and open assault. Naught but our own cowardice can take it from us."

He lifted his great ax. "They will set up their camp tonight and do no more. It is almost dawn now. Tomorrow night they may begin siege, but more likely storm. If it is storm, we will repulse it and sally forth in pursuit. Otherwise we will make the attack ourselves, having the fortress at our backs for retreat if things should go wrong."

His teeth gleamed snarlingly in the moonlight. "But I think we will carry them before us. We are more than they, and man for man stronger. Skafloc and I will seek each other out—there is no love between us twain. And I will kill him and get his victorious sword."

His voice ceased. The captain from Scotland asked: "But what of the Sidhe?"

"They are not all-powerful," snapped Valgard. "Once we have mowed down enough elves to make it plain that their cause is doomed, the Sidhe will be glad enough to make peace. Then England will be a troll island guarding the homeland from attack until we have mustered strength to return against the Erlking."

His somber gaze slanted down to meet Illrede's glassy stare. "And I," he muttered to himself, "will succeed to your throne—but what use is that? What use is anything?"

Freda sought to leave the house the day after she lost her child. She stumbled on the threshold and lay in blood until a carle found her and bore her back to bed. Thereafter she tossed in a fever, crying out things which caused the priest to shake his head, palefaced, and cross himself.

Twice in the following days she tried to slip away, and each time someone saw her and led her back. Her wasting form had no strength left to fight.

But there came the chill clear night when she lay alone and no one else was awake. She crept from her bed, shuddering in the cold, and to the chest where her clothes lay. Fumbling in the dark, she got out a long woolen dress and a hooded cloak.

She took the crucifix from about her neck and kissed it. "Forgive me," she breathed. "Forgive me if You can, that I love him more than You or Your laws. Evil am I, but the sin is mine, not his." Then she laid the cross on the chest and went out into the night.

The night bit at her with a silent fury of cold. The frozen ground crackled under her feet as she went toward the stable.

The dusky castle was still quiet as day waned toward sunset. Leea put her hands about Valgard's arm, where it was thrown across her breast. Slowly, carefully, she lifted it and laid it on the bed, and slid out onto the floor.

He turned, muttering in his sleep. His waking strength was gone, leaving only a skull over which a scarred hide was drawn tight, sagging under eyes and chin. Leea looked down at him, and a dagger taken from a hidden niche gleamed in her hand.

It would be easy to slash his throat now— No, too much depended on her. If she should make a slip—and he had a were-wolf's perception of danger, even when asleep—all was over. She turned away, noiseless as a questing shadow, Hung a cloak over her slim bare shoulders, and made her death-silent way out the door. In one hand she held the knife, in the other the castle keys lifted from the hiding place she herself had suggested to Valgard.

She passed another elf woman on the stair. This one carried swords from the armory. Neither said a word as they flitted on their ways.

The trolls tossed in uneasy sleep. Now and again Leea went by a wakeful guard who paid her no special heed. Elf women were often sent on errands by their owners.

Down into the dungeons she went, swiftly, soundlessly, a dim white ghost in the dank gloom. She came to the great cell door behind which was Imric, and opened the triple lock.

The imp looked up through the reddened dark. Leea was on him in one tigerish leap. His wings rattled briefly, but ere he could cry out he was flopping with his throat slashed open.

Leea scattered the fire and, reaching up, cut the ropes binding Imric. He fell heavily into her arms and lay corpse-like on the floor.

She carved healing-runes on bits of the charred wood, placing them under his tongue, on his eyes and burned feet, on his lame hands. The flesh writhed as it grew back. Imric gasped with the pain of it but made no other sound.

Leea put certain keys beside him. "When you feel recovered enough," she whispered, "release the elf thralls. They have all been locked into the dungeons for safety. There are weapons hidden in the old well-house behind the keep. Sneak out there and get them when the fighting starts."

"Good," he muttered with his dry throat. "Also I will get many kegs of wine and a haunch of meat. And vengeance on the trolls." His eyes held a terrible gleam.

Leea sped on soundless bare feet up an old and little-used tower. When she came to its top she stepped out, shielding her eyes against the sinking sun. A figure tall and brightly byrnied stood outside the wall, she could not tell who it was in the, to her, intolerable glare. A warrior of the Sidhe, perhaps, or—her heart beat faster—Skafloc himself.

She leaned over the battlement and flung the ring of keys upward and outward. In a glittering arc the ring looped on the warrior's spear—and among them were the keys to the main gates!

Leea sped back into the grateful dimness of the castle. Like a flying bird she raced for the earl's chambers. She sprang into the bed, and Valgard stirred and blinked awake.

He looked about him, out the dimming window. "It is almost sundown," he said. "Time to rouse the trolls."

He took a great horn from the wall, and, opening the door, blew a mighty blast, all unaware that it was the signal for every elf woman in the fortress who was beside a troll to plunge a knife in his heart.

Freda kept fainting, and waking up in a whirling red-spattered darkness just as she was about to fall off her horse. It was the pain, ripping sword-like through her half-healed body, that roused her, and she thanked it with dry lips.

The horse could go no faster. Unmercifully she flogged it. The hills and trees swam in an unstable half-dark before her eyes, like stones seen through a swiftly running river. Often they seemed unreal, somehow things of dream, they were impossible and fantastic. There was a rising roar in her ears, filling her head with its dark tumult.

She remembered the horse stumbling once and throwing her into a river. Its waters were like ice, and they soon froze stiffly in her dress and hair as she rode on.

Later, many eternities later, when the sun was dying as red as the blood in her trail, her horse fell again, nor did it rise. She went on afoot, crashing into trees because her swimming blurring eyes could not place them, falling, getting up, groping through bushes whose barren twigs clawed at her.

North—north to Elfheugh, to Skafloc.

The clamor of dark waters seemed to fill her skull. Her being drowned in their elemental madness, she knew not who she was nor cared—but north, north, north to Elfheugh—

28

At sundown Skafloc let sound the battle horns. The elves, who had slept and eaten within their tents, came forth into the dusk with a clashing of metal and a great vengeful shout. Horses tramped and whinnied, war chariots rolled brazen over the frosty ground, and a forest of shining spears and lances lifted among the flying banners and the head of Illrede.

Skafloc mounted his Jötun stallion. The demon sword seemed almost to stir of itself at his hip. His face was a mask, worn and gaunt and pitiless, as he spoke to Firespear: "There seems to be a great disturbance within the walls."

"Aye, so," grinned the elf. "The trolls must just have found out how the other castles fell so swiftly. But they will not catch the women ere we are at their throats."

Skafloc jingled the key ring at his belt. "Do you lead the attack on the rear," he said. "When we have opened the front gates, it will draw enough defenders for you to be able to ram down the rear ones. Flam and Rucca will lead assaults on the sides, diversionary ones which will swing to help us once we are in. I will go with the Sidhe and the Erlking's guard against the front gates and unlock them."

The moon rose, gleaming on metal and eyes and white horses. The lurs blew again and the host raised a mighty shout that rang between the crags and cliffs and frosty hills, up almost to the coldly glittering stars. As one, the elves charged up the steep hillside, up toward the sky-storming walls of the fortress.

A great twanging sounded through the night. Shaken the trolls might be, with a third of their number murdered in sleep and their slaves loose somewhere in the labyrinthine castle, but they were stout warriors and Valgard roared them on to battle. Now from the walls the archers sent a steady rain of arrows down on the elves.

The missiles rattled off lifted shields and metal-bound helms—but they also struck deep. Elf after elf toppled under the sighing cloud, horses screamed and bolted, corpses littered the upward way.

Only the narrowest of paths led up to the huge brazen gates. But these were elves, who needed no paths, they sprang over sliding talus and frost-slippery rocks, from crag up to next higher crag, their war-cries tearing from their throats. They threw hooks that clutched deep into creviced precipices and swarmed up ropes tied to these, they rode their horses where no mountain goat would have dared go, they stormed to the flat ground about the walls and fired their own arrows upward.

Skafloc took the path, so that he could lead the war chariots of the Tuatha De Danaan. Frightfully they rumbled behind him, wheels sparking and crashing, brazen bodies gleaming like the sun. The whining arrows rattled off helms and hauberks and shields, none of Skafloc's allies were hit. And he himself, thundering on his dark horse up a path of shadow and tricky moonlight, was not even approached by a missile.

Thus the elves won up under the walls. Now boiling water and blazing oil and ice-slick vitriol rained down, spears and stones and the lurid fire of the Greeks. Elves screamed as the flesh peeled from their bones, and their comrades drew snarling back.

Skafloc shouted, wild with wrath and battle lust, longing only to lose himself in the terrible game of weapons. To him the elves dragged a covered passageway on wheels, and under shelter of this he moved toward the gates.

Valgard, standing on the wall just above, shouted for the heaviest ballista to be brought forth. The brazen-bound gates could not be beaten down ere the shelter was crushed under huge hurled stones.

Skafloc put the first key in place and turned it, calling out the old rune words. A second key, a third, a fourth— Now Valgard himself helped load the ballista with a boulder under whose weight the engine groaned. Trolls were already winding it up.

Seven keys, eight—Valgard grasped the lever. Nine keys, and the gates were unlocked!

Skafloc leaped onto his horse and reared him back. The pawing forefeet clashed mightily on the gates, giant strength to swing them back. The gates flew open, and Skafloc galloped the tunnel-like thickness of the wall and burst into the moon-silvery courtyard. Behind him, the passage echoed to the wheels of the chariots of Lugh, Dove Berg, Angus Og, Eochy, Mananaan, Coll, Cecht, Mac Greina, the whole host of the Sidhe, to hoofs of horses and running of feet. The gate was taken!

The gate guards struck out with their weapons. An ax smote the leg of the Jötun horse. The stallion kicked out, snorting, trampling, treading warriors into bloody smears.

Skafloc's sword screamed forth. The blade flamed icy blue in the half-light, thundered, rose and fell, striking like a living snake. Clamor and clangor of metal belled under the grandly wheeling stars, shouts of warriors, whistle of cleaving glaives, thunderous rumble of sword-hubbed wheels.

Back and back went the trolls. Valgard howled, his eyes flaming wolf-green, and led a rush down from the wall to the courtyard. Mightily he smote at the flank of the invaders. An elf fell to his ax, he twisted the weapon loose and struck at another, smashed the face of a third with his shield—hewing, hewing, he waded into battle.

At the rear gate rose the roar of Firespear's battering ram. The trolls hurled stones at it, fire to set it ablaze, spears and arrows at the warriors around it. But now from behind leaped a crew gaunt and bloody and coldly afire for revenge, weapons singing in their hands—Imric's gang of freed slaves. The trolls turned to fight this new menace, and Firespear broke down the gates.

"To the keep!" Valgard's voice rose huge over the tumult surging between the walls. "To the keep—hold it!"

Some few trolls battled their way to where he towered gigantic and blood-streaming over the combat. They went in a tight ring, the clattering elf swords menacing them from every side, they hewed their way to a door in the keep.

It was locked.

Valgard hurled himself against it. The door groaned under his frightful strength. He chopped at the lock, it shattered in sparks and he swung the door open.

Bows twanged from the darkness inside. Trolls sank, and Valgard staggered back with an arrow through his left hand. Leea's voice jeered at him, sweet poisonous mockery: "The elf women guard this place for their lovers—better lovers than we have lately had, O you ape of Skafloc!"

Like a blind man, Valgard turned away, wrenching the arrow from his hand. He howled, gnawed the rim of his shield, froth at his mouth. His ax began to shriek and thunder, striking at all before it, he was mad with killing-lust.

Skafloc fought with a bitter flame of cold murder within him. The giant's sword was a living fire in his hands. Blood and brains spurted, heads rolled on the ground, guts were slippery under his horse's hoofs—he fought, he fought in a timeless whirlpool of death where only the icy lightning-swift workings of his brain were real. He scattered death as a sower scatters grain, and wherever he went the troll lines broke.

Swords blazed under the moon. Spears flew, axes smote, metal and men cried their pain. The horses reared, trampling, whinnying, their blood-clotted manes flying. Elves and trolls died in a storm of weapons and were crushed under the swaying struggle.

The moon climbed over the castle walls. Its light was ghastly on the clanging, roaring battle. It rose up until it seemed pierced by the castle's highest towers. It began to sink, and the trolls broke in fear.

Few of them were left. The elves harried them about the courtyard and out onto the white hillside, slaying them, hunting them.

"To me, to me!" Valgard's great voice boomed over the waning battle. "Hither, trolls, and fight!"

Skafloc heard the sound and wheeled about. He saw the changeling standing huge in the gateway, drenched with blood, a heap of elf corpses before him. The berserker's eyes still flamed with cold fire as he battled. And toward him some few trolls were making their way for a final stand.

For a moment, the black rush of his hatred blinded Skafloc. He felt the hunger of the sword and it was his own hunger. Valgard, Valgard, your weird is upon you!

As he spurred his horse, he had a sudden instant when he saw a hawk rising up toward the moon. The chill struck deep into his bones, and he knew he had seen his own fetch. He was fey.

Valgard saw him coming and grinned in hate. He put his back against the wall and raised his mighty ax. As the black stallion thundered down on him, he swung as he had never swung before. The weapon sank into the horse's skull.

That terrible rush could not be stopped. The stallion crashed into the wall, shaking its stones. Skafloc flew from the saddle, twisting elf-lithe even as he did. But he could not save himself from caroming off the wall and out the gateway.

Valgard wrenched his ax from the dead horse and ran after his foe. Skafloc, his right arm hanging limp, was reeling to his feet. The sword gleamed in his left hand. Blood dripped from his torn face and ran down the bright blade.

"Many things end tonight," quoth Valgard, "and your life is one."

"We were born nigh the same night," muttered Skafloc. Blood ran from his mouth with the words. "There will not be long between our deaths." He sneered. "When I go out, how can you, my shadow, live?"

Valgard screamed and struck at him. Skafloc lifted the sword in his left hand. The ax Brotherslayer hit the demon blade and in a tremendous clang and crash and sheeting of sparks burst asunder.

Skafloc staggered back, caught himself, and lifted the sword anew. Valgard stalked empty-handed toward him, growling deep in his throat like a maddened wolf.

"Skafloc! Skafloc!"

The cry rang and wavered in the night, and it was like a sword in his heart. The warrior turned to see Freda, haggard, bloody, in rags, but the most beautiful sight in all the wide world—Freda, his Freda, stumbling up the narrow path to him.

"Skafloc," she breathed. "Skafloc, dearest—"

Valgard rushed forward and wrenched the sword from the hand of his unseeing foe. A surge of strength and hate flamed icily in him, he lifted the blade and brought it screaming down.

Howling like a wild beast, he lifted the sword. It ran with unearthly blue fires under the moon, "Victory!" he shouted. "Victory and death are in the blade! I have won, I am master of all the world and I tread it beneath my feet— Come, darkness!"

His hands, slippery with blood, lost their hold. The sword seemed almost to twist in the air, it flamed as it fell point foremost down on him. Its great weight knocked him from his feet, drove through his neck and into the earth, and there he lay pinned with the blade gleaming before his eyes and his life rivering from his throat. He tried to pull it loose, and the edges opened the veins in his wrists. And that was the end of Valgard the Changeling.

Skafloc lay on the ground with his breast hidden in blood. His face was white in the moonlight, but he smiled as Freda bent over him and his eyes held their old merry gleam.

"I am sped, my dearest," he whispered. "But you have too much youth and beauty for a dead man. You are too lovely to weep. Forget me—"

"Never, never," she sobbed. Her tears fell like a spring morning's rain on his bloody face.

"Will you kiss me goodbye?" he asked.

His lips were already cold, but she sought them hungrily. And when she had opened her eyes again, Skafloc was dead in her arms.

Imric and Leea came out into the first bitter dawn-light. "No use to heal the girl and send her home," said the elf woman. Pain and sorrow twisted her lovely white face. "Better to send her screaming in torment to hell. It was she who slew Skafloc."

"It was his weird," replied Imric. "And helping her is the last thing we can do for our comrade. Elves know friendship, if not love, and I would fain see that done which would have gladdened him."

"Not know love?" murmured Leea, so softly he did not hear. "You are wise, Imric, but you know not all things."

Her eyes went to Freda, where she sat on the rime-white ground with Skafloc cradled in her arms. She was singing him to sleep with the lullaby she had thought to sing to her child.

"Happier was her fate than mine," said Leea.

Imric misunderstood her, on purpose or otherwise, and nodded bleakly. "Happier are all men than the beings of faerie—or the gods, for that matter," he said. "Better a life like a falling star, brief and bright across the dark, than the long, long waiting of the immortals, loveless and cheerlessly wise." He looked to the sword, flashing ominously in the throat of its prey. "And I feel a doom creeping on me," he muttered. "I feel that the day draws nigh when the powers of faerie fade, when even the Erlking shrinks to a forest sprite and then to naught, when the temples of the very gods crumble and are forgotten. I think man is fated to outlive the immortals."

He walked slowly toward the shining blade. "As for it," he told the dwarf thralls who followed him, "we will take it and cast it far out to sea. But I do not think that will do much good. The will of the Norns stands not to be changed, and the destiny of the sword has not yet run its course."

He followed the thralls out in a boat to see that they did their task well. When he returned, he and Leea went slowly into Elfheugh, for the cold pale dawn of winter was breaking.

Here ends the saga of Skafloc Elf's-Foster.

AFTERWORD

This is frankly a romance, a story of admittedly impossible events and completely non-existent places. Whether or not it is true must be settled by those scientists who argue the reliability of the annals of faerie and those philosophers who are trying to settle what truth itself may be. The historian can only set down the plain tales of the doubtful milieu of faerie and hope that they be found readable. He can scarcely debate their truth or falsity, especially in these latter days when so much of the patently absurd has become everyday fact and so many of the eternal verities been shown to be blatant fabrications.

For the benefit of the curious, however, it should be remarked that such parts of the story as deal with purely human beings are as accurate as the scanty records permit. There were many such half-converted Christians as Orm, many forcible exchanges of property, much violence, and, one suspects, much peace and tenderness at times. Our own age is not one which can afford to call its ancestors savage.

I am also well aware that the winters in England are not as cold as here suggested. But there is considerable evidence that at the time of this story the English climate was more continental, with warmer summers and colder winters than now. If that is true, then a few days of extreme chill are not unreasonable in the middle of such a winter.

Much of the culture of the time lay in the verses, which every well-educated man was expected to be able to make on occasion and which certain men, the skalds, made more or less professionally. The verses were not sung but recited—I have used the term "quoth" to replace one for which there is no real modern equivalent but which was cognate—and followed certain rules of meter and alliteration which I have also obeyed. But it seemed best to omit the elaborate metaphors of the skalds, and to keep to a minimum the conventional wolves and ravens of the poetic battlefield. It is recorded of Sighvat, skald to King Olaf the Stout (later known as St Olaf), that he spoke slowly, but made verses faster than most men could talk—indeed, he made a whole political speech in verse once, to good effect. So it did not seem incredible to me that the men of faerie, or even their human fosterlings, should have the same gift.

Likewise, it seemed only natural that the dwellers in the middle world would be technologically superior to their human contemporaries. Assume, if you will, that there really were races once which could do magic—that is, mentally control external phenomena by some means as yet unknown to our physical science. (But see some of the recent work and speculation on "parapsychology.") Assume that they could live indefinitely, change their shapes, and otherwise have mastery over the world. Such an alien metabolism might have its own penalties, in an inability to endure the glare and actinic light of the sun or in disastrous electrochemical reactions induced by contact with iron or silver. So—why should not these handicapped immortals compensate by discovering aluminum, beryllium, magnesium, and the steel-like properties of many non-ferrous alloys? They might have made other inventions as well, such as ships which could sail indefinitely fast because of having virtually frictionless hulls. Though castles such as we know them were not yet found in the Europe of King Alfred's time, the faerie folk might have been building them for a long while; and in the same way other apparent anachronisms would be simply the achievements of races older and wiser than man. But an aristocratic warrior culture, particularly with the conservatism induced by many centuries of life, would not be likely to develop science very far, and we should not look for gunpowder or steam engines in the ruins of faerie.

As for what became of the people of this story, and the sword, and faerie itself—which obviously no longer exists on Earth—that is another tale, which will perhaps some day be told.

ABOUT THE AUTHOR

Poul Anderson (1926–2001) grew up bilingual in a Danish American family. After discovering science fiction fandom and earning a physics degree at the University of Minnesota, he found writing science fiction more satisfactory. Admired for his "hard" science fiction, mysteries, historical novels, and "fantasy with rivets," he also excelled in humor. He was the guest of honor at the 1959 World Science Fiction Convention and at many similar events, including the 1998 Contact Japan 3 and the 1999 Strannik Conference in Saint Petersburg, Russia. Besides winning the Hugo and Nebula Awards, he has received the Gandalf, Seiun, and Strannik, or "Wanderer," Awards. A founder of the Science Fiction & Fantasy Writers of America, he became a Grand Master, and was inducted into the Science Fiction and Fantasy Hall of Fame.

In 1952 he met Karen Kruse; they married in Berkeley, California, where their daughter, Astrid, was born, and they later lived in Orinda, California. Astrid and her husband, science fiction author Greg Bear, now live with their family outside Seattle.

POUL ANDERSON

FROM OPEN ROAD MEDIA

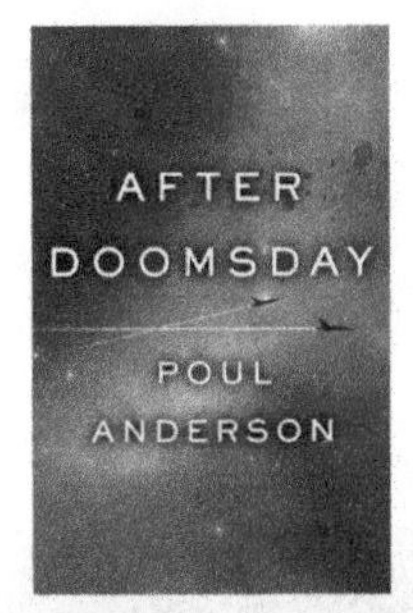

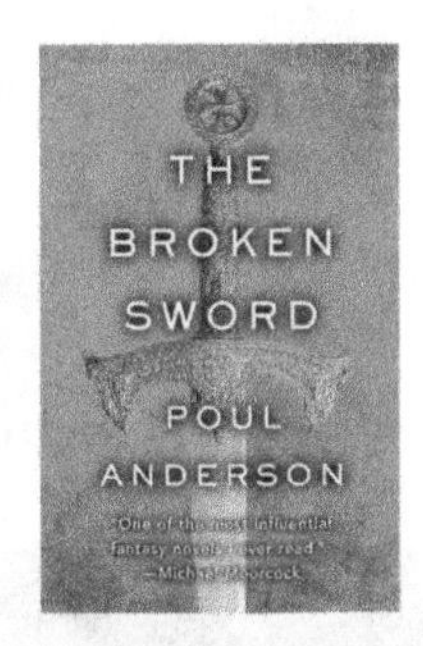

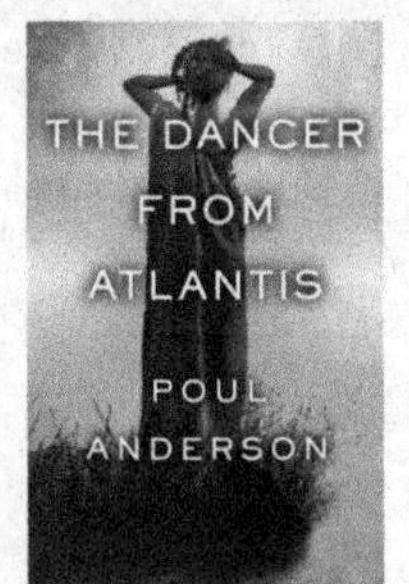

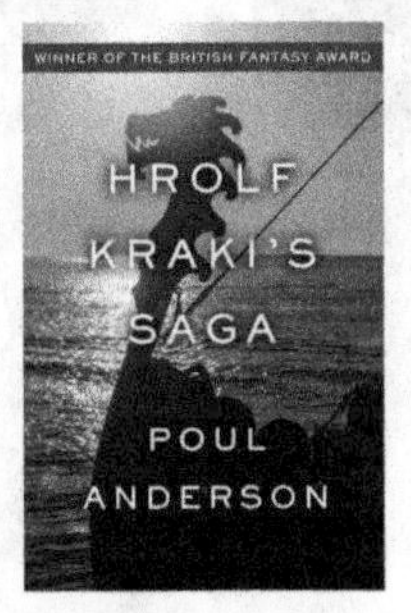

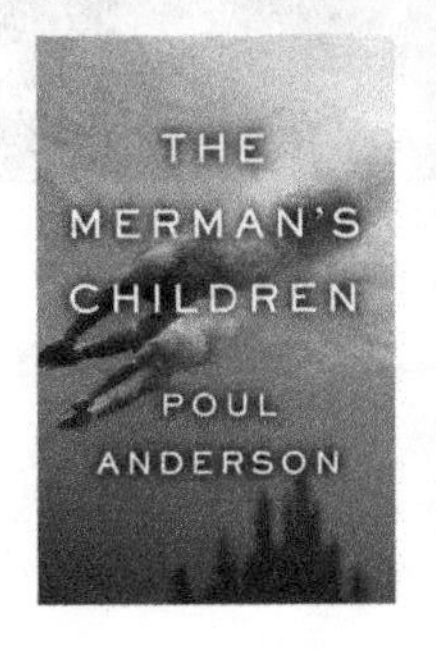

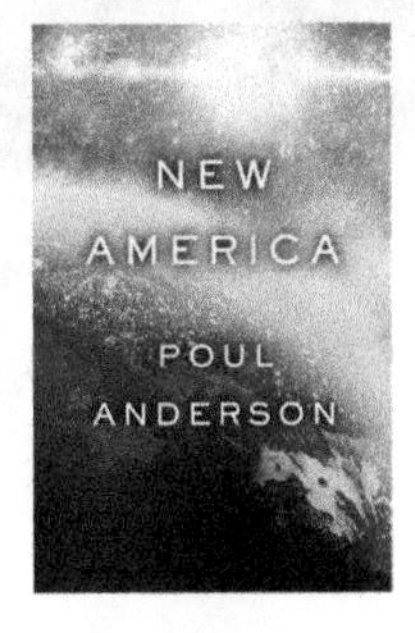

OPEN ROAD
INTEGRATED MEDIA

CPSIA information can be obtained
at www.ICGtesting.com
Printed in the USA
JSHW041049240321
12865JS00002B/257